BATTLE GROUND

CHRISTIAN BLACK

FOREWORD AND AFTERWORD BY BERNARD GLADNEY JR.

Cover swords photo copyright © 2024 by 100 Covers. All rights reserved.
Cover background copyright © 2024 by 100 Covers. All rights reserved.
Author's photo copyright © 2024 by Caleb Moss. All rights reserved.
Cover Illustration by 100 Covers
Edited by Cherry Jones

After reading, please leave a review of this book on the platform which you ordered it.

Library of Congress Data

Black, Christian
BattleGround/ Christian Black, Bernard Gladney Jr.

ISBN: 979-8-218-43758-9
Library of Congress Number: 2024908940

This book, this labor of love, could not have been done without my Father in heaven, Jesus Christ. Jesus, thank you for pouring every bit of this book and the entire series into my mind. Thank you for helping me through every event of this book that is part of my testimony. Though these events could have destroyed me, you made sure that those things did not kill me but could be used to tell someone about a man named Jesus that died on the cross so that they could be free, free from the bondage of insecurity, free from the bondage of perversion, freedom from fear and so much more. Thank you, Father, for delivering every soul that will read this book and find that their story resides somewhere in these pages. My prayer is that as you have grown me, taught me what being a man truly means, that the people who this book will reach will grow into a deeper relationship with you if they are part of the body of Christ. If they are not, I pray that this would convict them to be born again via water baptism in Jesus' name and filled with the Holy Ghost.

Thank you for every growing pain and every tear that I cried (both aloud and silent) because I know all those tears were for this moment. Thank you for giving me the drive to finish the first portion of the assignment you gave me. I pray that this is pleasing in your eyes and that ultimately, someone will know that they are not alone in their struggle. I pray that through seeing these characters and what they face, they will see that with you, Jesus, they can overcome anything. I pray that this will be more than just entertainment for them. Thank you for never abandoning me, for knowing my name and knowing everything about me, the good and the bad. Finally, thank you for being a "good, good Father." Because truly you are perfect in all your ways!

Acknowledgements

To my Mother, I want to thank you for being there for me through the years. Thank you for pushing me into this crazy world and taking care of me. I really appreciate your support. I love you very much.

To my editor, Dr. Cherry Jones, you have been nothing short of amazing in this process. Thank you for all your hard work and dedication. I cannot believe that we were able to collaborate on this project, but I am grateful for you to be on it.

To my artist, Chelsey Clay, your artwork is extraordinary! You took what was just an idea and made it into an incredible work of art. I am so happy with the work you have done, and I cannot wait to see what your next big work is going to look like. Chelsey, continue to be creative. Never stop using your God given talent to uplift those that are around you. Thank you for your friendship. Thank you for all the support you have given me from beginning to end.

To my friend, Bernard Gladney: When I first asked you to write the foreword and afterword, I knew that the work would be exemplary, but you exceeded every expectation that I had for this. So, for that, I say thank you. However, I want to take this moment to say thank you for your friendship and wise words. You inspire me, as a big brother, to strive to be the very best and to really be a student of God's Word. Thank you for being a willing vessel for this project and thank you so much for every discussion and words of wisdom you have imparted onto me.

To one of my best friends, Caleb Moss: For over a decade, we have had each other's backs and continue to pray for each other. Thank you for 10+ years of support, kind words and for pushing me even when I did not want to. From my catering to this book, you have helped me achieve whatever goal I had in front of me. In some of the times that will be mentioned in this series, you were there for me and I cannot thank you enough for that. You really are a friend that became a brother.

To Lorna, David and Miko: Without your willingness to be used by God, I would not have learned as much as I know now as fast as I learned it. Thank you all for imparting wisdom into me. Thank you for every hour, every minute and every second of prayer for me. You all made such a big impact on my life that I would never have imagined when I first met you. Thank you for giving me opportunities and pulling out the absolute best in me. I love all three of you very much and appreciate you.

To Keiara Gladney (or Beatrice is what I like to call her): We have been friends for a while, but it feels like I have known you a lifetime. You are an inspiration and embody what a friend should be. Thank you for having my back, for your honesty and your kindness towards me and my family. I tell you this all the time, but you are the sister I always wanted, but did not get until I met you.

To Brenda Barker, thank you for pushing me and encouraging me, every step of the way. I truly appreciate everything you have done to help me, as well as every prayer. Thank you for being my sister and being a part of this journey.

To my friends that has supported this vision and that continues to push me to be better, I thank you.

To my wife, Briana Black: You have been there for me, despite my past, and accepted the good and bad. Thank you for being my wife, for being my prayer partner. Thank you for every prayer of intercession, for listening to all my crazy ideas and helping me pursue the things that God has for me to do. You have been a blessing to me. Thank you for being the core of my support system. I love you so much!

Last and certainly not least, to my son, Thomas: You will never know how much I love you son. I am so thankful for you. You make me smile, laugh all at the same time. I pray that when you are old enough to read and understand the things in this book, both spiritually and naturally, that you see that with God, all things are possible. I pray that no matter what you go through, that you trust God. Trust Him in the process of you becoming more like Him. As you read through this series, some of the things happened in your dad's life, but know that your dad faced these things and overcame them because of Christ. facing these obstacles, I wanted to make sure that I did so that you did not have to.

Foreword

There are times in life when you run into situations where you have no idea why they are happening in your life. Oftentimes, it is mind-boggling that it heightens the stress level of the situation because there is no explanation for *"Why is this happening to me."* What we do not understand most is that these situations are always triggered by something in the spiritual realm. The Bible says that **in the beginning God created the heavens and the earth**. God is and has always been in control of what happens in our present; however, spiritual attacks will happen to you for one of two reasons. If you do not believe in God and His power, the fallen angels led by Satan love to influence the actions of your life because people who do not know God typically do not understand how the spiritual realm plays a key factor in the events that happen in and around your life. Those that have been baptized in the name of Jesus Christ and filled with the gift of the Holy Spirit will face trials, throughout, that will test and build you up, spiritually, for the purpose of God to use you for His glory.

Spiritual attacks are not fun and most people would rather not go through them. Whether it is sexual misconduct or the loss of life, these experiences are traumatizing to the point where they leave you in a state that could cause you mental and physical damage for the rest of your life. This book displays several scenarios of real-life trials that have happened and are currently happening to people. It is a testament for the reader to utilize the stories and apply them to their situations to understand that making the right choices is the key to keeping or losing your mind in this world. The Bible says that **the thief comes not, but for to steal, kill, and destroy**! The fallen angels want nothing more than for you to lose your mind and ultimately end up in a lake burning with fire and brimstone alongside them. Be encouraged to know that there is another choice because Jesus came to give life and that more abundantly. When one is going through the worst periods of your life it is the time to choose Jesus! He gives peace no matter what the situation. He provides solutions that you would never be able to come up with on your own. This series of stories are designed to help the reader to know that there is help in your situation.

Christian Armand-Alexander Black has dealt with or witnessed the series of stories that are portrayed in this literary work to inspire and encourage. He found out that when he had nowhere else to turn, he had to turn to Jesus, but what he found was nothing like he had ever imagined. I encourage every reader to be reminded that not only are the scenarios true stories but they are written to let you know that there is nothing too hard for God! Allow the power of the Holy Spirit to minister to you through this work as we pray that you find the answers that you have always desired to have.

— Pastor Bernard Gladney, Jr.

Table of Contents

Acknowledgements v

Foreword ix

Chapter 1 1

Chapter 2 11

Chapter 3 21

Chapter 4 31

Chapter 5 45

Chapter 6 57

Chapter 7 69

Chapter 8 69

Chapter 9 91

Chapter 10 103

Chapter 11 115

Chapter 12 127

Chapter 13 149

Chapter 14 159

Chapter 15 169

Chapter 16 183

Chapter 17 199

Chapter 18 209

Chapter 19 221

Chapter 20 237

Epilogue 265

Afterword 269

Let's Connect 275

Chapter 1

It is 2 a.m. The sound of thunder reverberates through the sky over Detroit, as a car races down the street with a man and his in-labor girlfriend making their way to the hospital. In pain and with her quick breathing, she tells her boyfriend, from the backseat, "The…. the baby……the baby is coming, Hun."

"I know…. I know, Bae," he says, focusing on the road and watching for police as he is going well over the speed limit.

The thunder continues to rumble and the lightning flashes as the rain begins to pour. The boyfriend begins to get worried because as they travel down the road, the rain begins to fall harder, with his visibility of the road dwindling.

As he looks into the rear-view mirror, he says "Babe, are you okay?" She does not respond.

"BABE!!" he yells.

She still has not responded. He begins to fear the worst, takes his eyes off the road just for a moment, and looks behind him to see that she is bleeding out.

With tears falling, he says, "Lola, stay with me… God, please. I know I do not pray like I should, and I know that my life is not right, but I am begging you, save Lola and my son!"

As he drives, he hears a voice that says, *"Fear not, only believe."* And as the voice speaks, he turns the corner and arrives in front of Meridian Hospital's emergency room where there are two doctors outside in a shelter smoking. He pulls up and yells "HELP!!…. PLEASE HELP!"

Choose ye this day…

"I'm over this Maria!" the man yelled.

"I'm tired of your crap and this kid…this freaking annoying kid, always getting in my way!" He yells in the woman's face.

She pushes him and says "Nobody told you to stay. You could have left and went to whoever that chick is that keep calling you."

As she continues to yell in his face, a shadow figure watches on the other side of the room, laughing.

It walks over to the man, whispering in his ear uttering, "you gonna let this…. this woman…this ugly woman disrespects you??"

The figure goes on to ignite the man's anger.

"YOU ARE WEAK!!!....and you need to show her you are a man and you don't treat a man like that. Just hit her."

She continues to yell, and the man's anger continues to grow. "HIT…HER!" the figure says to the man.

The man's anger boils over, and he hits her, knocking her into the wall.

"See what you made me do huh…SEE WHAT YOU MADE ME DO?!?!" the man yells.

He goes over to her in a fit of rage and kicks her. The figure stands in the corner laughing uncontrollably, being entertained as he watches what this man does to this woman.

A little girl runs into the room, saying "stop it daddy. Stop hitting mommy."

The figure walks to the man and says, "Now hit her too" and he hits the girl.

"You want this too?? I been waiting on this for a long time" the man says, chasing after the little girl.

"No, James! Don't you go near Maddy" Maria says,

struggling to speak.

Madison runs into her room, closing the door and locking it. She runs under the bed, weeping. She closes her eyes, whispering "please don't hurt me…please don't hurt me."

The man beats on the door, yelling like a mad man "MADDY!!"

Maria tries to run to James to try and stop him, but before she steps out her room, the figure steps in front of her and pushes her back into her bedroom, slamming the door shut. She turns the knob to open the door but it wouldn't open. The figure goes to James, inciting his anger even more until he kicks open the door. The figure watches and laughs with a manic laughter as it observes what transpires.

The figure leaves the house and goes walking about the street. It turns a corner, walking down an alley.

"Did you finish your assignment?" Jim asks.

"Well, if you mean did I get that weak man to beat on his woman and daughter, then yes…yes I did" the figure says.

"You are not done. The office is sending some friends to go back with you. In the meantime, you have new orders."

Whom you will serve

As the doctors go to take Lola from the backseat of the car, they notice the paleness of her skin and one doctor notices the amount of blood on the seat.

"Dr. Cho, look at the seat" the other doctor says. Dr. Cho looks at the seat and it is drenched in blood.

"Let's get her in, now!!" Dr. Cho says.

"Is my girlfriend alright?!?! What is going on??" the man says.

As two male nurses approach them, one comes with a gurney,

they all lift her up onto it and rush her into the ER, with the man following.

"Does she have any medical allergies??? What is her blood type?? How long has she been bleeding out??"

He hears the doctors asking him, bombarding him with more and more questions. The words from their questions and sounds of the ER flood his mind. He tries to make sense of everything, but all he can seem to do is aimlessly follow them. As they go through these massive metal doors, he is stopped by a mid-height, older, heavy-set female nurse.

"Sir…" she says, holding him back. He struggles with her, trying to get past.

"Sir!! You have to wait out here" she says.

"No, I need to get to Lola. She needs me!" he cries in a panic.

With tears falling down his face, he goes to say, "Lola…my son…they have to make… They just have to make it." As he sobs and is falling to the floor, she catches and holds him tight.

"It's going to be alright, Sir. There are some things you can do to help the doctors in the back. Let's get you cleaned up and sit down. The doctors need to know a few things."

So, they go over to a small desk in the waiting room.

"Thank you for everything, Miss…"

"Marlinda…just call me Marlinda" the nurse says.

"Thank you, Marlinda, for being here for me. You do not know how much this means to me. I just want them safe" he calmly speaks.

"What's your name sir? I usually don't let strange men just cry all over my scrubs" she jokingly said.

Smiling, he says "Samuel…my name is Samuel."

"Oh baby!! You don't know how powerful your name is."

He does not reply to her comment. She begins to ask him questions about Lola's health history, but before she can get her last question out, a doctor walks out of the double doors. Based on the look of his face, she tells him to stay sitting at the table while she sees what is going on. He waits with bated breath to get the news as he watches Marlinda and the doctor speak. She walks back to him and from her look, he knows something is wrong

"Samuel, she lost a lot of blood and they are taking care of that; however, she has to have a C-section."

"Will she and my son be okay???"

"The doctor said it was a lot, so they are hoping that with the blood transfusion, she will come to."

Samuel hugs Marlinda tight, crying tears of joy, thanking her for everything she did.

"Oh child, don't thank me. Thank God, for it is Him that gives life."

Wiping the tears from his eyes, "By the way, what does my name even mean?"

Smiling, she says, "God has heard."

They both sit down talking for hours, like they have known each other their entire lives. They spend that time talking about God, telling their testimonies about how they entered into a relationship with Christ. They connect in a way that only a long-lost brother and sister can. Marlinda tells Samuel about how she used to live out on the streets for five years because she had nowhere to go, mother and father had died and family was just too far, but it was in those years that she came to know that Jesus would never abandon her and that He loved her more than she could possibly imagine. He is amazed at the life this old woman has had.

"Wow you have definitely lived an extraordinary life."

"Baby that is not even the half of it."

Her parents were southerners, from a little town in Mississippi. She is not only the youngest, but the only one of 12 kids to even go to college. She tells Samuel about how the dynamic of her family began to change once her mother died.

"Once momma died, things began to really change. Our family began to really drift apart. Most of my older siblings began to move away and go west and up north. My oldest sister went so far as Canada. My father, on the other hand, just couldn't take my mother not being there. She was like his anchor."

She went on to talk about after he died and she basically had to hitchhike her way to Michigan to find a job since there were no offers where she was.

"I am sorry for your loss."

"Aww, it's alright, Baby. My father and mother in the hands of Jesus now. After getting here, things went from bad to worse as I finished nursing school here just to not be able to find a job. I started feeling like I went to school for nothing. Eventually, I was not able to pay my rent, so I lost my apartment and my car was repossessed."

She goes on to talk to him about how during those five years, she went from shelter to shelter until there was no shelter that would take her due to them being full. She talks to Samuel about these experiences like it was something that just happened yesterday. Samuel looks amazed. He thinks about how he used to complain about the job he is at, how it is not enough money for him, Lola and the baby, but at least he had something. This woman here had nothing. Her words really help put things into perspective.

"Through it all, I just kept trying to believe that things would end up better. I was trying to believe that some way, somehow, Jesus was going to make a way just like daddy always said. However, one day I was just fed up."

Reminiscing about the event and what Jesus did for her brings tears to her eyes. It really did not hit her before that this moment was the moment that her life changed for the better.

"I remember one time when it was snowing, and you know

Detroit has some baaaaaad winters. It was snowing and I was struggling just to get warm. Every shelter I went to turned me away. So, I sat on these church steps, crying, saying 'Jesus, why would you do this to me?!?! This is all your fault. You took my parents away and left me with nothing but debt, misery, and the clothes on my back.' Out of nowhere, these two guys tried to attack me. So, I did the only thing any sane person would do…. I ran. I ran all the way down this street and turned down this alley, but it was a dead end. So, I stand there in the cold, in the dark, panicking because I just thought this was going to be the day that I died. As they turned the corner, I fell to my knees, bowed my head, screaming 'Jesus save me!!!!!' As they ran up to me, I lifted my head to see them stumbling and running away from me. I didn't understand why until I looked behind me and I saw these two massive angels with their swords drawn out. I walked out that alley comforted knowing that there was someone that cared enough about me to watch over me. I ended up at some church, sleeping on the steps and to my amazement; the angels stayed watching me the entire night."

"Wow……I truly do not know what to say."

"Sam, I just knew I was dying that day, but Jesus had other plans. Just so happen that very next morning I met the Pastor of that church where I was sleeping. I will never forget his name: Pastor Davis. He allowed me to come inside and offered me a hot meal. He was asking me all these questions about who I was, where was home for me and how did I get there?"

"You told him the whole story, I gather…"

"Oh yes!!! He was shocked and said that God had a calling on my life and to be able to see angels and stuff is a gift from Him. He said that this was God not only answering my prayer but showing me that He never forgot about me. I broke down and cried like a newborn baby."

Samuel smirked as he drank his coffee.

"I asked him now what to do and that is when He explained to me the importance of water baptism in Jesus' name. I told him that as a kid I was baptized in the name of the Father, the Son and the Holy Ghost. Boy, he broke that thang down for me!!! He explained how all those are titles and he walked me through some scriptures in St. John showing me that the name of all three titles was Jesus. He also explained the baptism of the Holy Ghost too and what it really means to have God in you. He said 'you think that is something, wait until you have His Spirit in you. You will be able to do the impossible. You will be able to lay hands on the sick and they will recover. However, more importantly, you will have a bond with Christ that nobody will be able to take away from you. I jumped in that baptism water so fast, it shocked me. As soon as I came out that water, I just remember saying a bunch of words that I did not understand. I know that it was another language that I did not know. I had to be talking for at least 30 minutes because when I was done, I was exhausted. I asked the Pastor about it and he said "that is the evidence that His Spirit is within you. That is a language that is spoken somewhere on earth, but you just did not know it before now." We talked for hours about speaking in tongues and what it is. He even gave me some scriptures about it. I just was happy that now I had someone that would never leave me."

Samuel was in awe of her testimony. It really made him see the value of a relationship with Jesus. To think that He stepped into her life, saved it and then brought her to repentance was a sight to behold. He could clearly see that she was a changed woman because of this encounter. This causes him to reevaluate his and Lola's relationship and just his life in general.

"Wow…that is one powerful testimony. I had an interesting experience too."

As Samuel goes on to tell her his testimony about how he was born again, he sees Dr. Cho come out from the double doors.

Smiling, he says, "We are about to deliver the baby and I thought you would like to be in there. We got the bleeding under control and are preparing to do the procedure now."

"Don't be afraid baby, for He has not given you a spirit of fear."

Samuel stands up quickly, with a smile on his face fixing himself up as he prepares to greet his new son and Lola. Samuel walks into the observatory room, watching as they are performing the procedure. He is there in a blue scrub, as the doctor prepares to make the first cut on Lola. He waits, nervously, thinking about his son and how he wants to always be there for him, as his father was not there for him due to him dying fighting for the freedom of the people of the United States in the Iraqi War. He thinks about all the football games he wants to attend with him. Samuel has his whole life planned for him.

He would go to a nice elementary school and middle school and make sure he got admitted into Cass Technical High School. He wants all the best for him. Even spiritually, Samuel thinks about what his son could be in the kingdom of God. Samuel thinks to himself, *This is the best moment of my life.* He even wants to marry Lola after this. They are both born again believers with each of them having received the gift of the Holy Ghost in their freshman year of high school. He wants to do things right. Samuel starts to see where the baby is slowly coming out. He begins to get more and more excited. God really heard him and He saved both of them.

Samuel hears the baby cry, and the doctor says "Congratulations, you have a baby boy."

Samuel is elated. Hearing his boy's cry and seeing that Lola is alive is everything that Samuel could have asked for. Dr. Cho looks over at him, with the baby in his hands, asking him if he wants to hold his son once they are finished with Lola.

"Absolutely doctor!" Holding his son, tears begin to fall

down his face. "Thank you…Thank you Jesus for my son. I would not have either of them without you."

The nurse then asks about the boy's name. Samuel looks at him, trying to think of a name, as he and Lola were still torn on what to name him. She wanted some super long, complicated name, while he wanted something that she did not like. There was a long pause for a moment and that is when a name suddenly came to him.

"…. Elias. My son's name is Elias."

The nurse takes him and tells Samuel that the doctor wants to run a couple of tests and to go to the waiting room until they are done with Lola's C-section. He leaves the room where he was watching the procedure take place and the nurse begins to walk out of the room with the baby. He walks back to where Marlinda waits to hear the good word. Samuel tells her everything and how the C-section went according to the plan, but the doctor wanted to run a couple of tests on the baby.

"Wait…that is what the nurse told you? Hmm…that seems weird on the account that the doctor told me that your boy was perfectly fine. Well, maybe he changed his mind or something. Who knows? I am just so happy for you two!"

Marlinda hugs him. She then speaks to another nurse and tells Samuel that he can go into the room where Lola is resting. Barely able to contain himself, he and Marlinda walk into Lola's room. As they walk closer to the room, they hear tumultuous sounds coming from her room. They walk in, confused, as the nurse tries to calm Lola down.

"Baby, what's wrong??"

Lola, in a state of panic, looks at him asking, "Sam, where is our son??? You need to find our son!"

"Baby, he is fine."

"No…he is not okay. You have to find our son, Sam!

Chapter 2

Lola continues to fuss, trying to get out of the hospital bed as the nurses, Marlinda, and Sam struggle to calm her down.

"Baby, baby. Lola!" Sam yells, grabbing her arms to get her attention. "You're going to hurt yourself."

"Who are you yelling at?" Lola questions with a stern voice, looking him in his eyes.

"Lola, you are not going anywhere. You just had a C-section, and you are going to tear your stitches if you're not careful. Now, what do you mean our son is not okay?" He demands.

The nurses are astonished by the way Sam is able to calm Lola down, as they are concerned that she would reopen her incision. Marlinda pulls the nurses aside to reassure them that she wouldn't allow Lola to leave the bed.

"Are you sure we don't need to administer a sedative director?"

"No, she'll be fine." Marlinda reassures them, keeping an ear out for Sam and Lola's conversation.

Marlinda approaches the couple as the other nurses leave the room. Seeing the look of horror on Lola's face, as she begins to retell the dream she's had, Marlinda could tell that it was either a very believable dream, or there was unforeseen danger present in the hospital. Whatever it is, Marlinda begins to feel that something is very wrong.

"Sam, you have to find our son. Where is he?"

Lola asks shakily, tears slowly rolling down her face.

"What makes you say that he's not okay?" Sam questions.

With a look of pure terror on her face, Lola begins to tell Sam what she saw in her dream.

"Sam, I saw this dark room with an altar in it. I have no clue where it was, but the only source of light came from these candles that were around. It was like I was there watching, but I wasn't there at the same time, you know. I saw these people dressed in these monk-like robes and then there came this woman with a baby. Our baby."

Tears continue to stream down her face as she continues.

"I could see the woman's face when she took the hood off, and she was holding our son. The people that were around her were chanting these words that I couldn't understand. Then she placed him on an altar, and she held a knife up and—" she could not finish as she began to sob.

Marlinda places a hand over her mouth in total shock. God has allowed her to see everything that Lola has dreamt in her mind. "Jesus!" she yells, as she begins to go into spiritual warfare on their behalf, interceding for baby Elias.

"The room they were in got so cold, it was freezing. Listen, if you don't find that woman before she leaves this hospital, we'll never see our son again Sam!"

Sam, conflicted, feels a mixture of emotions; part of him is frozen solid in fear of Lola's dream coming true, another part feels angry with himself for allowing his son to fall into such danger. He blames himself for allowing the nurse to take his son.

"Sam please find our son!" Lola cries.

Emboldened and full of courage, Sam remembers the scripture 1 Timothy 1:7, that God has not given a spirit of fear. Holding Lola, he places a kiss on her forehead and reassures her that he would find their son. Finishing her prayer, Marlinda looks at Lola and comforts her.

"Child, that witch won't take your baby. Not on my watch! Do you remember what she looked like or her name?" Marlinda asks Lola, returning to the conversation after her bout of prayer.

"No. No, I don't. I just remember her voice."

"We gotta find this woman now! Time is running out! Do you remember what she looked like?" Marlinda asked Sam, grabbing a hold of his arm.

The nurse tries to muffle the infant's cries, as she rushes down the hospital hallways. Being careful not to draw attention, she hurries to the 12th floor elevator and presses the button fervently. As a doctor turns the corner, she darts over to the stairwell door, entering abruptly. She stops on the steps to catch her breath, as the baby begins to let out a loud cry.

"Shut up!" she yells, frustrated.

She begins to get nervous, as she feels that someone will soon discover what she has done. Walking outside with a newborn baby in broad daylight and impersonating a nurse is already risky enough. The loud sound of a door slamming startles her out of her thoughts. Nervously, she looks over the railing to see the apparition of a woman with pasty, bleached skin in hospital garments motioning her to come down the stairs. As she begins to follow the apparition down to the 8th floor, the woman's arms begin to tire. This small baby was beginning to feel as if he was twice his size. She knows that if she does not escape quickly, her arms will give out.

Meanwhile, Sam gives Marlinda his best description of the nurse that took baby Elias. They walk over to the nurse's station outside of Lola's room to see if the nurse knows who the mysterious woman could be, but to no avail. No one has seen her or even knows of a nurse that fits the description. Exhausting all their options to find out the identity of this nurse, Sam's frustration begins to set in.

"You gotta be kidding me. You telling me nobody has seen this nurse?"

"There can only be so many nurses here and we are running

out of time. They could be anywhere by now!" Marlinda explains.

She tries to calm Sam down, but her words just make the situation worse. Suddenly, a still, small voice tells her to quickly go down to the 8th floor. "Sam, come with me."

"Where are we going?"

"Sam, please!" Marlinda says, losing her patience.

"Tis not the time to be lookin' at stuff with them natural eyes. If you would just start listenin' to the voice of the Lord, ya would've heard the same thing I heard, which was go down to the 8th floor. Now let's go!"

They run down the hall towards the elevator. As Sam reaches to press the button signaling the elevator, a power surge causes a brief blackout throughout the hospital.

The 12th floor is thrown into a state of panic as medical staff rush to check on patients that are on powered equipment. Loud beeps and alarms blanket the halls, as doctors and nurses scurry about in every direction. The wave of noise coming from all around is deafening. With everyone else panicking, Marlinda knows that their time to save Elias is coming to an end. Invigorated with strength, she grabs Sam's hand and they dart down the stairs to find the missing nurse.

Stopping abruptly as the lights flicker, the nurse quickly snaps into action, this being an opportune time for her to escape the hospital. With baby Elias in tow, she runs down the stairs, floor by floor, the strength in her arms wavering. Huffing and puffing, she continues down each flight of stairs finally reaching the 2nd floor. Noticing that the exit to the main floor is by elevator only, she hesitantly steps through the door and sees that people are still trying to recover from the power surge. She walks down a seemingly empty hallway and presses the elevator button, finally at ease since the baby has gone quiet. Stepping inside, like a chameleon, she blends in with the passengers on the elevator as she prepares to make her grand escape.

Running down various hallways and stairwells, Marlinda and Sam desperately try to catch up with the missing nurse. Marlinda thinks to herself that this is the most exercise she has ever gotten, but quickly pushes the thought aside, refusing to allow the baby to be used as a weapon for the children of the devil. Finally, arriving on the 8th floor, they check around to see any signs of the missing nurse.

"Tabbi!" Marlinda shouts after spotting a familiar face, a nurse she has worked weekends with previously. Huffing and puffing, Marlinda and Sam rush to meet Tabitha.

"You know that is not my name! My name is Tabitha and I have no time for your shenanigans Marlinda" Tabitha says, irritated.

"And I don't have time for your smart mouth! We need your help. You help me first honey, and I might try to learn your name."

"No, you won't Miss Marlinda. What can I do for you?" Tabitha chuckles. "We're looking for someone," Marlinda begins explaining the situation of the missing nurse to Tabitha.

"Oh God, does this nurse have blonde hair and silvery eyes?"

"Yes!" Sam says.

"Please tell me you seen her," Marlinda begs.

"Yes, I saw her running down the hallway in a long coat. She had something in her hands. I thought it was strange, but then you know, all hell broke loose".

Sam, feeling worried that they might have missed their only window of opportunity to save his son, hangs his head. Marlinda grabs his hand, sensing the heaviness of his heart. "Don't worry baby, she won't get far," she reassures him, giving his hand a squeeze. Tabitha runs over to the computer behind the counter, trying to look up the missing nurse's information to no avail since the generators are just beginning to kick in.

"The computer won't load properly!" Tabitha yells, pondering what she can do to help. She notices a security guard rushing down the hall to help a doctor. "Hey! Excuse me!"

Hearing a voice, the guard turned to see who yelled but could not distinguish the one voice amongst the chaos. Tabitha yells once more, but this time incorporates hand motions with her voice, getting his attention.

"What's up? I can't sit here and talk," the guard approaches the counter, impatiently.

"Quick, is Larry here? We have a huge problem".

"Ya think?"

"Is he or isn't he?" Tabitha demands, glaring in response to his sarcasm.

"Yes he—" The guard begins but is interrupted as a doctor calls out for help.

"Yeah, just call extension 3469".

Tabitha thanks him as she quickly dials Larry's extension. Marlinda and Sam stare impatiently, hoping that Larry would pick up. The ringing subsides as a deep voice answers the phone.

"Yo, this is Larry".

Tabitha hands the phone over to Marlinda, "Larry, this is Marlinda. Listen, we don't have time for small talk. There is someone in this hospital posing as a nurse and she's using this chaos as her meal ticket. To make the situation worse, she ran off with a couple's newborn baby. Can you please help us?" Larry and Marlinda speak for brief moment before she hangs up the phone.

"So, what did he say? Does he know where my son and the nurse are?"

"From what he saw, they were last on the second floor. He radioed in to all the guards on duty and they are on the lookout— where are you going Sam?" Marlinda asks abruptly as he walks off. "We need a plan".

"I'm done with chasing after a shadow. I'm going to get my son." He says firmly. Tabitha stares at him as he walks down the hall. "Wow. Ain't nothing like a man that can take charge!" she exclaims, eyes bright.

"How the kids today says it? Don't be thirsty." Marlinda snaps, side-eyeing Tabitha.

Exiting the elevator on the first floor, the nurse begins to rush down the corridor, as the baby cries. Each turn she took, she began to see signs pointing to the main entrance. Turn by turn, she becomes more confident in her escape. Making the final turn into the main lobby, she sees a guard walking towards her, glaring and speaking into his walkie. Feeling as though she has been found out, she steps back slowly, pivoting to retreat back the way she came. *"I will head to the south exit"* she thinks aloud as the baby cries, drawing more and more attention. Quickly walking down the corridor, she sees another guard, and frightened, makes a break for an office. Keying in the code, she waits for the guard to pass.

Slipping inside the office, she peeks through the small glass window waiting as guards walk by. Realizing that it is now or never, she muffles the baby's cries and darts out the office. She runs, following the signs that direct her to the south entrance of the hospital, but stumbles to an abrupt stop. Her eyes grow wide in awe of the sight unfolding before her; a grand figure stands blocking the exit, blinding light shining as bright as the sun in all its glory. Terrified, she shakily recites a chant call for help as the angel unsheathes its large sword. Bystanders began to look on worried, as this woman clutches this newborn baby. Struck with fear, she looks around to find a way out.

"Give us the baby ma'am!"

"No!!!"

God gives Marlinda the sight to see the angels, wielding swords, surrounding them. She slowly lifts her head and sees an angel at the door. She is terrified as the angel unsheathes the sword on its back. She whispers some words, trying to call on some help but nothing happens. Bystanders begin to look on in worry at the woman on the ground clutching the newborn baby. As they try to help her, a guard approaches the forming crowd, causing her to flee back towards the way she came, only to be halted by the presence of another angel standing behind her. Pale with fear, she realizes she is surrounded by angels, frantically turning in circles trying to find an out.

Sam, Marlinda, and their entourage of security rush into the south entrance corridor, slowing to a stop as they see the scene before them. Sam looks on, his mind flooded with all sorts of thoughts as he sees the woman with his son. Is the baby dead? Why can't he hear the baby's cries? How will this end?

"What are you doing with that baby ma'am?" a guard asks.

Looking around, Marlinda realizes they are surrounded by sword-wielding angels.

"No harm will come to the baby, Sam." she reassures him, relieved.

"What are you doing with my son?" Sam demands, taking a step forward.

The nurse remains unresponsive, staring at the doors. Marlinda begins to quietly pray in the spirit as she watches Sam.

"I am only going to say this once. Let. Go. Of. My. Son!"

"You take one step and I will kill him!" she hisses.

"Stand back sir!" the guards stand at the ready, their guns drawn.

"No! No, you won't. I don't know why you won't, but this is the end of the line for you. You see, Jesus told me that everything will be okay. So, he had to have known that this was going to happen. That being the case, you have already lost. So, give me my son."

Fearfully, she glances around, shaking like a leaf. She goes to put a hand on the child, but the angel behind her takes a step forward. "Here just take the boy. I just want to make it out of here alive." she pleads, sticking her arms out towards Sam as he slowly approaches her to take the baby.

As he turns to walk away, the nurse hastily reaches into her pocket, only to be tackled to the ground by a guard. Securing her hands in cuffs, the guard reveals from her pocket a sinister-looking, curved knife. Confiscating it, the guard sits her down in a chair as they wait for the police to arrive.

"Who are you? I want a name" Marlinda demands, but the nurse says nothing.

She just sits there frozen, watching Marlinda speak. Observing the woman's disheveled appearance further, Marlinda gasps, as she notices a bizarre tribal tattoo on her chest. Her study of the woman is interrupted before she could say anything else as Sam calls out to her.

"Marlinda? Is Elias alright? Why isn't he crying?"

"Baby, that boy slept through this whole thing. I guess he knew that Jesus had his back and that his dad being the tough guy that he is, would never let anything happen to him" Marlinda said laughing.

The doctors arrived to check Elias out as the group made their way back to Lola's room.

"Thank you! Thank you!" Lola tears up, having feared the worst. She holds her son and kisses Sam. "I love you so much."

"I love you too Lola."

Marlinda looks on smiling, as they interact with their son for the first time. Glancing upwards, she thanks Jesus softly for looking after them all. With tears in her eyes and a smile on her face, she begins to head out of the room.

"Marlinda, wait! You're not getting off that easy. Thank you for being there for us" Lola calls after her.

"Child, to God be the glory! I was just doing what any good

southern, Christian woman would do for another follower of Christ."

"No, you did more. I know it. I don't know how, but I do," Lola says looking down at Elias before looking back up at her. "Would you like to hold him?"

"No, no" Marlinda protested, not wanting to ruin their family moment. "This is family time baby, y'all be with each other."

Sam and Lola laugh, looking at her, "But you are family".

Chapter 3

A gentle wind blows through the window as the little girl plays with her new Barbie dolls. She runs over to her closet, grabs a dollhouse, and begins to pretend that the Barbie she had named Alice, and the male doll, who she had creatively named Paul, were a family. She places the two into a toy car and races it across the floor. The wooden floors creak, as the toy car runs across the floorboards. She has created a perfect family with a beautiful home.

"Quiet down!" her mother says. She hears her mother yell from downstairs to stop making so much noise.

"Yes momma!" the girl calls from the top of the stairs.

With the window open, warm air blowing, and the sun beaming in, she thinks to herself, "*the setting was perfect! Daddy would be so happy to see how this looks.*" She rushes to the bedroom door, as her mother comes up the stairs.

"Is it time momma?" she asks with excitement.

"Yes, it is. Hurry up, I don't want to be there all day," her mother says, irritated.

"It's already bad enough I gotta see this man," she murmurs.

The girl rushes to grab her jacket from the closet and leaves her room. Quickly, she walks back and snaps a picture of the dollhouse and playset she has made for her dolls, using her tablet. The girl and her mother go into their car and begin to drive to the airport.

"Can you roll down my window a little, momma? It's hot!"

Her mother cracks the back windows, allowing a breeze to

come in. She looks on in amazement of what she sees on the countryside. She sits back, relaxed, and let the cool breeze blanket her. The mother glances in the rearview mirror and smiles seeing her daughter was fast asleep. She rolls her window down as well. *"There is nothing in this world like summer Memphis weather"*, the woman thinks to herself.

Several hours later, she pulls the car into the arrival parking at the airport, her daughter seemingly unconscious in the backseat. She looks at the doors and then into the rearview mirror. Her irritation begins to set in as she thinks about seeing him again.

"I'm doing this for her. I am doing this for her." She tries to convince herself but can't stop thinking about the situation. She stops briefly to compose herself, but her feelings begin to surface again as she speaks to her daughter, "Candice!"

"Yes, momma…" Candice says as she wakes up.

"Wake yo butt up and let's go. We here."

Candice unbuckles her belt with excitement, this is a momentous occasion for her. They enter the airport and Candice, ready, takes off running towards the gate.

"Girl, you don't even know what gate to go to," her mother called after her. Pausing, Candice, realized that her mother was right. "There's more than one gate momma? This is confusing."

"Well don't you run off. You stay with me. Last thing I need is to look like another Black woman that can't keep her child under control."

As they pass each gate, Candice becomes antsier. She watches and looks at everyone passing her by. To her, the people walking by look like giants walking through the busy airport. The plane has just arrived from Rome as they approach gate number 37. As people are coming in, Candice stands with wide eyes. She looks, anticipating the sight of a particular person, who in her eyes, is her knight in shining armor. Candice watches as 15 people come and go, but her knight has yet to appear. Just as she is about to give up hope, a tall Black man with a muscular build in a US Marine Corp uniform appears from the gate. She watches as he walks in with authority. Her eyes light up and her smile widens. Candice snatch away from her mother and yells so loudly that everyone within earshot turn to stare.

"Daddy! Daddy! Daddy! Daddy!" she runs to him and jumps into his arms. His deep voice reminds her of a rumbling tank.

"Heeeeyyyy! You have gotten so big! Let me see you," he says, holding her in his arms. He is filled with joy, as he sees his beautiful daughter. He looks past her to see the scowling face of her mother but does not pay her any attention. He puts Candice down, as he reaches to grab the diaper bag sitting beside him on the ground.

Candice looks up and sees a short woman with red hair, who has a funny accent, steps out from behind him. She hears the woman mention to her father that she needs to find a restroom. Her mother looks at the woman curiously and quickly becomes infuriated when she notices the ring on the woman's finger. Her anger turns to pure shock, as she sees the woman is carrying a baby in her arms.

"Candice, Daddy needs to talk to you." He says before kissing the woman and looking down at his daughter.

Choose ye this day…

In the small town of Poughkeepsie, near the shopping district, the shadow figure walks up and down the streets, looking at the people. It sees them walking about, doing meaningless tasks, going to different stores, and playing basketball at a local park. It sees all the other spirits that are at work, placing thoughts of deception, perversion, lust and other malevolent thoughts into the minds of people. Just looking at the people there, fuels its hatred for all of mankind. *"These insignificant people. They are weak and easily influenced"*, it thinks. As the figure continues to stand and watch the people around, it sees a man approaching. Unbeknownst to the man, he walks past the figure; he is not able to see it with his physical eyes. Just looking at the man angers the figure. Its contempt for humanity grows and grows. It watches as the man stops at the corner, waiting for the light to turn green and crosses the street, but as it turns to follow him, it sees angels flying around the man.

"Hey, hey, look, I don't want any trouble," it says, nervously.

The angels glare at the figure until it slowly backs away from the man and runs off, too weak to even attempt to stand toe-to-toe with one angel, let alone four of them. It runs away, back to the alley where it meets up with Jim, the demonic spirit that resides inside the body of a tall, slender man in a dusty, tan trench coat. Jim walks into the alley following behind the figure. From the perspective of those that see the man, he appears only to be a homeless guy that is a nuisance and a total eyesore to those whose storefronts he frequents. The neighborhood kids made up stories about how he became a deranged lunatic that always repeated the same phrase "ashes to ashes, dust to dust" over and over. Some of the kids believe he is a Vietnam War veteran that went crazy after all the things he had seen. Some even think that he was an escapee, a mental patient from upstate. No matter what the story is that people have, most of the locals try to avoid him.

"Why are you so jumpy?" Jim asks.

"You didn't see what I saw. I mean this place is craw—"

"Enough! Your new orders from the office are in. This is of the utmost importance. There is a woman, not too far from here, that could be a problem down the road. She's kind of at a crossroads right now and I want you to push her over the edge. Get. The. Job. Done!"

The shadow figure leaves Jim in the alley to strategize over ending the woman. It sees the woman and monitors her for hours, trying to pick out the right opportunity to strike. As the woman leaves the grocery store and begins to drive home, it listens to her speak as she drives down the road.

"I'm working all these hours at this dumb job and I barely can buy food to eat."

Frustrated, she parks her car behind the small apartment building, grabbing the one, lonely bag of groceries she is able to afford. As she makes her way to the front door, she looks across the street to see three men shooting dice. Seeing the fear in her eyes, the shadow figure sees the perfect opportunity to strike. It scurries over to the tallest, Black man holding a pair of dice, and whispers in his ear.

"Yo, my bread gettin a lil low. Tonight, we hittin' that building" he says suddenly to the group, eyeing the woman as she walks through the door.

Madison wakes up in the middle of the afternoon to the silence of the apartment.

She looks over to her window and sees that the sun is shining, and the birds are chirping. She rolls slowly out of the bed, in pain from the beating that James had given her. She glances at her arms and waist to see that the bruises are still there. She leaves her room and looks around to see that nobody was home except for her. This is normal for her, being left alone in the apartment for days without seeing her mother or James. She walks into the kitchen to make herself a bowl of cereal and watch cartoons. She sits in front of the TV with her bowl of cereal and bows her head to say grace.

"God, thank you for waking me up. Bless my food in Jesus name. Amen!" She laughs and laughs at her favorite cartoon but begins to worry about her mother because of James hitting her just days ago.

As she stands up, pain shoots through her small body and she falls back down onto her butt.

"Ouch!!!!" she cries.

With tears flowing down her face, she begins to sob, wondering why she had been beaten. Was her momma and daddy mad at her? Is it her fault that she has gotten beaten so badly and so often? Madison remembers seeing her granny crying and calling out to God. And so, that is what she does.

"God, what did I do? Why do momma and daddy hate me?"

She cries in the middle of the room, hoping that God will hear her and speak back, but she hears nothing, only the sounds coming from the TV. She lays on the ground, curled up in the living room with tears flowing down her face, too sore to move. She slowly begins to drift off to sleep.

By nightfall, the three men have been watching the woman all day, looking to break into her place. The three approach the building looking for a way to sneak in with the shadow figure watching not far off, thinking how easy it has been to influence them to terrorize the woman. *"This might actually be the easiest assignment the office has ever given me. This is such a waste of time!"* It thinks. Reluctantly, it follows them into the building, seeing as it could not afford to have the fools screw things up. Silently, they go up the stairs to get to the woman's apartment.

"What floor is she on, man?" one of them asks, out of breath.

"The sixth," replied another.

"Are you serious? Man, she better have some stuff in there worth stealing!"

While the other two thieves continue to banter, the leader looks back annoyed and tells them both to shut up before they wake up the sleeping residents. The figure looks at them in utter disgust, as they bicker about what they are going to do with the money they find. Finally, the three thieves arrive on the sixth floor, looking for her apartment number.

"Are you sure this is her apartment number?"

"Yeah man. I made sure to case this floor to make sure," one of the thieves whispered. They approach the apartment unit. One of them put his ear to the door to determine if there is any movement inside.

"Yo, I'm hearing total silence. We can pick this lock and be right in there." "Are you sure this is her unit?"

"I think. I mean, I didn't come up with the idea to do this. I just agreed to it. Mike is the one who said we were robbin' this lady. Ask him."

In a fit of rage, the shadow figure slams its hand on the wall.

"Oh, what the— what was that sound?"

"Man, dude I'm not feeling this. This is like some scary movie type stuff." Looking at his two boys acting like some little punks, Mike decides to try and pick the lock.

"These guys are some idiots!" the figure says to itself. Frustrated, instead of guiding the thieves to the right unit, it says nothing as the three breaks into an empty apartment.

"An empty apartment!" Mike yells as his voice echoes down the hallway.

Mike's yell inadvertently wakes up the woman they meant to rob, who lives across the hall from that empty unit. She looks through the peephole.

Seeing them, she dials 911 on her cell.

"Yo Mike, thanks for waking up the whole floor." "Fool, shut up! We gotta go!"

Just as they try to escape, they hear sirens from outside of the building. They rush out, only to be met by the Poughkeepsie police. The shadow figure watches as they are arrested. "This was a waste of my time. At least I got a good laugh out of these idiots."

The woman down the hall looks out of her window as the men are arrested. She thinks to herself that they could have broken into her apartment had she not woken up in time.

"I don't know who was looking out for me, but whoever you are, thank you." The shadow figure's eavesdropping is suddenly interrupted as it is yanked out of

the building and dropped onto a random street. Prepared to fight, it looks around only to be greeted by Jim again. "Oh. Hey, I thought you were something—"

"Silence! I thought I told you that you were to push the woman over the edge? Not make her thankful! We wanted her to be depressed and to hate the life that God has given her. Now, if you couldn't pull this simple task off, why is it that I should assign you to that Madison child?"

Unable to speak, the figure stares at Jim in silence.

"This is the part where you speak."

"Oh, my bad. Listen, the only reason why that was a bust was because of the foolishness of those three guys. They had one job, and they blew it! That's not on me. They were boring and a waste of time anyway. Trying to destroy them and that woman was a waste."

Jim glares at the figure, infuriated.

"Look, you know my talents are better suited with that family. I mean, look at the damage I've done already. That little girl's life is going to be trash. It's her thoughts of worthlessness and low self-esteem, which keeps a door open for me."

Jim nods in agreement with the shadow figure, as it pleads its case.

"You keep me on that girl and I will make sure she destroys her life and the lives of everyone she touches."

"I'm glad you think so, because the office is sending someone to assist. That spirit is already working on James."

Jim approaches the figure and, in an instant, they are in the same location as James. They arrive at a bar called Tony's, where they see James with a woman. He is completely mesmerized by her beauty, looking upon her as if she was a goddess. He tries to form the words to praise this goddess, but cannot form them properly, as he is totally drunk. James only sees the woman, Jim and the shadow figure, on the other hand, seeing the demonic entity that has taken possession of the woman.

"Oh, she is good." The shadow figure says, as it watches the two converse.

"You have no idea. This is who you will be working with. We're ramping things up with Madison. It's time to execute our plan."

Chapter 4

As the doorbell rings at a house in Brooklyn Heights, New York, the little boy steps out of his room to see who is coming. He peers between the bars of the railing at the top of the stairs to see a group of people, hugging his mother as they enter. As she looks up, their eyes lock briefly before she smiles and begins climbing the spiral staircase toward him. He runs into his room, hiding behind the door as his mother walks into the bedroom, looking for him.

"William? William, I have no time for games. Where are you?" Rebecca calls. "Boo!"

Expecting his surprise, Rebecca turns and tickles him.

"Stop! Stop mom! I give, I give!" William shouts, laughing uncontrollably.

"See, that's what you get!" Rebecca says, hugging him tightly. Brushing his hair back, Rebecca looks into his eyes,

"Mommy loves you so much, Bill."

"Stop mom," William says, blushing.

"Hush. Listen, you know the rules. No matter what you hear, you do—"

"I know, I do not leave my room, if I have to go to the bathroom, I go to the one on this floor and back to my room and follow everything my sister tells me to do no matter what it is. I'm not dumb."

"I never said you were, but your mommy and daddy are about to take care of some things with our friends, and you cannot get in the way. I don't want you to get hurt."

Not fully understanding, William agrees, nodding as Rebecca kisses him on his forehead.

"Rebecca, stop messing with the boy and let's go!" "Coming, Damian," Rebecca says annoyed.

As she leaves the room and shuts the door behind her, William overhears his mother speaking to his sister, Lilith. Not able to make out what is being said, he hears his mother walk down the stairs. Lilith steps into William's room, pulling the curtains shut. She frantically walks throughout the room, making sure he has everything he needs.

"Lilly, are you okay?"

".... Yes. I'm fine. I just need to keep you safe."

"Why would I not be safe? I want to get a snack. Let's get some ice cream!"

"No! We cannot go downstairs under any circumstances."

"But why? This is stupid."

Irritated by William's whining, Lilith picks up her headphones and turns on some music from her phone. William plays with his robot action figures in silence, the rumbling of his stomach brings his play to an abrupt stop.

"Lilly, I have to go to the bathroom."

Lilly nods, waving him off before looking back at her phone, not paying William any attention. William quickly walks out of the room, shutting the door quietly behind him. After his trip to the bathroom down the hall, a loud crash causes him to carefully peer over the banister and look out to the main floor, but he sees nothing. William begins to think about the ice cream he wants. *"Mommy told me to listen to my sister and to stay on this floor,"* he thinks to himself. Deciding not to listen to his mother and sister, he decides to venture downstairs to the kitchen. Back in William's room, Lilith calls out to William, just to look up and see that he is not in the room anymore.

Whom you will serve

Samuel hears the baby crying on the monitor. He groans and Lola looks at him.

"What?" Samuel asks, exhausted.

"Go ahead and get him. It is your turn anyway." "When did it become my turn?"

"It became your turn after the last three times I went into his room, and you were playing like you were sleeping."

Sam agrees, though he is exhausted and not in the mood to argue with Lola. He goes into Elias' room and picks him up. With the baby in his arms, he walks over to the chair in the room and begins to talk to him.

"What is wrong, Son?? You just refuse to let your daddy sleep huh?"

Elias just stares at him, slightly whining. Sam begins to tell his son all about how he plans for them to play video games together, go to football games and how he is going to teach him all about how to be a good man of God.

"You know Elias, me and your mother have had our issues…. really big issues, but one thing I can tell you is that Jesus be really coming through for us. I've learned that He really is a counselor."

Elias just looks at Sam and smiles.

"And I'm sitting here confessing my thoughts to a baby that doesn't understand a word I'm saying……great Sam, shows you ain't got no type of friends."

Sam begins to tell Elias all of the issues he has had and how he and Lola really struggle mentally, because of the choices that they have made.

"I was in love with your mother from the day I met her at church. She was….and still is I might add, the most beautiful woman I've ever seen. Now don't get me wrong, your mother is extremely feisty… like this woman is a firecracker, the very definition of sass. Maybe that's what really drew me to her…"

Sam looks and notices that Elias is looking at him so attentively, as if he understands every word that he is saying.

"Wow…I see you are going to be a great listener. Anyway, I…I didn't always do right by her. I didn't do anything crazy like put my hands on her or anything, but I failed her in other ways, ways that are just as bad. Honestly, I feel like I failed her as a leader. I feel like I failed her as a man. Honestly, I feel like I failed Jesus because of what I have done."

Tears begin to swell up in his eyes as he rocks Elias in his arms.

"I know in God's Word it says that if I confess my sins, then Jesus is faithful and just and will forgive them and cleanse me of that wickedness, but if I had to be honest, I don't feel all that clean. I still feel dirty. I wasn't so scared of losing you back at that hospital, but I am terrified of failing you too."

Sam just continues to talk and while he is talking, he looks down to see that Elias is knocked out cold and seems to have been out for a while. Sam looks at Elias and smiles.

"Jesus, I guess you were the only one listening huh? I want to do so much better. I will do better and I will do right by you, Father."

He goes back to Lola's room to see that she is also sleeping. He stands in the doorway looking at her, reminiscing about all the times they had argued about the dumbest things, the times where they were just mad at each other, and Jesus had to get them both together. He thinks about how much he appreciates Jesus making sure that she and Elias were safe during that whole hospital incident. He hears his phone vibrate and looks to see that it is a text from Marlinda saying:

"Hey Sam! I hope all is well! I was in prayer, reading first John chapter one and I love this book. It brings me so much joy, but as I was studying it out, God just began to speak to me and while He was talking, I just began to cry and I don't even know why. I know what you are probably thinking, 'Women problems' right? Well no. To make this brief, He told me to tell you that baby, He has already forgiven you and He loves you so much. You need to forgive yourself now. He also said that as long as you stay connected to Him, you will never lack nor will you ever fail. Yo Daddy ain't raise no failure! Now pick yo self up by the bootstraps and keep movin'! You got too much kingdom work to do to be cryin' ova spilled milk. He forgives you, Lola forgives you, now move on! God has more for you baby!"

He smiles and laughs. "Thank you, Jesus…You are so faithful to me!"

He replies to Marlinda's text. Before he hits send, he looks back at Lola and smiles, finally feeling free. He goes into Elias's room, grabs the baby bag and begins to pack it. He packs the bag and writes a note to Lola saying that he is going to the store, and he is taking Elias with him for a while. He also tells her that he wants to see her at 8 tonight to take her out to dinner since he knows she always wakes up from a nap hungry. With Elias in hand and the baby bag across him, Sam quickly straps Elias in the car seat and gets in the car himself. He calls up Marlinda.

"Hello Sam…You could have just replied to the text, you know. I was just about to watch some football."

"What you know about football, Marlinda?"

"More than you do…so what's wrong baby? Is Elias okay??"

"Oh yes yes…He is fine. However, I was calling to see if you could come with me and Elias to the mall? I need some help with ring shopping."

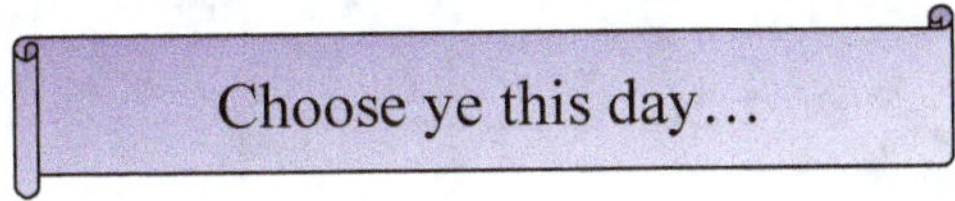

In a panic, Lilith snatches out her headphones and runs to the bathroom that is on that floor. Poking her head in, she calls out to him. However, she hears no response. She looks over the railing of the stairs to see if she sees him, but still nothing. She rushes down the stairs and sees that the front door is still locked so he did not leave the house. This is not a good sign, considering the alternative. She looks to the left and the right, trying to surmise which way he could have gone. Her worry slowly turns to fear as she hopes he did not go towards the basement, as they are forbidden to go near the basement when mom and dad have company. Lilith turns right and searches every room she comes across.

"Bill…..BILL!!!" she says as she goes in and out of rooms.

She hears this banging sound come from the direction of the kitchen and she runs into the kitchen to see that he is not there, but there is an open pack of cookies on the countertop. As she stands in the kitchen, she begins to feel weird. She notices that the air in the kitchen is totally different from the upstairs. As she knows what goes on in the house when her parents have "company", she knows that if she and her brother are caught down there, then their father will not be pleased. These fears are all but confirmed as she hears voices and the commotion of people coming up the stairs. She rushes out the kitchen and runs past the study to find her brother in there picking up random books to read.

"Look Lily! These are some funny looking books. Why do they look so old?"

Lilith snatches William off their Dad's desk.

"Have you lost your mind?!?!" Lilith whispers.

"Do you have any idea what will happen if Dad finds us down here?"

"I just…"

She looks down at the book he opened and realizes what it

was, closes it and tells him to never pick up that book or come in here ever again. He agrees and she grabs his arm to run out of their father's study, but just as they are about to leave, they are met at the door by their mother. She pushes them back into the study and slams the door.

"Are you two trying to get in trouble??" Rebecca whispers.

As Lilith tries to explain what happened, Rebecca cuts her off.

"I do not want to hear it. You know the rules, young lady!"

Rebecca remembers to lower her voice, as she does not want to alert their father.

"Mommy don't blame Lily. It was me. I just wanted a snack and she had told me not to come down here, but I did it anyway," William explains to their mother.

She embraces them both, apologizing for being upset. She raises her eyes, as she notices one of the books on the shelf missing.

"Um…Where is that book that was up there??? Rebecca says as she runs to the shelf.

"I caught William reading one of the books."

Looking at the book he opened, she is in shock. "Don't ever open this book again…. either of you. Am I clear?"

"Yes," Lilith and William say, looking at her.

Rebecca puts the book back on the shelf and walks them both to the door of the study. She cracks the door and peeks out as she sees her husband speaking to one of their friends. She never had any interaction with this friend in particular, but she knows that this is one that is extremely influential and powerful. As she hears them talking, she pushes the kids behind her and closes the door slightly. She leaves the door open just enough so that she can hear them speak, but they will not see her. While she is listening, Lilith and William begin to argue. She turns to them, telling them to be quiet as she is trying to get them out of there. As she is listening, she is shocked by what she hears.

Lilith notices how shaken she becomes, as Rebecca almost collapses.

"Mom, are you okay?"

"No…he wouldn't…He would not agree to something like that…"

"Mom!"

Rebecca comes to, reassuring her that she is fine. She eases them out of the study through another door that connects to the kitchen. Their father closes the front door and heads to where he hears people talking and runs into his family eating cookies.

"Why are you kids down here? What did I tell you both about…"

"Damian, please the kids and I just wanted a snack." Rebecca says, cutting him off. As he looks at her, the kids bid him to come into the kitchen to join them. He passes and walks out of the kitchen. William asks his mom why their dad did not join them, but she makes up some excuse about him being tired from their meeting and tells him not to worry about it. As the kids and Rebecca enjoy the cookies, she cannot help but think to herself, *"Could Damian really be capable of something so terrible?"*

Whom you will serve

"How about this ring, Sam?" Marlinda says gazing at the brilliance of the diamond at the center.

"No, that one won't do either. This is really frustrating."

"No child, what is frustrating is you got this old woman out here in the mall for an hour and a half and you cannot even find one that you would even consider as being the one," Marlinda says with an irritated tone.

"Sorry, Ms. Marlinda. I just want to find the perfect one. It has to be the one that just screams **Lola**."

Marlinda laughs as she grabs Elias out of the stroller to hold him. She plays with him, making some funny faces as Sam continues his search in the store. Sam bids the lady behind the counter farewell and leaves out to the new jewelry store in the mall. As they walk, Marlinda begins to talk with Sam about how he is going to propose to Lola and if he has a dream scenario.

With sarcasm, he responds, "My dream scenario is for her to say yes."

Marlinda just side-eye glances Sam, as he laughs.

"I'm kidding. However, I really don't know."

"I'm sure you'll think of something."

Elias starts crying, as they continue to talk.

"I think he is hungry," she says and then her stomach begins to grumble.

"And apparently so are you," Sam says to her, as she laughs.

They stop at the food court in the mall to grab some food. Marlinda places Elias back in the stroller with his bottle as she and Sam sit to enjoy their food. They begin to talk about their journey with Christ and reminisce about the highs and lows. Sam talks about how he never thought that he would be here in a mall buying a ring to propose to Lola. Marlinda laughs as she explains to him that Jesus can give you the unexpected, but it will be the thing that is good for you.

"I can agree with you there because honestly, Lola didn't like me when she first met me at our church." Sam said laughing.

"Really??? Now that is a surprise, considering how dat girl look at you. That's all love right there baby."

"Well…it wasn't always like that Marlinda. I remember the first time she came into the church with her parents and her best friend Carla. We both were in College. Heck, I didn't even know we went to the same university until I noticed her at lunch. At the time, I was in a complicated relationship with someone else."

"Aww, look at that! College sweethearts! What was with the other relationship?"

Blushing, Sam brushes her off and continues with his story.

"That story is complicated….however, I was at church and she was sitting in the aisle across from me. Me being me, I couldn't help but to keep looking her way from time to time. I think she even noticed that I was looking at her. I was trying to keep my cool and everything."

Marlinda smirks, trying not to laugh as he can do anything but keep his cool. "What church do you go to?"

"Tabernacle of Faith. It is right here in the city on the west side. What's crazy is that it was the same day she gave her life to Christ. I was even there for her baptism. I wouldn't find out until later that she received the Holy Spirit that same day. I remember seeing her walk out and I was trying to reach her but I didn't. I asked the Lord that day to allow me to meet her again and would you know, I found out that we had the same class together."

"Look at God!"

"Right! We were both freshmen at the time. The next time I actually got to meet her was at church. We ended up sitting right next to each other. I finally introduced myself to her and she told me that her name was Lola. Marlinda, I promise you, I had never seen eyes as beautiful as hers. I mean they are like this golden brown, but when you look at them, you can tell there is something deeper and I was just amazed."

Marlinda just shakes her head as she listens.

"Why are you shaking your head?"

"Because y'all are so cute, but why did she not like you at first?"

"Because she said, I entertained a lot of foolishness in the church…of the female kind. She ended up going to a different school after our first year. Not to mention, I was finally getting moving on from the space and place I was in."

"Ooooh so the plot thickens…okay."

"It was not like that. I became a minister at our church and she sang in the choir. Lola has the most beautiful voice. It is so sweet, while being powerful at the same time. Oh, and the girl can hold a note. However, she didn't like the fact that I would have a lot of ladies around me and that I would always allow them in my space. I remember this one time I was with all my friends and it was a gathering for someone we both knew. She came in with this beautiful red and black dress. She had curly black hair with these highlights. The woman was bad! She was gorgeous, but she wouldn't give me the time of day. It wasn't until I prayed about it that God really showed me why. He had to show me that she did like me, but she refused to be just a random chick that flirted with me. She desired more and I had to make a choice."

"Between the legion of Jezebels…I mean the young women that were no good for you or the woman that God has for you."

Laughing, Sam says, "Legion of Jezebels?? Oh, that is a good one. I gotta tell Lola that one, but yes you are right. So, I chose her and we started dating and made everything official and stuff. That's when I saw people, both in the church and in the world, who were so jealous of us. People would do some of the meanest things, everything from starting rumors to lying to actually trying to set us up to cheat."

"Oh, my goodness! Are you serious?!"

"Yes ma'am. It really came from my friends, but we stayed close to Jesus and continued to press forward. However, that's when things started turning left."

"Turning left? What does that mean?"

"Oh, I'm sorry, turning bad."

"Oh, I see…Talk next time. You know I don't know yall millennials' slang." "Things got bad because Lola started noticing that the women that would try to come my way were my friends and it started making her jealous. She allowed jealousy to get in her heart and that attitude of hers came out. Don't let her fool you, she is nice, but baby girl got some fire. So naturally, we started arguing a lot and we started growing distant. I didn't know that she was struggling with jealousy, and I never cheated."

"So, you thought that she was being insecure?"

"Um…perhaps, but there were things that I could've done differently to make sure she didn't feel like that. We got over that and then there was the faithful night that we…well you know."

"Boy, if you don't just say yall had sex?! You act like we kids. We all grown at this table…well, besides the baby, but you get it."

"Sorry. Yes…we did and everything changed after that because the whole church knew that we were dating and she ended up pregnant."

"So, she hated you because she got pregnant?"

"No, it was because people started saying some really awful things about us, specifically her and….and I didn't defend her."

Marlinda was stunned to hear this. As he talked about it, she could see tears swelling in his eyes.

"You would be surprised at the names that they'd call her or the things that they'd say about her behind her back. She became furious with it because she felt like how could I let her be disrespected like that and she was my girlfriend and the mother of my child? Marlinda, I really regretted not being there for her like she wanted me to, but I was just trying to keep the peace. She was so heartbroken by what they were saying that she even quit being in the choir because of it. I mean I was happy about my son, but between the guilt of our sin against God and my guilt for what I did to Lola, I…I question if I should even marry her or if she would even say yes. I don't feel like I deserve her. I mean she put up with some terrible things and essentially I abandoned her."

Marlinda reaches in her purse, handing Sam some tissue.

"I am so sorry that you and Lola had to deal with that, but you have to forgive yourself. First John 4:9 says that the Lord is faithful to forgive our sins as we confess them. Did you repent?"

"Ye….yes."

"Then you gotta let that go baby. Remember what I messaged you and keep reminding yourself of it. God loves you so much. He knew you and Lola were going to make mistakes and that you were going to do this before y'all even met. You gotta let that go. If you don't, it will destroy you and Lola and will eventually cascade to your son. Now…. dry dem eyes and let's go get dat ring!"

Sam dries his eyes, grabs the stroller with Elias in it and they make their way to continue their search. As they are making their way to the center of the mall, Sam looks across at this small jewelry store and his eyes light up.

"I found it!" Sam and Marlinda walk over to the counter, where the ring is. Elias begins to fuss, being strapped into the stroller.

Sam takes him out and Elias points to the ring they are looking at saying, "Mmmmmm."

"Looks like Elias agrees with you Sam." Marlinda says, smiling at them both.

"Okay son, let's get mommy this ring."

Chapter 5

Candice's mom looks on in shock as she cannot believe that he would have the nerve to not tell her about this woman, not to mention this was a moment that should have been about Candice. The wife of Candice's father reaches out to Candice to greet her.

"Hi Candice! My name is…"

Before she can finish her sentence, Candice's mom pulls her away from the woman and looks at the father.

"How could you bring this…this woman here?!? This was supposed to be about you seeing your daughter, not you trying to flaunt this woman and your new baby around. You could have said something!"

"Enough, Diana," Candice's father whispered.

"Stop making a scene. You are very disrespectful to my family and to our daughter. We can talk about this more in private."

"No…. Bruce…No we aren't because this arrangement between us is done! You

never are around to take care of her anyway. Do you even know that she had a singing competition coming up?"

With a smile, he looks at Candice saying, "Wait, our daughter can sing?? When did this happen?"

"Well, you would know if you were around!" With tears in her face, Candice's mother says, "I loved you and you do this?!?"

She grabs Candice's arm and tells her that they are leaving and to say goodbye to her dad and his new family. Candice begins to cry as she wants her dad, begging not to go. One of the

TSA agents hears what is going on and comes over to make sure they are okay. Bruce tells them that they are fine, but he looks on with tears streaming down his face as he must watch his daughter be yanked away from him once again.

Choose ye this day…

Rolling over in her bed, Lola looks at the clock to see that it is almost 7pm. She quickly sits up, as she did not mean to sleep that long. She goes to Elias's room to see he is not in his crib. *"I guess you decided to go with your daddy, huh?"* she said to herself. She goes out of the room to get back in the bed when she notices a note written by Samuel. She smiles as she reads the note.

"Meet up for dinner 8pm."

"He knows me oh so well…" She said.

Realizing how close it is to eight o'clock, she runs into her room to get dressed.

Sam gets out of the car to give Elias to Marlinda as he is about to go pick up Lola for dinner. Marlinda looks at Sam as he hands her the carrier.

"Oh baby, you lookin' mighty fine! If I was just 20 years younger and you were single…."

Sam interrupts her, "Um…please stop. You're making me feel weird." Marlinda laughs at him, "Just kidding. So, are you ready? This is going to be a good day for you. I am so excited!!"

"Um…I will let you know after I tell her."

"Did you at least tell your friends that you were proposing to her?"

"Yeah, I did. They were super excited and wanted to see the engagement firsthand instead of just hearing about it, but I needed this to just be me and her, you know?"

"Yeah baby I do…Just remember to breathe," Marlinda said as she smacked him on the back.

"What was that for?"

"Go on ahead now. Me and Elias got some soaps to catch up on. I haven't seen them all week."

Sam waves bye to them and drives off. As he is driving down the entrance ramp to get onto the freeway, he rolls down his window to feel the summer night breeze. He begins to reflect on everything that he and Lola have gone through to get to where they are now, all the fights and all the tears they cried. Smiling, he realizes just how much he is in love with her and that he could not see himself with any other woman on the planet.

Whom you will serve

That evening, Bruce and wife, Alexandra, drive to Diana's house to try and speak with her again about the situation. They park in front of the house, and he cuts the car off. He stares at the house that he was once fond of, as he built that house from the ground up before he went back into the service. Alexandra grabs Bruce's hand, as she can feel how tense he is right now. With a soft voice, she reassures him that she loves him very much and knows how hard this must be. She reminds him that he is doing all this for Candice and not her mother.

"Thank you, Sweetheart. It is just…there were a lot of good times in this house, but there were too many bad times as well. I want Candice to have some sort of relationship with Bella, but I do not want to bring her and you into this."

She tells him that they will be fine and offers to pray for him before they go into the house to speak with Diana.

"You know, I would love that."

Alexandra begins to pray, "Father, we thank you for

goodness. We thank you for being so kind to us and keeping us through the good and the bad. Lord, Bruce really needs you. Give him the right words to speak to his daughter and Diana. Lord, I even ask that you would soften her heart to listen to what he has to say to her. Cover Candice and Isabella. I pray that as they grow up, that they will be there for each other. Allow Bruce to be receptive to what Diana is saying and to understand how she feels. We love you Father God and ask these things in Jesus name, Amen!"

Smiling, Bruce kisses Alexandra and they get out of the car with Isabella in the carrier, walking up to the door. Bruce takes a deep breath and rings the doorbell.

Choose ye this day…

For days, the shadow figure has watched James, studying him. It watches him fall further and further into depravity. In a twisted way, it finds his struggles entertaining. James has spent several days and nights away from his family, as he spends most of his time in a drunken stupor. James finds himself at this local club. He looks on as one of the women dances, gazing into James' eyes. The figure sees all the spirits that are at work in each person there. Some are influencing the people to make certain decisions, while others are fully possessed like the woman dancing. It looks on, as it sees that the opportunity will be coming soon to seal James' fate.

It walks through the club to sit beside James. It watches as James is mesmerized by the dance of the young woman. The woman approaches James, as he lustfully looks at her. The figure looks through the woman to see the perverse spirit that has taken refuge in her body. It laughs, as James has no idea what he is in for. "*If he only knew...see, this man is alright by me. He makes my job easy. Now, all I need is for this spirit to do its part so that I can execute on my end."*

James pushes the woman off him, as he feels himself getting sick. The woman sits beside the shadow figure and the spirit in the woman converse about how they plan on achieving their goal. For their plan to work, James must make all the right choices. Meanwhile, James is in a stall of the men's restroom vomiting violently due to all the liquor he has consumed. As he sits in the stall, he hears a whisper.

Terrified, James falls out of the stall and crawls to the wall. With his back against the wall, he looks around to see that there is nobody there. He slowly gets up and looks at himself in the mirror. He notices the long bags on his eyes and the roughness of his hands. *"This is stupid. All of this for that stupid woman and her miserable brat of a child. She is not even mine anyway."* Again, he hears the voice call out to him. The still, small voice tells him to leave now. James, still unable to distinguish the voice, stumbles out and leaves. Meanwhile in the club, the other spirit notices James. "You have to act now!" the figure says. "If you fail, me and you are finished." The other spirit assures the shadow figure that it has everything under control, as the woman goes over to James. James takes the woman by the hand, as she leads him to the back of the club.

Whom you will serve

Sam pulls up to the front of Lola's apartment. As she walks out of the front door, he sees her come out in a red and blue dress with some high heels to match. Sam breaks his neck to get out the car to open the car door for her. She giggles, as she gets in the car. They begin to make their way to the restaurant, recollecting on what they have been through since they found out they were having a baby.

"To think that we are actually parents…I don't know whether to be excited or to think that Elias is in for trouble with us, Sam."

"You are a great mother Lola. Your dad would have been so pleased with the woman you have become."

Lola looks down, as she begins to think about her father and how close they were. Sam places his hand on her lap.

"It's okay, Babe. He would not think any less of you."

"No…. but he would've killed you," She said, chuckling a little.

"Killed?? I would have met Jesus that same hour, like straightway, I would have been before the throne like 'see Jesus, what had happened was….'"

They both laugh as they pull up to the restaurant. She looks in amazement, as she sees the lights that trim the top of the establishment. They walk in and Sam tells the greeter that they have reservations. As they walk to the seats, she sees their whole table pre-staged with a dozen roses waiting for her. Tears begin to swell up, as she hugs Sam tight.

"Thank you so much Sam!" Lola says with tears. "This is so beautiful. I cannot believe you did this for me."

"Only the best for you."

The waiter comes to take their order. Lola looks around just to take in the scenery. She is amazed at how much thought he put into this date. They are sitting in the patio seating area that resembles a garden. The way the lights are surrounding them is refracting on the glass containing them makes this mesmerizing shimmer that blows her away. She looks down into Sam's eyes and smiles, as she has never been this happy before. She begins to see that through all their arguments, all her frustrations with him and herself, she is truly in love with him.

"What are you smiling about Lola?"

"Nothing…just taking in the moment. I don't want this

moment to go away.”

“Okay Sweetheart, but what if we could have moments like this forever?”

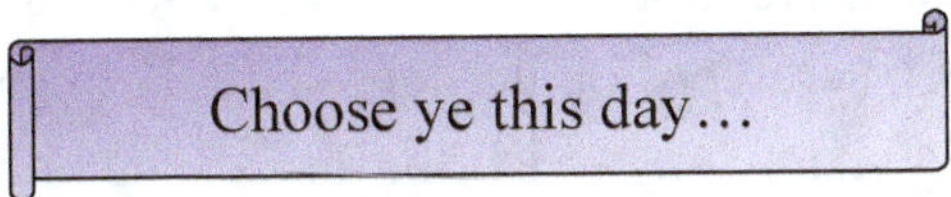

Still in shock from what she heard from Damian, Rebecca lays wide awake next to her husband, who is sound asleep. She knows her husband is not perfect, but he is not heartless. She begins to really dig deep into what is really going on with her husband. She climbs out of bed and walks down the stairs, going back into his office. Quietly, she closes the door, so as to not alert the rest of the family. She begins to search through his desk to find anything that would give her peace of mind. She looks at the bookcases and is amazed at the number of books he has. Most of the books he has not touched, but instead just collects. She picks up the book that her son had grabbed. She opens it and begins to feel strange as she begins to read it. She closes it quickly and continues to look around. She hears some footsteps coming down the stairs. She closes the drawer she opened and looks up as Lilith comes in.

“What are you doing here?” Rebecca whispers.

“I was walking to the kitchen and you got this bright light on. If you are trying…” “Lower your voice.”

Lowing her voice, Lilith says, “If you are trying to sneak around, this is a terrible way to do it.”

“What do you know about sneaking around young lady?”

“……no comment,” Lilith said nervously.

“Thought so. You need to leave.”

“No Mom. What is going on in this house? What are you and dad doing and why is it that I keep hearing footsteps in the house?”

"Nothing…wait, what do you mean footsteps?"

"Outside my bedroom, I can hear these steps and…."

"And what Lily? You can tell me."

Lilith sits down and pulls her pajama pants' leg up slightly to show these deep scratches on her legs. Totally in shock, Rebecca does not know what to say to Lilith. Inside, she knows what they probably are, but she chooses to disregard Lilith and just tell her that it is her scratching her legs in her sleep. She tells her not to worry and that she will just have the maid change detergents.

"Mom, you cannot be serious! These are not scratch marks that have come from my nails. My nails are not even that long. What is really going on here? What type of demonic stuff are you all into??"

"Demonic? You've been watching way too many movies and you need to keep your voice down."

As they continue to go back and forth, they hear a loud bang on the door that scares them both. Lilith grabs onto her mother, petrified. Rebecca tells her to stay behind her, as she walks toward the door. As she goes to put her ear to the door, she hears some more footsteps coming down the stairs.

"Mom, what was that??" Lily asks in a state of terror.

Rebecca says nothing to her.

"MOM!"

She shushes Lilith and motions her to go out the other door that leads into the kitchen. Rebecca follows behind her and tells her to keep their conversation between them.

Damian comes down the stairs, following the sounds he hears. He looks down the hall to see nothing, but notices that his study door is cracked open. He walks to the door, ready to yell at the kids to notice nobody was there. He cuts out the light and hears talking coming from the kitchen. He walks over to see his daughter and his wife eating ice cream and laughing.

"Um…why are you two up eating ice cream?"

Lilith pauses and looks up at her mom, "Oh, you know…just having a little girl talk, daddy. Are you trying to join us?"

"Oh no," Damian says, chuckling.

"You will not trap into your conversation about boys."

"Oh dad, you are always welcome into our conversations."

"Yes, Sweetheart. Come join us."

Damian smiles, walking over to them.

"As long as I get the big spoon and we don't wake up Bill."

They all sit, talking, and laughing all night long.

Whom you will serve

Lola sits there, speechless, as she does not know what is happening. "What do you mean about having moments like this forever?" Lola questions.

Sam looks at her smiling.

"Yeah, what if we can share moments like the one we are having now forever? Lola, I love you so much and I…"

Right before Sam could finish his statement, the food that they ordered comes out. Lola gazes at the food, as the aroma from it has her salivating. They pray over their food and Lola begins to eat when she stops to listen to Sam.

"Sam, I'm sorry. I got so distracted by this amazing food that you were in the middle of speaking."

Sam takes a deep breath and looks at Lola, smiling at her.

"Lola, we have known each other since we met in church during our college years and our relationship has not always been the best, but from the beginning, there has been a bond between us that has been undeniable."

"That is so sweet Sam! I love you very much."

"I love you too."

Sam pulls a small box out of his pocket and gets down on one knee. Tears begin to slowly fall down Lola's face, as she is in shock.

"Lola Sophia Martinez, will you marry me?"

Jumping out of her chair, she yells yes! All the people around them begin clapping, as they congratulate them both. Sam puts the ring on her finger, kissing her.

Two Years later...

Chapter 6

Smoke clouds fill the sky as the sounds of bombs are going off all around a small town called Baghran. People storm out of their homes filling the streets as they try to flee the explosions. The streets are littered with the bodies of those that died in the gunfire and car bombings. Armed men begin to storm each home in the town, dragging people out. Ali rushes to check on his kids as their mother struggles to pack their remaining bags.

"We must hurry! They are searching house by house," Ali says with a trembling voice. He goes back to the window as he sees his neighbors pointing to his house.

"We have to go now!! Talia, are the kids…."

Before he could finish his sentence, he hears banging on the door. Ali runs to his wife and kids to take them out of their home through a small hole that was made in the back. As the men kick down the door, Talia pushes her husband through the hole, kissing him goodbye with tears in her face. The men grab her and pull her outside. Ali quickly covers his mouth to muffle his yelling. Micah yells for his mom, but Ali puts his hand over his mouth, making him quiet. The men that raided the village put Talia in a line up in the middle of the village. The men came there in search of resources and to control the village.

Talia looks down the line that they have and begins to pray, as she knows the real reason they are there. One of the men comes to her and hears her praying. He makes a joke about her praying. Ignoring the brash comment, she tells him that her savior will come. The man hits her, telling her to shut up. Ali shuts his eyes and the eyes of his daughter, as they watch her being hit. However, Micah looks on crying. The men tell them in the line that they are to renounce Jesus Christ and His teachings or die. One by one, Talia watches as they senselessly kill those that are in the line as an example to the others.

Once the killing begins, Ali quickly grabs the kids and tells them to hide. Talia looks up, as her neighbors just watch. She knew that the people in the village knows that she is a Christian and believes in the Bible, as the inspired word of God; however, it breaks her heart to know that the same people that she laughed with, whose kids she fed when Jesus blessed her family with more than enough in times of famine, are the same people that led those terrible men straight to them. She just prayed that God would keep her family safe. She looks on as one by one they go to the people, some of them died, while some of them really denied Jesus and go back to follow Islam. With tears falling down her face, she looks up saying "Jesus, if this is really my time to go, please take care of my family and forgive those that turned from you out of fear." She sees a little boy and his sister next to him. She begins to intercede for them both, speaking in a different language that nobody around her understood. She looks at the boy and comforts him.

"You and your sister will not be harmed on this day."

"Ho.....how can you be so sure?" the boy says crying, as he grips his sister's hand.

Gripping his hand tightly, she says, "Because that is just what I believe. Jesus will save you."

The men finally get to her. Not being able to watch carnage any longer, he grabs his daughter and tells Micah that they must leave. Micah, still gazing over a broken wall, decides to stay. He feels compelled to stay, believing that the God his mother served will come to the rescue. He is torn between his desire to help her and his fear. He kneels hidden behind a broken wall, as he watches her being punched and kicked. After beating her, the men hold a gun to her head making her the same offer: to renounce Jesus Christ and His teachings or die. Talia, for a moment, looks past the men to see her son's eyes. She is overwhelmed with sadness, as she knows that this is the end, and this will be the last time she sees her son's beautiful brown eyes. She is overtaken with grief for a moment and begins to pray.

As Ali continues to run away from the village with his daughter, he turns to see that Micah is not with them.

"Where is your brother, Aiya?"

She shrugs her shoulders and asks for mommy, but he says nothing to her.

Realizing that Micah is still in the village, he picks up Aiya and heads back.

The men see that she is praying, but do not understand what she is saying, as she is praying in a language not known in that region. Out of frustration, the men kick her in her back and her face hits the dirt. She looks up at them and quotes Romans 8:27-28.

"And he that searcheth the hearts knoweth what is the mind of the Spirit because he maketh intercession for the saints according to the will of God. And we know that all things work together for good to those that love God, to those who are called according to his purpose."

The men are still confused, as she continues to pray in this unfamiliar language to them. One of them points his gun to her. With her final words, she says "I forgive...", but before she could finish her sentence, the man pulls the trigger. Micah watches as his mother lies motionless on the dirt in a pool of her own blood. Running back to the village, Ali hears the loud bang. It echoes through the desert. He falls to his knees crying while holding his daughter. His daughter, still confused about what is happening, wipes the tears from her dad's eyes and hugs him.

"It's okay poppa, don't cry." Picking up his daughter, he gets up to go after Micah.

Micah stares at his mother's body as he hopes that she will get up, that the God that she prays to every night will get her up. The men walk over to the little boy next to Talia's body. Right before they are about to take the children, a jet flies over the village, grabbing everyone's attention. The men begin to get nervous, speaking in their native language. The leader of the men motions to kill all the rest of the people there. Just as the men prepare to slaughter the people left in the middle of the village, an American military tank and soldiers storm the village. The men invading the village begin to fire on the soldiers, as they come from both sides of the village. Micah takes this chance to run back towards his house to hide from the gunfire. Meanwhile, Ali and Aiya approach the village to see it in total disarray. There is so much sand being kicked up from the gunfire and the tank that it makes seeing virtually impossible, but Ali still believes that his son is there. One by one the terrorists fall, as those that are not mortally wounded are taken by the Americans. Ali and Aiya arrive at the village, frantically looking for Micah while trying to protect Aiya from the gunfire. They hear a loud boom coming from the tank that is deafening. He covers Aiya's ears and covers her with his body. As he looks up to see his home in rubble, the Americans gather up the remaining villagers to get them to safety. A soldier walks up to Ali, asking him if he and his daughter were hurt. He tells him that he is fine, but he is looking for his son. The soldier explains that they had to get out of there, as the village was in ruins from the mortar fire, and they were wounded. Ali looks around to see nothing left of the village he once called home.

Aiya looks up with tears in her face asking, "Poppa, is Micah dead??"

Fighting to hold back his tears, he says "Aiya, Micah is with your mother now…they are in a better place."

The Americans help those that are left living out of the village and help bury the dead. The boy looks at Ali and says, "Micah's mom said me and my sister would be okay and she was right." Ali, reluctantly, follows the soldiers out of the village thinking of all that he lost in his home to a god he did not even believe in.

As day turns to night, Micah finds himself beneath the rubble of his old home. He thinks to himself to call out for help, but he is afraid as he does not know if those men are still out there. Micah looks at himself to see he is covered in dirt and blood. In pain, he lays there crying, wishing that his mother was there to help him.

Choose ye this day…

A car pulls up to the front of the Huntington residence, as Damian prepares to go into the office for a couple of days. The maid knocks on the door of Damian's library.

"Sir, your driver is here. Would you like for me to gather your things at the door?"

"No, Celeste. That will be all."

Damian grabs his briefcase and a book from the shelf. As he is walking out of the door, Rebecca stops him.

"Look Becca, I will only be gone a few days. I have some business to take care of. Make sure those kids stay out of my library," Damian says with an irritated tone.

"I do not want you to go. You hardly spend time with the kids as is and I cannot remember the last time me and you spent some alone time together. After all, it is Halloween. You should stay here with us and pass out candy to the neighborhood kids tonight."

Annoyed, Damian explains to her how important these meetings he is going to are. He tells her that now that he inherited his father's company, a lot more is on his plate and especially today, their friends are going to require his presence. Rebecca becomes frustrated, saying "Those are your friends, not mine." As the two of them continue to discuss this, Lilith looks over the railing to see them going back and forth. Damian and Rebecca look up to see her watching with hesitation. Damian waves Rebecca off and walks to the front door. Dressed like a power ranger, William runs over to Damian to hug him.

"I will be back, Son."

"Don't worry dad, my powers will protect you. Just carry this."

William gives Damian a little crystal that he says will protect his dad from the monsters. Damian walks out the front door and approaches the car. The driver steps out to take his things and open his door for him. Damian gets in to see a woman with flowing blonde hair already sitting inside. She is wearing a short, white, fitted dress with velvet color lipstick on. Damian is captivated by the aroma of her perfume and her beauty.

"Hello," the woman says.

"Well, hello ma'am."

Damian's attention is stuck on her until he hears the voice of an older man. "Good morning Damian, I see you met Tiffany."

Damian looks over to see that his mentor, Lucius, is there as well. Damian is shocked to see him considering the last time they saw each other was at the funeral of his father.

"I'm…surprised to see you here."

"Well, it is not every day that your mentee goes from Vice President to CEO and Owner of a multi-million-dollar corporation. This is a momentous occasion that deserves all the attention. Now, things are going to be moving fast so we must stay focused. We want you to take the company to places your father could only dream of."

"We…as in…"

"Yes…one in the same. We plan to take it to places only a few have gone. You know a lot of the inner workings anyway. Therefore, we feel that it is about time that you move up. Furthermore, we need to discuss the situation with this Board of Directors."

"What is there to discuss? They didn't want me to succeed because they felt I was not good enough to lead. We won, they lost. They should be glad that they all still have jobs."

"Whoa Whoa! Easy tiger. Don't pull out the claws just yet. We can finesse this situation. We need some of them. In fact, a few of them have some pretty big ties to the Senate. So, until we can get some of our guys in, you must play ball. We hold majority shares anyway and if they do not play ball, we will handle things accordingly."

"Is that what happened to my father?"

Drinking his Cognac, Lucius stops and looks up at Damian.

"Low blow, Damian…even for you."

"Well, I know he made some……unpopular choices that the group did not like and caused some things to get exposed that probably should have stayed in the dark."

"Yes and…," Lucius says sitting his drink down.

"And I know some did not take too kindly to that. I might have been low on the totem pole, but I was not low enough not to hear the whispers among us."

Lucius looks at Damian, admiring his tenacity and fearlessness.

"Listen, if you are asking me if I killed your father, then the answer is no. Were there people that wanted your father dead, considering how careless he was? Yes. However, your father's death involved him being careless and shortsighted. He did not see that he was not helping anyone. Your father was a good, close friend of mine. He helped me make some choices that in my younger years, I was too afraid to make on my own. Your father got sloppy in his old age, and he paid the price with his life. I warned him time after time, not to do certain things, but he went over the edge."

Damian turns and looks out the tinted window, as they are driving down the expressway.

"If I could bring him back, I would. However, his death served a greater cause."

Damian looks over and asks about the things that he exposed. Would this endanger exposing them? Lucius expresses that all it did was give internet conspiracy theorists something new to talk about. As Damian, Lucius, and Tiffany continue to talk more about the state of affairs in Damian's takeover, Lucius' phone rings. Lucius answers, speaking to someone on the other end. Meanwhile, Damian looks over at Tiffany. Still in awe of her beauty, Damian hesitantly begins speaking to her about how she knows Lucius. Tiffany explains that Lucius hired her as a "helping hand", expressing that those were the words he used.

"Well, I see you two are getting acquainted," Lucius says as he hangs up.

"No no…I mean…," Damian shutters.

"It's fine. I won't tell. You now have a meeting with the Senator."

"What?? Are you serious?"

"Yes, I am. This is your chance to get a Senator in your pocket. Impress him and he might even help you get your foot in the political door."

"Congratulations, Mr. Huntington." Tiffany says.

"Please, call me Damian."

"Yes, Damian."

"First name bases I see. This brings me to our next topic Damian."

"Yes, Lucius…"

Lucius drinks the last of his drink and sits the glass down.

"Did you bring the book?"

Damian opens his bag and pulls the book out. He goes to hand it to Lucius and Lucius grabs it.

"We will be needing this tonight. You will be there, correct?"

"Yes sir. Same location?"

"Yes, I will send you the time. We need to discuss your wife, Damian."

"What about her?" Damian says annoyed.

Lucius can see the change in his demeanor. He presses him about what is going on at home. Damian expresses how things have changed ever since some of her friends have her volunteering at this church. He expresses that she has not been the same in a long time.

"Well, Rebecca has always been a do-gooder ever since you two were children."

"Yeah well…I don't do charity cases."

"Didn't you have a friend once that was like that? I remember you two were close."

Damian looks over to the window, saying "that was a long time ago…"

"Yeah well, apparently Rebecca is turning over a new leaf. We also need to discuss her actions when we last met up. We won't stand for that to happen again."

"Like I explained before, there were some things going on in our old home that she was concerned about and…"

Interrupting, Lucius says "And that was the wrong time to speak. We warned you about marrying that woman. I even suggested someone for you to court since you wanted companionship that bad and you refused her over being with the quote 'love of your life'. Well, your 'love' is causing problems. Do I need to step in?"

Nervously, Damian responds, "No sir."

"You keep going down this road and we will have no choice but to rectify the situation for you. You should not be with that woman in the first place."

"Listen, Becca was once a part of us and I know with some persuasion, she can come back. At the very least, she will stay out of our way. You all will not make a move on her!"

With anger, Lucius exclaims, "Know your place boy! We do what we see fit for the whole. You have not yet reached a place where we are equals. Therefore, I am still your superior and even after tonight, I will still hold more power than you."

Tiffany advises that Lucius calm down, so as not to make the driver nervous. Damian has never seen Lucius this angry and felt cold all the sudden when Lucius was yelling. Lucius fixes his tie and puts his hand on Tiffany's thigh, thanking her.

"Listen Damian, get Rebecca together or we will. We cannot afford to mess up now. We are at a crucial stage, and we are preparing to make some moves that will change the world."

"I hear you. You worry about your crap and let me be concerned about my family."

To break the tension in the car, Tiffany begins to ask Lucius about what Damian will need for his meeting. Tuning them out, Damian looks out of the window gazing at the lights of Midtown Manhattan. He begins to reflect on just how much of a threat Rebecca is becoming and what steps he might have to take to protect her. The car that they are in pulls up to the building adorned in lights. Getting Damian's attention, Tiffany places her hand gently on his lap, calling out to him.

"Yes, sorry. I seem to have let my mind drift. What were you saying?"

Smiling, Lucius motions for him to step out of the car, as the driver was holding the door open for them. They all step out, with Lucius and Damian looking up at the mere size of the building.

"This whole building once belonged to your father. He said that he wanted it to dominate the landscape to show the strength that he held. All that power is now yours Damian. Show those board members that you are king and you have come to assume your rightful place."

"Thank you," Damian says

As Damian is approaching the steps to walk up onto the plaza, he notices that Tiffany is also with him.

"It was nice meeting you, Tiffany."

Lucius informs Damian that Tiffany will be his new assistant from here on out and that she will do everything he needs and more.

"Thank you, Lucius. I appreciate the opportunity," Tiffany says.

Lucius kisses her on the cheek, holding her close for a while.

"Are we going to stand here and sing Kumbaya or are we going to get some work done?"

Both laughing, they walk quickly to Damian's side. Lucius tells Tiffany to take his things and head to the elevator, while he has a quick word with Damian. While she is walking, Lucius expresses his fondness of Damian in this new position of power and how he is going to be the company's golden boy.

"You are going to do some great things."

"Thank you. I just hope to live up to the expectation."

Lucius' demeanor instantly changes. The look Damian sees in his eyes is the same cold, menacing look he saw in the car. It was like he had become a whole different person.

"You better. I put too much work into making sure you got this position for you to screw up now. So do what is asked of you."

Lucius walks up close to him and whispers,

"And if you ever raise your voice to me again, it will be the last time you ever speak. Just nod your head if we have an understanding."

Terrified, Damian nods.

"Good. I'm so glad we had this talk. I will see you tonight…oh one last thing, enjoy Tiffany."

"It is not like that."

Before Lucius walks back to the car, he pats him on his shoulder saying, "sure it isn't." Damian watches Lucius' car drive off. He looks to the building, walking up to the plaza as a triumphant king finally taking his throne.

Chapter 7

As the chill of the night begins to set in, Micah starts shivering, as he is still inside the remains of what was once his home. As he is getting up, pain shoots across his body. He feels like he was just hit by a bunch of rocks. Micah falls back down, screaming out in pain. *"I have to get out of here,"* he thinks to himself. He musters up the strength to move what he can in order to make a way out. As he is climbing out, he can feel the pain in his arms worsening. It feels as if his arms are about to give out, but he manages to pull through and climb out of the small hole he made for himself. He looks around to see what is left of his village but remains on alert for anything suspicious. He slowly goes out to the middle of his village, with no clue where to go next. Micah looks up to the glow of the stars in the night sky and is awakened by the cold wind of the night. He looks around for something to cover himself up with, as the temperature is dropping. Micah finds this old, tattered cloth and puts it around his shoulders. With no idea as to where his family has gone or if his family is even alive, he begins making his way west with the hope of being rescued.

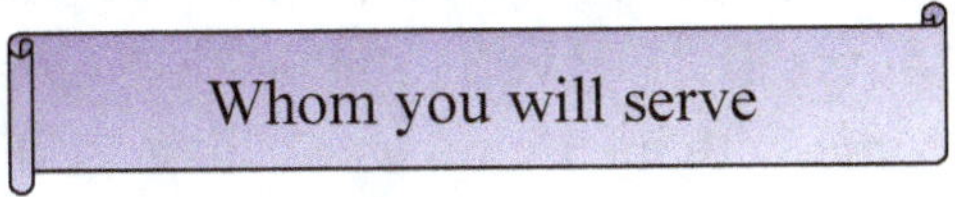

Rebecca sits in the kitchen to prepare dinner for Lilith and William. She begins to reflect on the choices she has made in the past and her recent involvement with the local church. Though she never identified as a "Christian", she does believe in a higher power. She found herself mixed into whatever Damian is involved with and began to turn a blind eye to everything that is happening. She thinks back to the night that Lilith showed her the scratch marks on her legs and the horrified look her daughter had. She denied it, even made excuses and tried to justify what she and Damian were doing; but it was the more recent events that brought to light the reality of the situation at hand. The shame she has felt over the last two years has broken her to the point where she feels lonely in her own home. Between separating herself from her previous affiliations to volunteering at a church and really connecting with those people, she still feels empty and divided between her loyalty to her husband and doing the right thing for her kids. As she is over the stove cooking, she begins to quietly weep. "I just do not know what to do anymore," she says.

Moments later, Lilith walks into the kitchen to see her mother crying.

"Mom, are you okay?"

Wiping the tears from her face, she looks at her smiling.

"I am fine, dear. Is everything alright?"

"Yes…I just wanted to tell you that Bill left already with his friends to play some games and go trick or treating."

She turns the eye on the stove off and unties her apron. Rebecca looks down at her watch to realize she is late to meet up with the women at the church to help them out.

"Shoot! I have to get out of here. Are you sure you will be okay here by yourself? I gave the maid the night off and you could always come with me if you would like." Lilith laughs and hugs Rebecca.

"Mom, I will be fine. I am glad you have found yourself some friends to spend time with."

"If anything happens or you need anything, do not hesitate to call me."

"Mom, I will be fine. Now go, I have some delicious food to eat and some scary movies to watch. I mean, it is Halloween after all."

Rebecca walks out of the door, driving off to go volunteer at the church tonight. With her Mom, brother, and father all gone, Lilith realizes how big their house really is. She walks into the kitchen. She peers into a pot on the stove to see what her mother made her for dinner. She sees that her mom made some gumbo. Lilith's mouth begins to water, as the aroma of all the flavors hit her face. "This is going to be amazing!" she says. She runs over to grab a bowl. She fills it to the brim and walks over to the entertainment room to watch some movies while she eats.

Choose ye this day…

Sitting in the living room, Candice looks out of the window seeing all the kids dressed up in their costumes. She flops down on the couch pouting, thinking how much she wishes she were like those kids. Her dad, Bruce, walks out of the kitchen and notices the look on his daughter's face.

"What's wrong sweetie?"

"Dad, why can't I…" Before she could finish her sentence, her half-sister, Isabella, starts crying.

"Hold that thought, I will be right back."

Candice rolls her eyes and continues to click through the channels. The sound of her sister crying annoys her, making her angry. *I wish my mom would hurry up! I hate coming over here,* she thinks to herself. Bruce goes in to check on Isabella to see that Alexandra is already attending to her.

Laughing she says, "Sorry dear, looks like you are a little late."

"As I can see. Is she okay?"

"Yes, she is fine. She was just a little hungry."

Bruce sits on the bed next to them and starts playing with Isabella's feet. Candice looks out of the window to see her mother is pulling up. She runs to her Dad to tell him that she is about to go, but she stops when she hears her Stepmother and her Dad talking to Isabella. Candice stands in the hallway, peeking around the corner into their room. She sees him holding Isabella. As she looks at her Dad holding Isabella, she begins to burn with envy. With tears in her face, she storms back into the living room to grab her things. She gathers her belongings and slams the front door shut.

As she is walking to her Mother's car, she whispers, "Isabella, I hate you. I wish you were dead."

She gets into the car.

Watching and listening, the shadow figure says "Oh, that can be arranged."

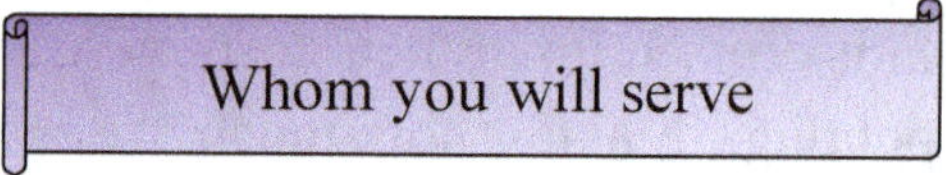

Damian walks around his new office as the sun finally sets. The lights from the city illuminate the skyline. *"I finally did it. I took my father's place."* He thinks to himself. He walks over to the window to look at the city. He stands there, as a king overlooking his kingdom. As he stares outside the window, there is a knock on the door and Tiffany walks in.

"You know, if I did not know any better, I would have thought I walked into the throne room of pharaoh."

Damian laughs, looking at her, "Did you change?"

"Yes, you need to get ready as well. It is about that time."

Damian and Tiffany walk to the elevator. As the elevator is going down, Tiffany explains to him all that he needs to know to prepare for tonight. She expresses that he needs to be 100% sure that he is willing to do this because once it happens, there is no turning back. The elevator stops and they walk out of it. As they are leaving the building, she stops him.

"Are you sure you are ready for this? Don't chicken out on me when we get there. I have just as much on the line as you do."

Chuckling, Damian looks at her and places his hands on her shoulders.

"Look, I assumed my father's place in the company because I knew I was the best one for the job. I am taking this because I want it. I have never been so sure about anything else in my entire life."

"Okay Damian." The two of them get inside of the limo and drive off to the undisclosed location of the meeting.

Meanwhile, Lilith sits on the couch pondering on how things have changed so much in her life. They left their home, her mother and father are more distant than ever, and her brother seems to be more distant than usual. As she continues to watch the different horror movies that come on, her mind cannot help but to go back to what happened to her in their old house. She still has some of the scars that were left by whatever attacked her in her sleep. It seems to always peak whenever mom and dad's "friends" would come over to visit them. She never wanted to cause any contention amongst her family, but she could not be silent about what was happening to her and risk her brother being targeted as well. A scream from the movie snaps her out of her deep thought, scaring her so much that she feels herself almost jump off the couch. *"I've been sitting here watching this stuff for too long."* She thinks to herself. She goes to get a snack from the kitchen when her phone goes off. She sees that it is a text from her mother checking on her. She responds saying that she is fine. Going back to the living room with her snack, she notices the light from William's room is on. She walks into his room to cut it off and walks back to the couch. She sits down and continues to watch the film. Tiffany expresses to Damian the importance of keeping everything that is about to take place a secret.

"Who am I going to tell Tiffany?"

"Your wife. She cannot know what is about to go on or what you are about to see."

Damian laughs, "You act as if we even talk like that. Furthermore, you continue to treat me as if I am new to this and I do not appreciate it."

"My apologies sir, I just want all the best for you. You are truly one of a kind and I would hate for you to fall like your father did."

"Wait, what do you know…" Before he could finish his statement, Tiffany says that they have arrived. As Damian is going to open the door, Tiffany stops him.

"Wait, before we leave this car, there are some things you need to know."

Sitting on the couch, Lilith begins to get cold. She walks over to the thermostat to see that it is getting a little cold, seeing that it is the end of October. It has dropped to about 48 degrees. She turns the thermostat up to 65. She runs up to her room to grab a blanket. As she is grabbing it, she is overcome with this strange sensation. She begins to feel as if someone is watching her. She quickly turns around to see that no one is there, but this feeling that she has is undeniable. Slowly, she walks out of the room to look down either end of the hallway. With her seeing no one, she walks back to the room. As she walks back into the living room, the sensation comes over her again. She stops and looks around. Still, she sees no one. *"It must be all these horror movies I am watching. I am freaking myself out here. Lily, get it together!"* she thinks to herself.

After Tiffany speaks with him, Damian is left shocked.

"Why would you tell me that?"

"Because I…I did not want you to do this and not know what happened before. Your family has always been important and very powerful. I should not even have told you that in the first place. I could be reprimanded or worse for saying that; however, the amount of power and influence you are going to have, it will supersede anything you could imagine. Your father made a mistake. Do not follow in his footsteps. Be the leader I know you are."

"What do you think I should do?"

Tiffany pauses, kisses him on the cheek, and says "You are a king, right?? Kings do not ask for permission to take what is theirs. They just take it!"

With these words, Damian and Tiffany get out of the limo and walk into the building to meet the others. As they are walking in, they are greeted by someone behind the door that leads them down a hallway. They go down into the basement of the building. While this should be a momentous occasion, the only thing that is on Damian's mind is what Tiffany has told him. He ponders how everything he has known has been a lie.

"We are here," The man says, as he opens this large metal door for them.

As they walk in, Damian is perplexed by what he sees. He has done things with these people before, but for the first time, he is able to see the people with real power. He sees the faces of world leaders, US politicians, musicians, billionaires, and other people of great influence. His heart flutters at the thought of finally having some skin in the game. As he walks around, he captures the attention of everyone there. He walks around in what appears to be a huge open space. He notices the change in the air from outside, but he disregards it as just him being in some sort of basement. The walls reflect the light from the torches, giving off a radiant heat. As he walks through the crowd, he is greeted by Lucius.

Slapping him on his back, he says, "Hey my boy! Are you ready? All these people here came to see you because they believe in you."

He sees a woman walk up to him. She greets him and kisses Damian's hand. "That woman is the Senator of Wisconsin," Damian says in shock.

"Yes, well you will be quite surprised when you find out who is really in our little club."

Lucius continues to talk to him, but the sound of his voice is drowned out by thoughts of what Tiffany told him before they entered. With every moment that passes, he thinks about what she told him, and Damian's anger is kindled. Tiffany, noticing the demeanor of Damian changing, grabs him by his arm. "Sir, excuse me, I remember Damian offering to get me a drink before we get started." Noticing her eye contact with him, he nods.

"Oh, well…Hurry up. It is almost time we got started with the ceremony."

Tiffany takes Damian by the hand to get a drink from the server.

"You need to change your face now!"

Tiffany sternly says. "I refuse to let you get me and you killed here."

"After what you told me, Lucius is lucky I don't kill him here and now."

"Listen, you even try to do something here and you will never make it to see your kids again. You need to be strategic about your next move. You want to get back at him?"

"I want him to suffer."

Tiffany looks at him and can feel how tense he is. "Suffer? We can do suffer. Do this, strip him of his power and he will do a lot more than suffer."

Lucius walks over to them. "Are you all done?"

"Yes…yes we are." Damian says with a stern tone.

Damian walks over to the circle that is formed. He sees everyone, but his gaze is set on Lucius as he is speaking. As the ceremony begins, Damian feels that cold chill again. As he hears Lucius speak, his only thought is to make sure Lucius pays for what he has done.

Choose ye this day…

Micah begins walking through the desert, looking up at the night sky. Thoughts begin rushing through his mind, like the winds of a hurricane. He wonders if he is even going in the right direction to get help. His mind then drifts off to his mother. The wind howls in the desert and his thoughts begin to betray him, as he thinks he hears the voice of his mother calling him. He falls to his knees and weeps. To think that his mother died just because of what she believed in, he finds it heartbreaking. He picks himself up and continues to walk. As he is walking, he remembers that his mother used to pray. However, when she prayed a lot of times, it would look like she was talking to herself. She explained to him that God can hear everything and that he was everywhere. Thinking about this, he begins to speak.

In a timid voice, he says "Um…God, are you there??" He waits to see if he hears an answer, but all that his ear catches is the sound of the wind pushing and pulling the sand. He waits longer to hear something back, but still nothing.

"I…I do not know if you can hear me, but please bring my mommy back. I miss her so much." He continues to talk as the tears begin to swell. "Why did you have to let her die? I want my mom and dad back. I wish I knew where my dad and sister were." As he continues to talk, he notices his vision becoming blurry and starts feeling weak. His speech begins to slowly fade as he falls into the sand. The winds blow and Micah lays in the desert, helpless under the mercy of the unforgiving cold.

Micah starts coming to and he finds that he is lying on a red blanket. It is rough against his face, as it is seemingly worn with several holes. He looks up to see that it is almost dawn, yet the cool of the night is still in the air. He sits up to see that there is a fire going and there is a tent that is pitched. He looks around to see no one. He crawls up to the fire to get a little warmth. He looks over to see that there is a canteen next to the tent. Micah runs over to it, in the hopes that there is water in there. He grabs the canteen, twisting it open. He voraciously drinks the water without a second thought. As he drinks, he looks to his right and sees a tall man smiling at him. The man appears slender in size with worn clothing, short hair, and a bushy beard. The man's voice was deep, but friendly. Micah began to be frightened, as he did not know if this man was with the people that killed his mother. Micah drops the canteen and tries to run away. The man chases him and gently grabs his hand.

"I will not hurt you." The man says. "The desert can be a real unforgiving place. You are hurt and it is not safe for a boy like you to be alone."

As Micah turned to look at him, he began to calm down as something about the man did not cause him to be afraid like the other guys did. It was something about this man that made him feel at peace and safe.

"There is no need to be afraid. I will not hurt you."

"Sss…sorry about the water."

Laughing, the man says "It is okay! When I found you, you were about to die from thirst. I had just been out trying to find stuff to make a fire for the night. So, I brought you here and gave you a little water and you were sound asleep. For you to have survived for as long as you did, is nothing short of a miracle. You were pretty banged up when I found you, hopefully you are feeling better."

"Thank you, sir. I am from one of the villages west of here. It was raided and..."

The man places his hand on Micah's shoulder, "It is okay, I know. It is the same story all around here. People are dying, senseless deaths. It is sad."

"I watched my mom die."

"I am so sorry." The man said heartbroken. "Where is your father?"

"I do not know. My father took my sister and I away from the village, but I wanted to go back for mom, so I ran back. Some army guys came in and there were a lot of bangs and I was in my house when the shooting started. After that, I do not remember much."

"Do you remember a lot about these army men?"

"Um...no. Just that they had these big metal things."

"Tanks...They could have helped your father and sister escape. How about I help you find them?"

Smiling, Micah thanks him for the water and helping him. Micah asks the man his name. "My name is Jabril." He said smiling.

Chapter 8

Damian walks over to what would look like a large platform. Standing with Lucius are three other men in suits. They sit onto these large thrones on the north end of the platform. As the ceremony begins, Damian begins to feel strange. He cannot describe what it is that is changing, yet he realizes that the room is different. He walks to the center of the circle, where he is asked to begin reciting their oath. Tiffany looks on at Damian. She can see the anger and hate burning in his eyes. Her heart gradually beats faster with every waking moment, as she is unsure of Damian's actions. She ponders on whether she made the right decision to even tell him the truth. As she watches Damian take his oath and perform the ritual, she looks over to Lucius. She begins to recall all the things Lucius has done to her including the embarrassment and shame she has endured just to have a little something. As these thoughts race through her mind, she becomes more nervous that Damian might try something during this ceremony. Everyone outside of the circle kneels reciting their words. As she is fixated on Damian and Lucius, she almost forgets to kneel as well. With bated breath, she looks up to see Lucius walking up to Damian. With every step Lucius takes, her heart beats faster and faster.

The howl of the wind echoes through the entertainment room, as Lilith watches her movies. The very sound of the wind causes her to jump. She looks over at the window to see that flurry of leaves being tossed around by the wind. *"I have to calm down. It was just the wind."* She thinks to herself. She looks at the clock to see that it is almost midnight. Lilith gets up to check to see if her mom might have come back. She walks to a window near the entrance of their home to peek at the driveway. She sees that it is empty and goes to text her mother to check on her. Her phone beeps and she read the message from her: Hey Lily, I am okay. Wow…I did not realize that it was midnight. I am at the church, but the power went out here. So, I am helping the people here get the generator up and running then I will be home. TTYL.

"Mom knows nothing about getting generators to work, but whatever works to get her to stop worrying about me and Bill so much."

Lilith flops back into the couch and scrolls down the channel guide to see what is on. As she goes down the channel guide, she finds herself slowly falling asleep.

Lucius walks over to Damian. Every step Lucius takes towards him makes him angrier. Damian has never felt this kind of anger towards anyone. It was as if his very being was burning with wrath. Standing face to face with Lucius, all he could see in his mind was killing him where he stood. It takes everything Damian has inside of him to not kill him right there. Tiffany, seeing all of this, is ready to make her way to the door if anything is to happen. Lucius sticks out his hand and on his hand is a dazzling ring. Light hits the ring in such a way that it would almost blind Damian. It was large with diamonds, surrounding the large stone in the center. The central stone was a ruby. The ruby was the heart of the ring.

"As we are here tonight, we have come to see the rise of our brother: Damian. Damian has done nothing but devote himself to our cause to change the world. This will be the night that Damian is enlightened."

With his hand out, Damian takes him by his hand and says he is ready. Lucius recites and begins the next part of their ritual. As he begins, the atmosphere in the room begins to change again.

Holding Lucius's hand, Damian feels the wrath within himself just bubbling up by the second. He feels like a volcano just waiting to erupt. As he looks around the room, he notices that there are now more people in the room than when he first came in, but they did not appear to move like everyone else. He looks over at Lucius to see the two other figures at his side. He cannot make out their faces, but in their presence, his heart begins to feel heavy.

Tossing and turning, Lilith becomes very restless in her sleep. In her dreams, she is at her old house being chased by something she cannot see. As she runs through each door, each one brings her back to another memory of her life she is not so fond of. She hears the footsteps of someone coming. She closes the door and continues to run, looking to exit her house. She finally reaches the front door, when she is stopped by her father. She tells him that something is after her, but she looks to see that her father does and says nothing. Hearing the footsteps approaching from behind, she slowly turns to see something in the dark grab her.

Screaming, she calls for her dad to help her, but not a single sound comes out. She watches as her father walks out the door. Struggling and screaming, she tries to wake up. She does everything she can to at least shout for help, but nothing comes out. She feels like she is stuck between a dream and reality, as she struggles with whatever is in the dark. The terror of this lucid dream begins to overtake her, as she finds herself unable to move. She can feel the figure grabbing her, trying to take her into its embrace. As she struggles and fights, all that she can think to herself to do is yell out Jesus.

Slowly she feels herself being enveloped and she begins to yell out "Jesus"; however, there is still no sound. She tries it again, "Jesus, Jesus, Jesus!"

The more her mouth formed the word, the more the darkness

moved away from her and she was able to move. She continued to yell it more and more, "Jesus, Jesus, Jesus!" With this, the darkness finally flees and she wakes up, freely moving. As she wakes up, all she could do was sob on the couch. Just as she starts sobbing, Rebecca comes running through the door.

"Baby, Baby, It is okay. What happened?!?!?"

With tears flowing from her face, in a state of panic, she says, "I do not know. It was like I could not move and something was trying to take me. I could not speak, nor could I move. It was like something had me. Mom…please help me!"

Rebecca holds Lilith close, apologizing over and over for not being there for her again.

As Damian finishes the ritual, Tiffany looks on, concerned as if something feels off. She knew what was supposed to happen; however, it seems as if things took a turn. She wonders if he has done something wrong, or if maybe they were wrong about Damian. She looks up to see Lucius speaking to everyone.

"I would now like to present to you, our newest member, Damian Huntington."

Damian is greeted with a thunderous applause. Tiffany smiles. It seems, at least for now, her worries are ill placed. Lucius looks at Damian, shaking his hand.

"Congratulations and welcome into the inner circle," Lucius whispers in Damian's ear.

"I am sure you saw some things during the ceremony that were…how should I say this, out of the ordinary."

Damian interrupts him, "Do not worry, I am well aware of the stakes now."

"Great, now let us make this world into our image," Lucius says smiling.

Whom you will serve

Jabril and Micah begin their walk through the desert, as the hot sun looms over them like a hawk watching its prey. Right before they leave camp, Jabril makes sure that Micah has enough water to last him several days. Micah looks at Jabril and is surprised that a man with a size like his was even able to survive. He has so many questions for him but is afraid to ask in fear that it would anger the man that is helping him get back to his family. His father always told him and his sister to never trust strangers, especially now with all the wars going on in their country. While he knows what his dad taught him, he cannot help but feel at ease with Jabril. It is almost as if he is protected by him. Jabril looks down on him, smiling.

"Are you okay, Micah?"

"Yes, it is just really hot."

Laughing, Jabril says, "Well it is called a desert for a reason."

"We should be coming to an area where we can rest. Until then, tell me about your mother. You were calling out to her while you were unconscious."

Micah looks down, pondering on what to say about his mother.

"I'm sorry. I didn't mean to bring her up so soon, considering. She just seemed…"

Micah suddenly stops Jabril mid-sentence, "My mom was the most beautiful mom ever."

"Really now? That sounds just lovely. What was she like?"

"She was really nice too. Though people used to look at her strangely because she was so nice, people used to always say hi and help us when my dad was out working. There was this one time when she even cooked for all the kids in our village. She made this really good, sweet bread for us."

"She sounds like quite the lady."

"Yeah, my mommy was the best.," As quickly as the joy came in Micah's voice, it quickly faded. "Then people started acting weird to us. My friends did not want to play with me anymore. I started hearing people call my mommy bad words. I asked my mommy one day 'why were people acting weird?' She told me that sometimes people do not like change and when that change comes, people are not kind to that change."

Jabril stops, looking at Micah.

"Micah, your mother was a very wise woman."

As they continue walking, tears begin to fall down Micah's face. Jabril kneels to look Micah in his eyes.

"Listen, I know that you are sad that your mother is gone, and I am so sorry that you had to witness that. However, what I can tell you is that where your mother is now is far better than where we are now. She is at peace now, not crying anymore and not being sad."

Jabril wipes the tears from Micah's face and tells him that everything is going to be okay. As they continue on their path, they stumble upon a transport van. As Micah prepares to make a run for it in hopes of seeing his dad and sister, Jabril grabs him and hides behind a cliff. He covers Micah's mouth and motions him to be silent. Jabril then tells him that those people in that van are not friendly. Jabril looks over to see the men with guns forcing people into the van. Micah looks over to see that it was the same guys that were in his village. Micah begins weeping as he whispers to Jabril that those were the guys that killed his mom. Jabril looks over to Micah, assuring him that no harm will come to him and that they just need to be still until there is enough distance between them and the van.

Micah grips Jabril, using the strength of every muscle he has in his small arms. Jabril says, "Don't be afraid, just believe." When Jabril speaks these words, Micah could feel his sense of fear leave him. It is as if the very words that Jabril speaks has the power to push the fear away.

A few hours later, Jabril looks over to see that the van is gone and that they were kept hidden from those that would do them harm. He looks down to see that Micah is still holding on, but only not as tight.

"It's okay now, Micah. We can keep going. We have to leave this area quickly though. It would seem that things are getting progressively worse."

Micah and Jabril walk into the camp where the men were. They pick up any spare supplies that were left there and continue their way to the military base. While they are making their way, Micah cannot help but to think about how much he misses his mom and wonder where his dad and sister are. He pictures how upset his dad is going to be to find that not only did he disobey him and almost get himself killed, but that he has followed a stranger. The very thought of this conversation makes him regret even disobeying in the first place, but by walking with Jabril, he feels safe. He feels as if there is nothing in this world that would hurt him. Just Jabril speaking those words earlier gave him so much peace. He could tell that his words carry so much weight.

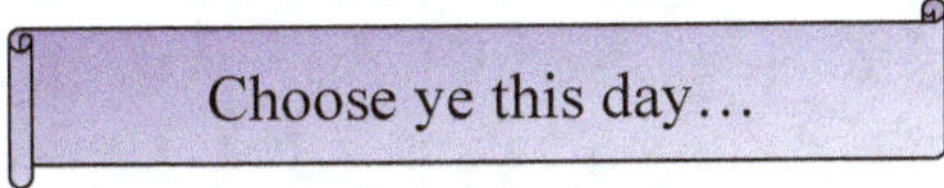

Still confused by what she hears Lilith say to her, she paces the kitchen floor. Nothing about anything that has happened in their family the last several months makes sense. Things have been falling apart in their family and somehow, Damian has been at the epicenter of it all. Rebecca looks over at Lilith to see a look of a frightened child wanting to be in the embrace of her father, the man that is supposed to protect her. However, Damian is nowhere to be found. She calls his phone again and there is nothing but the voicemail.

The world around her seems to move at a snail's pace, as she tries to formulate the words that describe how she feels at this moment. She tries to comprehend it, yet all that she feels at this moment is fear. Scratches were one thing, but to not be able to move or speak while she is sleeping is something that she wishes on no one. All she can think about is how powerless she feels at that moment. She hears a faint voice calling out to her that suddenly wakes her out of her trance.

"Lily…Lily…Lily!"

"Yes, mom? I am sorry."

"Are you okay? Do you need anything? I am trying to reach out to your father, but his phone keeps going to voicemail. I hope he is okay."

This response does not surprise her, as she does not expect her dad to come to her aid. Lilith has known for a while that her and her dad's relationship has become somewhat scarce. It is almost like they are complete strangers. Her dad seems to have a life outside of the family and will only come to her out of obligation or to get clothes for an out-of-town stay. He would always use "work" as an excuse. At one point, she even thought that her dad was cheating on her mom but never had the proof to back it up. Nevertheless, she still loves him so much.

Just as Lilith begins to think upon her experience, she hears the front door close. The sound of the door breaks her concentration, and she notices her mom already beating her to the source of the sound. Lilith quickly hops out of the stool to see who it was and as she turns the corner, she is shocked to see that it is her dad coming in with William and next to them stands a young woman with him dressed in white. For some reason, she feels like something is off. "Tiffany, the bathroom is upstairs to the right," Damian says. Lilith looks up at the woman and as they lock eyes, she knows that this woman will be trouble. Lilith turns to see Rebecca approach Damian.

"Bill, go upstairs and get in the bed."

"But mom, I want to…"

"Now William!" Rebecca said sternly.

Damian kneels, kissing William on the forehead, and tells him that he will be there soon to tuck him in. William rushes upstairs and shuts the door.

"Where have you been Damian??? I have been calling you for hours. We need to talk. Furthermore, who is Tiffany?"

Damian walks past her to head to the kitchen, as if she was not even there. Rebecca looks on in shock. She follows him.

"I was talking to you. Where were you? Something happened to Lily!"

Damian, taking a sip of whiskey, walks over to Lilith kissing her on the forehead.

"Are you okay?"

Lilith freezes, as his lips touch her head. It is as if she does not recognize her dad. She doesn't know how to describe it, but something happened to her dad. She answers him that she is fine but she is about to go into details, Tiffany walks into the kitchen. Tiffany sees them and she experiences something that she has never felt before. It is like a lump forming in her throat that will not go away. It is an internal blaze under her skin that is out of control. She sees Lilith and Rebecca and the feeling becomes unbearable.

Damian sees Tiffany and arrogantly answers Rebecca's question, "Oh and to answer your previous question, this is my assistant Tiffany."

Tiffany wonders if she should speak to them. She quickly nods her head and races out the door. As she goes into the car, the driver begins to make his way to the house and suddenly the phone rings and she sees that it is Lucius. She decides to answer the phone.

"Envy, it is a power thing, huh? To see someone have what you have always desired and be willing to do whatever to whomever to get what you want."

She begins to panic and questions in her mind how he knows this. Lucius assures her that he knows what he needs to know and that she should do something about her little issue. Before she can get out another word, the phone drops the call.

Chapter 9

It has been two days since Candice had last been with her new sister, Isabella, and her dad. She still struggles to understand why they cannot be a family again, without Isabella and Alexandra. As she plays with her dollhouse, she hears the voice of her mom downstairs. The sound of her voice echoes through the house. Candice puts her dolls down and walks to the stairs to see what is happening. As she gets to the bottom, she hears her mom yelling at someone over the phone, screaming that she hates them and hangs up.

Candice walks up, calling out to her mom. "Mommy, what's wrong?" she says.

Diana yells, "Get away from me!", pushing Candice down to the ground, causing her to cry.

"Oh my…Baby, I am so sorry. I am just really upset right now."

Diana grabs Candice, holding her close.

"Were you talking to dad?"

"Yes…Yes I was. I was angry with your father and I should never have taken it out on you. Your father is just a horrible liar. Sometimes…Sometimes I wish I would have had you with someone other than him. He is a liar and a cheat."

As Diana says these words, she does not see the seeds that she is planting within Candice.

Whom you will serve

Things around the house have been silent since the incident on Halloween. It appears as if the whole house was divided and distant. Lilith is distant from both of her parents, Damian seems to spend more time away from home, William does not seem wiser, and Rebecca is trying everything she can to keep the family from imploding. She finds herself retreating to the only place where she has found peace, the church. She has seemingly found solace in knowing that there is an actual God she can pray to that cares about her every need and struggle. She walks into the sanctuary to find that it is completely empty. As she walks closer to the altar, she finds it harder to hold back the tears. Sitting in the front row, she begins to weep. Hearing something in the sanctuary, Martha, one of the office workers of the church, comes in to see Rebecca weeping.

"Re…Rebecca, is that you?"

Wiping her eyes, Rebecca looks up at her. "I'm so sorry if I should not have been in here. I was…"

Before Rebecca can finish her sentence, Martha embraces her. She asks Rebecca what is wrong, but Rebecca cannot help but cry. To Martha, it has seemed as if she has been holding back all the tears, all the pain for so long that she just broke down crying.

Looking up, Rebecca says, "I…I am sorry." She begins to gather herself together.

"It is okay. You are in the right place. God loves you and He wants you to cry out to Him."

"Loves me?" Rebecca scoffs.

"Yes! Loves you," as she points to Rebecca.

"God could not love me, especially after what I have done to my kids."

"Listen, God's love for you is unconditional, meaning that no matter what you have done, He loves you. He loves you even when you have messed up time and time again."

Wiping her tears, Rebecca looks up and says, "Even if you caused your family to be divided and done…"

"Nothing can separate you from the love of God," Martha says, interrupting her. Rebecca looks up at the altar, seeing the cross that is on the wall. She looks at Martha, hugging her. She has not had anyone there for her in a long time, especially since she was disconnected from her childhood friend.

"So, what is going on with you Rebecca? I have seen you in church a few times and you seem so distant."

"I…It is hard to explain. I have done some things, been involved in some things that I am not proud of. More and more, I am seeing that those things were not right."

"When you confess those things to God, He is faithful and just to forgive you. I see that you are married."

Rebecca chuckles, "Don't get me started on my marriage. I feel like that is pretty much done. I only did those things because of my husband. I love him, but I cannot allow my kids to be hurt."

"Rebecca, do you feel that your children's lives are in danger?"

"Honestly, I do not know."

"Rebecca, if you do not do anything else, you have to make sure that your children are okay."

"I know, but I just do not know what to do."

Martha places her hand on Rebecca's shoulder, saying, "Listen, you are not your mistakes. Whatever it was that you and your husband were doing, you separated yourself from it. So that is a start. Next, try giving your life to Christ. He loves you so much and wants you. Do not allow your past to be the thing that keeps you from Him."

"Honestly, I have been thinking about that very thing."

"What seems to be holding you back? You can do that today if you like. The water is ready. We can baptize you now."

Rebecca contemplates what Martha has been telling her, as

she realizes more and more that praying to God has been the only thing that has been keeping her sane. She hugs Martha telling her that she will think about it, but she must make a trip to the city first. Before she leaves, Martha asks if she could pray for Rebecca. When they are finished praying, Rebecca leaves the church to head to the city to find Damian.

Choose ye this day…

It seems, to Micah, that he and Jabril have been walking through the desert forever. Micah begins to wonder if he will ever find his family. Walking through the desert has been rough. The only thing that has been giving him peace is Jabril. Micah still is not sure how he even found him but is glad that he came to his rescue.

"Please tell me we are almost there, Jabril." Micah says sluggishly.

Smiling, Jabril just nods his head.

"We should be there very soon."

"I wonder what my dad will say to me when I see him."

"I do not think you have to wonder any longer," Jabril says as he points to the base in the horizon.

Micah looks up with such excitement, as it seems like forever since he has seen his sister and father. Jabril motions to take Micah's hand and they walk to approach the base.

Whom you will serve

She has always enjoyed the drive into the city; however, this time is different. This time she feels a sort of dread come upon her like a lion stalking its prey, waiting to pounce. She cannot help but feel like she is not going to like what she is about to find. So many thoughts and regrets plague her mind. She should not have ever gotten involved with this stuff Damian talked her into. The attacks on her daughter, the emotional damage done to the family, she should have stopped it all; however, she allowed what she thought was love for Damian to put them in harm's way. As all these things are going through her mind, she looks up and finds herself already in Manhattan. She continues her drive until she arrives at her destination. She drives up to the building where she is greeted by a valet.

"Good Afternoon, Mrs. Huntington."

Looking stunned she responds, "You…you know me?"

"Of course, we know you Mrs. Huntington. You are Mr. Huntington's wife. Unfortunately, you just missed him. He had a car brought here, but I am sure he will be back soon."

"I will wait for him in his office."

Choose ye this day…

Micah runs towards the base in excitement. As he is running, he finds himself stumbling over his own feet. He picks himself up and calls out to Jabril; however, to his surprise, Jabril is not behind him. He looks around yelling for Jabril, but there is no answer. He looks towards the base and sees soldiers running towards him with guns. He begins to flash back to what happened in the village with his mother. The fear that he felt then begins to rush over him like a wave in the ocean. He cups his face using his hands out of sheer fear, when he begins to hear a still small voice say that it is okay. He looks up to see who was talking, but there is no one around. He looks up to see two soldiers armed with rifles approaching him. One of them kneels to Micah while the other one covers them both.

"Son, are you okay? Who sent you here? Were you followed?" the soldier asks. Micah hears all the noise that is around them and becomes disoriented, as a few more soldiers come out from the base.

"Pat him down. He could have a weapon or device attached to him," A soldier says.

Micah yells at them that he does not have a weapon and he is looking for his family. Still suspicious of him, some of the soldiers follow him back into the base while others hang back to make sure he was not followed. As they bring him into the base, he looks around at all the people that have been displaced due to the violence in the area. He begins to get a little discouraged, wondering if his family is even here. The soldier with Micah takes him to his commanding officer. Micah hears some of the conversation between them. He sees the soldier walk back to him and he gets this feeling in his stomach that he is about to be disappointed.

Whom you will serve

As Rebecca looks out of Damian's office window, she begins to reflect on her life, the good and the awful mistakes she has made over the years. *"Where did it all go?"* she wonders to herself. She gave Damian so much of herself and she gave him two intelligent, beautiful children. So why would he do anything to harm them? She knows their marriage has not been the greatest, but has it really gotten this bad? She then wonders if maybe it was her. Maybe she could have done more to protect them. Those scratch marks on Lilith's thigh did not look human, nor did the encounter she had this past Halloween seem fake, but Damian does not seem phased by it at all. He has not even addressed it to her. Not to mention this Tiffany woman that he started bringing around the kids. She always thought that it was like a frat or a sorority, but as she has been attending this church, more and more she realizes what they were doing in the dark was far from right. While being a part of this cult, it provided a means to dabble in some very dangerous things.

Rebecca looks over to see that Damian has left his computer logged in. She sits at his desk and begins to look through different files on his computer. She searches through everything, as she really is not sure what to look for. Suddenly, she hears the door of the office open. To her surprise, she sees Tiffany walk into the office.

"Um…Can I help you, Mrs. Huntington?" Tiffany says, trying to hold back the combative tone in her voice.

Rebecca looks at her, trying to think to herself what she could say that would not draw Tiffany closer to see what she is doing.

"I'm waiting on MY husband. Can I help you?"

"Well, you are not supposed to be here. Damian does not like people in his office and most certainly not at his desk. Wife…or not."

Rebecca walks up to Tiffany, saying "What my husband does or does not like is not your concern. If he doesn't like me here, let him be a man and tell me. He's a big boy, trust me."

Tiffany smirks and walks out of the office. Rebecca knows that she will now let Damian know that she is here and in the office. She rushes back to the computer to finish her search when she sees a file labeled LB. She goes to try to open it, but it is protected with a password. She thinks to herself, "What could possibly be the password?" After moments of contemplating, she realizes that his password could only be one thing: his mother's given name. She puts this in and begins copying the file. As it is copying, Damian walks into the office.

"What are you doing here? And why are you at my desk?"

"Oh, so you are actually noticing me for once?"

She continues to strike a conversation with him to buy herself some time for the file to finish copying.

"What are you talking about? I have always noticed you. I mean it isn't like I could miss you. So, what do you want?"

"We need to talk. What has been going on with you lately? You have been extremely distant and treating your kids…treating me terribly."

"I have been busy."

Frustrated, Rebecca raises her voice at Damian and says, "Too busy to see what is going on with your daughter, the scratch marks she…"

"Lower your voice," Damian says sternly, as he grabs her arm.

At that moment, she had never felt so scared when she looked into his eyes. She looks in his eyes and does not even recognize him.

"The man I married, would never have done that."

"Things change, so do people. Now, we will finish this conversation at home."

"Are you kicking me out?"

As he walks over to his desk and sits, he looks at her with a look of just pure anger and says, "What do you think?"

As Rebecca walks out of the office, she makes eye contact with Tiffany for a moment and cannot shake the weird feeling she feels from her. As she gets on the elevator and the doors close, she sees Tiffany walk into Damian's office.

Choose ye this day…

The soldier walks over to Micah and explains that they are not sure if his parents are here, but he is not going to give up just yet. There are a lot of refugees here and they are going to try their best to find them. Doubt begins to set in, as Micah is starting to feel a little hopeless. He starts to think that his family has left him behind or maybe something has happened to them; however, he is reminded of the still, small voice he heard that said that everything would be okay. The soldier takes his hand, and they go walking around the base. Micah is shocked at the number of people that are there. The soldier asks Micah if he can identify his parents. Micah, not really understanding what the soldier is saying, just looks up at him.

As they get to the main area of this large base that was made in the middle of the desert, it looks as if there are people from all over. The faces of all the different people, some with a look of despair like they left all that they knew behind because it was no longer safe; yet there are some who appear relieved that someone is willing to help. As they are walking, Micah looks through the crowd of people and sees someone that looks a lot like Jabril walking. Micah breaks away from the soldier, running towards Jabril.

"Kid, stop! Where are you going?" the soldier says.

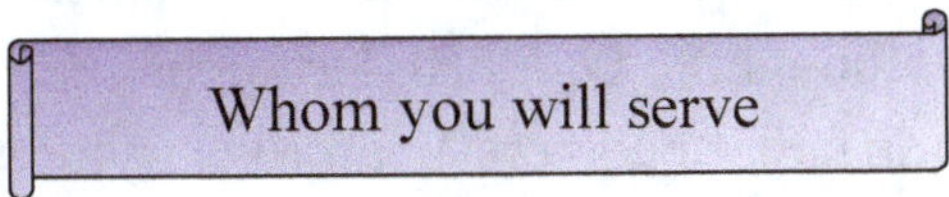

As Tiffany walks into Damian's office, she feels the atmosphere of the room shift. Damian instructs her to shut the door.

"How long was she up here alone?"

"I do not know. I was just coming from a meeting when I noticed that your office door was open, and I saw your wife at your computer."

In a panic, Damian checks his computer and notices that a file was copied.

"She took a file with her. She cannot see what is on that file."

"What was on it?"

Damian looks up at her and explains it is everything he needs to make sure that he brings Lucius down. In shock at what that file holds, she tells him that he was crazy for even having something like that on his computer.

"Lucius has people all around. You have no idea what he is capable of…how powerful he is. If he finds that you are coming after him for killing your father, he will not be pleased especially after vetting you to the rest of the organization. I saw things in that room that would leave a normal person shook."

Tiffany continues to talk, as she walks closer to Damian.

"I just would hate to see you come this far, just to fail or even lose your life over a vendetta."

She kisses Damian on the lips, as she tells him, "That is why if you are going to go after the king, make sure you don't miss."

Choose ye this day..

Micah runs through the crowd of people, attempting to follow what he thought to be Jabril. He keeps seeing him just go in and around different people. Micah runs trying to catch up to him, thinking maybe he knows where his father and sister are. Meanwhile, the soldier that was once with the boy is chasing after him. He continues to yell out to get the boy's attention, but Micah doesn't hear him.

"Kid…Kid! Wait! Where are you going???" the soldier yells.

People from all around bare looking at this soldier running and yelling.

"Jabril…Jabril! Where are you going? Stop please!" Micah says, desperately trying to get his attention.

As Micah is running as fast as he possibly can, he sees the end of the white robe that Jabril was wearing when he last saw him disappear into a crowd of people. He looks around and does not see Jabril anymore. Just as he was going to break down and cry, he hears this deep, heavy breathing voice that says "Micah?!" Micah turns around to see his father, with his sister in his arms.

"Dad!" Micah exclaims.

With tears in his eyes, Micah runs to his father hugging him. His sister, resting on their father's shoulder, looks over with tears in her eyes as she calls out to her brother. They all embrace each other like they had been separated for years. The soldier, finally finding the boy, looks on with a smile.

"Sir, I assume you know him."

"Yes," The father says with tears in his eyes.

"This is my son that I had been looking for."

"I am glad you all have found each other again. Did you spot your dad or something?"

Micah looks up at the soldier, not really understanding him. His father translates the question for the soldier.

"I'm sorry. My son is just starting to learn English and really does not fully understand. However, he said he did not see me. He was following someone named Jabril. He saw him and ran after him. He was the one that had led him here."

The soldier looks shocked as he explains that he must check security, as there is no one on the base that is named "Jabril". He takes Micah, his father and sister to security to see if Micah can spot him on camera.

Chapter 10

Rebecca walks out of the building, as the driver brings her car around. She gets in and calls Lilith, as she drives off. She rushes home as she knows that she is not going to have a lot of time to find out what is on this drive before Damian comes home. As the phone rings, she fears that Lilith will not pick up the phone. Lilith's phone goes to voicemail. Just as she is preparing to leave a voicemail, she sees that Lilith is calling her back.

"Hey Mom, how are you?"

"Listen, are you at home?"

"Yes, why? What's wrong? Are you okay??"

"I took a file from your father's office and I need you to help me find out what is on here."

"Please tell me you are not serious…"

"Yes, I did. We need to figure out what is on here."

"Mom, you are aware that illegally obtaining files from a company is a federal crime. Dad could send you to prison for that."

"Let me worry about your father."

Rebecca ends the call with Lilith, as she makes her way home.

Whom you will serve

Micah, his father, and his sister go with the soldier as they try to find the person that led Micah back to his family. They walk over to the commanding officer of the base. The soldier explains to her that they are looking for the person that helped Micah find the base. Micah's father has him describe the man that he was with and that led him to them.

"My son said that he was tall, skinny with short hair and a very bushy beard," the father says.

The commanding officer looks at the soldier, appearing irritated.

"Ma'am, we just want to see if we can find this person," The soldier says.

She explains to him that it could be a needle in a haystack, trying to find him. After a back and forth, the soldier finally comes to them and says that they can look for him. For what seemed like hours, they sit with the him to see if they could find him on camera, but to Micah's surprise, every place where he saw Jabril, as he was chasing after him, there is nothing there except a little light that the soldier chalks up to be just electromagnetic interference maybe. Micah explains to his dad that Jabril was there and he was the one that led him to them. His father, still not sure what to believe, is just glad that his son and daughter are safe. He thanks the soldier for his help and takes the kids over to a bench to take a seat. He sits them both down, telling them how much he loves them.

"Our home is gone, and I do not want to lose either of you again. So, how about we go someplace that would be better and safer for us all?"

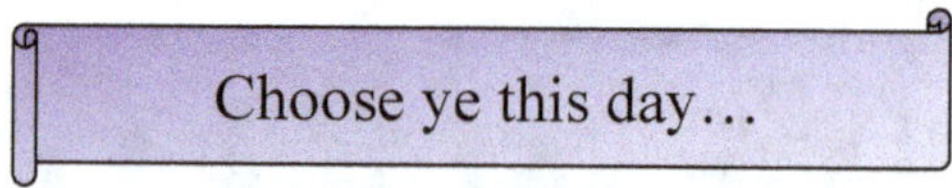

Rebecca walks into the house, calling out to Lilith. Lilith says that she is in the kitchen. She walks in and sees that there is a young man sitting at the bar table with her.

"Hi, Lily can I talk to you in the hallway please?" Lilith rolls her eyes.

"Robyne, I will be right back. My mom is freaking out."

She follows Rebecca into the hallway. Lilith can tell her mom is angry.

"What is he doing here?"

"What do you mean? You want to find out what is on that flash drive? This is how we do it"

"This is a family matter, Lily. I do not know what we will see on it and I do not want to put anyone in any danger."

"Mom, you took a file, illegally I might add, from dad. You then copied it and now want to view it. You have no idea what could be on this file, it could be anything on there, from a virus to encrypted files within whatever you copied. If there is something hidden on there, my friend Jamie is the perfect person to open it or make sure this virus does not destroy my laptop. Plus, I paid him."

"Wait, how much did you pay her?"

"I gave him $200 for the job and I promised her you would pay her another $250 for keeping her mouth shut."

"Seriously?? Let's just get this over with."

They walk back into the kitchen. Rebecca apologizes to Robyne. She explains to them both that this is going to take a couple of hours to check for anything harmful or to break anything that is encrypted.

"Whatever is on this file, whomever you got this from, they do not want anyone seeing what is on here."

"It is my husband."

Shocked, Robyne asks if this is really what she wants. Rebecca opens a wine bottle and grabs a glass.

"Yes, I am sure. Just open it."

Holding each other, Damian looks at Tiffany, wondering what just happened. He loves his wife, but Tiffany is just perfect.

She meets his every need, beautiful, assertive, and stands by his side.

"I'm sorry. I should never have…"

Stopping him, Tiffany says "No. It is okay. I should not have done that, but I will not lie to you that I…"

Right before she can finish, there is a knock at the door. To the surprise of Tiffany and Damian, Lucius walks through his office door. Lucius looks at them, with a look of an approving father.

"Lucius, Welcome. I did not know you were coming here."

With a smug look and taking a seat, he tells Damian that he wants to stop by to talk to him and that he does not need an invitation the last that he checked. As Tiffany is looking down, walking towards the door, Lucius stops her and says that she does not have to leave. What he has to say they both need to hear.

"Damian, we are putting our trust in you. You are aware of that correct?"

"Yes sir."

"Tiffany, I had you to stay with him because I was trusting you to make sure if anything were to happen, you could do damage control."

With a look of irritation and annoyance, Damian says, "What's the point Lucius? Stop being cryptic."

"My point is that you two have screwed up. I was on my way here to congratulate you on all that you have done and get word that some very important files that pertain to us have been copied from a server in this building. Care to tell me what happened?"

Damian and Tiffany look at each other, wondering what to say. They both wonder how Lucius even knew about the security breach.

"Come now Damian, there's nothing that goes on in this office that I do not know about. That still does not answer my question about how such an egregious mistake could happen.

This happened due to either your incompetence or your sheer stupidity."

"Excuse me?"

Tiffany grabs Damian's wrist as he goes to approach Lucius. She looks at him, shaking her head. Regaining his composure, Damian buttons the top button of his suit and leans against his desk facing Lucius.

"Lucius, we are aware of the situation, and I am going to fix this."

"You know, there is a reason why I chose you to lead this company into the future. More than that, there is a reason why I chose you to take your father's place with us. I did it because I knew we could trust you…that I could trust you. Was that trust misplaced?"

"No, it was not. We just found out about this not too long ago ourselves; however, we are going to do everything we can to make sure we find the culprit in this matter."

Shaking his head, Lucius tells him not to worry about it because he already did that. He walks up to him, hitting his chest with a file folder. Tiffany looks at the folder, curious about what it contains. Tiffany walks up to Damian, as he opens the folder. To their surprise, they see a photo of Rebecca at his computer.

"Finally!" Robyne shouted.

Rebecca walks up behind Robyne and Lilith sitting at the bar counter in the kitchen. She looks at the screen, hoping all her suspicions were wrong. She just does not want to believe that her husband is the terrible, cruel man that would do things to put them all in danger.

"Mom, do you know what we should be looking for exactly?" Lilith asks. Right when she is going to answer the question, the sound of the doorbell causes all of them to jump. Rebecca begins to become paranoid, as she knows that it will not be too long before Damian realizes what she has done and Damian knowing was the best-case scenario. She takes out her phone to see if she can see who it is via the camera on the doorbell.

"It is just the nanny bringing William home from practice," Rebecca says.

They all take a sigh of relief. She tells them to keep searching while she goes to the door. She walks over to open the door, getting William from the nanny. She thanks her and shuts the door.

"How was your day, William? Did you win your basketball game?"

"Yes mommy! The coach says that my skills have gotten better. Why did you and dad not come to the game?"

Feeling bad for not being there for her son, she hugs him and promises to come to his next game. She asks him if he has any homework to do. He shakes his head and says he is about to do it. He runs upstairs and she says she will be up there soon. Lilith walks into the foyer. Rebecca turns to Lilith, asking her if they found anything. Lilith tells her that they are still looking. As they both walk back to the kitchen, Jamie motions for them to come closer. Jamie explains to them that he is looking through multiple files to find what they might be looking for. As Rebecca looks at the screen, she notices that there are two files that she feels drawn to. One of them is labelled "LB" and another "Eden". Rebecca begins to think to herself what she would find if she opened either one of these files. Fear and anxiety overshadow her, as she stares at the screen. Fighting against the fear that this is what she thinks it is, she takes a deep breath and says, "Open the file that says "LB."

In absolute shock, Tiffany realizes that things have just gone from bad to worse. Her mind begins to go straight into damage control, as she sees this situation going south. She looks over at Damian and can see the anger on his face. Damian looks up at Lucius. Tiffany can see that he is trying to control his anger, internally.

"How long have you been watching me in my office?"

"Oh Damian, I watched your father. We always keep tabs on our own. Just in case one of us blunders like you just did. Did I not warn you not to be like your father? How could you be so foolish to let this happen? I..."

Furious, Damian says, "Who do you think you are filming me? Get one thing straight: I am not your child. So, you will treat me with the respect I deserve!"

"Oh, silly boy. Do you have any idea who you are speaking to?" Lucius walks up to him, standing eye to eye with Damian.

Tiffany goes between them, to separate them. "Listen, you two! We need to keep it down. Also need I remind you both that you are on the same team. We need to do damage control."

"No. You two need to get this situation under control. I warned you Damian about his wife. She should never have been part of this, nor should you have married her."

"You have no idea what she even took. It could be anything. Either way, I will take care of my wife. Do not go anywhere near her."

"I have extended my courtesy as far as I am going to do so. You exposed us. Now I have to fix your error. I told you that you should have never married her."

"Don't go anywhere near her."

"Please! Based on what I just walked in on, you have long since forgotten about your wife."

Just when Damian is about to say something, Lucius receives a phone call. He steps to the side to answer the call. Tiffany whispers to Damian, "We need to get your house in order." Damian stops her before she can say another word.

"Did you know that he was watching us? And don't you dare lie to me!"

"No! How do you think I feel?! The fact that he and the rest of them can see us at any moment is a huge problem. Listen, what Rebecca did also put me in Lucius's crosshairs too. Someplace I do not want to be. Understand this Damian, we are in a bad way right now. These people have no problem killing you, me, your kids and your wife if it means keeping them a secret."

"I know that."

"Okay well we need to talk strategy. Let's get this under control."

Lucius hangs up the phone and goes back to Damian and Tiffany.

"Lucius, me and Damian have talked, and we are coming up with some damage control tactics, maybe even some ways to spin some things if anything leaks to the public. We will just relegate things to just being another conspiracy theory by another wacko on the internet."

Lucius smirks. "There is no need. I am taking care of the problem, as we speak."

"What does that mean Lucius?" Damian says frantically.

"Don't worry about it. We will be cleaning up your mess. I must bid you adieu. I have another situation that needs my attention."

As Lucius leaves, Damian begins to fear the worse. He picks up his phone and calls Rebecca. As it rings, he begins to wonder if it is too late.

Robyne waits for the large file to open, Rebecca sees that her phone is ringing. She looks down at her smart watch to see it is Damian. Seeing his name causes her to begin to panic, as she believes he knows what she has done. She knows by not answering the call, it will further anger him.

"Listen, I need you to get that open now!" Rebecca says.

"I am. It is taking a while because this file seems to be very large."

"Mom, what's wrong?"

"It is your dad. I think he knows what happened."

As they are talking, Robyne tells them that she has it open. She explains to them that she initially thought there were multiple files in there, but it appears to only be three and they are dated for Halloween. Fear begins to overshadow Rebecca as she begins to connect the dots between what happened to Lilith that night and where Damian might have been.

"Lily, I need you to go upstairs to check on your brother."

"I'm sure he is fine."

"Do what I say!" Rebecca yelled.

Lilith reluctantly goes up to check on William. Meanwhile, Rebecca tells Robyne to hit play on the video. As the video begins, Rebecca sees these people in what appears to be red cloaks. Rebecca pauses it a third of the way through. She goes into her purse and gives Robyne the remainder of money she is owed.

"Thank you, Mrs. Huntington. What is this anyway? Are you all involved in some cult or something?"

Just as she asked this question, the sound of thunder seemingly rocks the house causing the lights to flicker. Rebecca thanks her and instructs her to see herself out. As the front door closes, Rebecca hits play on the video. As the video plays, she watches her fears take shape.

Damian seems conflicted, torn between anger and concern. He is almost certain that she has opened the file. Hearing the torrential downpour outside, he knows that it will take forever for him to get home from the office.

"Damian, did she answer?"

"No, it went to voicemail. Why would she do something like this?"

"I...I cannot answer that. What I do know is that you need to get to Rebecca before Lucius does whatever he is about to do."

Damian grabs his coat and makes his way to the door;

however, right before he does, he stares at Tiffany. He looks at her as one that is preparing to leave a long-lost lover. He tells her that they will continue their conversation they started earlier when he gets back.

As the door closes, Tiffany walks to the window. She watches the rain fall and lightning flash, wondering if she made the right choice sending him after Rebecca. Her phone rings and she see that it is Lucius calling her. She reluctantly answers. She begins to try to appease Lucius, to maybe try to stop him from harming Damian's family.

"Let me stop you right there. Don't sit there and act like you suddenly care about Rebecca. I mean you just got through kissing her husband. I could see your lust for him the moment I introduced you to him. So, you can stop it with the altruism. You know that since he is now part of us, that sacrifices must be made."

With tears in her eyes, Tiffany tells Lucius that he loves his kids and begs him not to harm them.

"I am not concerned about his son, as he can be molded. His daughter will become a nuisance and Rebecca is a problem that needs to be fixed."

"Leave his daughter out of this. This is about Rebecca, not her."

"And there it is. Your only stake in this situation is having Damian to yourself, not to save his family. You could care less how this goes, just as long as Damian isn't broken in the process. Hmmm…. What if we could both get what we wanted?"

Quickly drying her tears, she asks Lucius what he means by both of us getting what we want. She fears that she is about to make a deal with the devil again. She is torn between her loyalty to Lucius, but her love for Damian. Lucius explains what he means and says that it can all be done, but it will require nothing but a simple yes from her. Tiffany looks out, seeing this thunderstorm rage. She never thought that she would be at this crossroads, knowing that there would be huge ramifications for both her and Damian. She takes a breath and says the one word that will seal their fates.

Rebecca watches this video and cannot help the terrifying feeling she is getting. It feels as if someone or something is coming through the video, as her husband appears to be joining some cult. As she watches on, Lilith comes into the kitchen and sees the video. Lilith is confused by what she is seeing. It seems like something from a horror movie. Chills begin to shoot up her arms, giving her the same feeling that she felt on Halloween and night before that. It is this haunting feeling she gets, as if whatever is on that video is of the same kind of thing that attacked her once before. Rebecca looks at Lilith's face. Lilith seems to be stuck in this horrific trance. Rebecca slams the laptop shut and goes over to Lilith to snap her out of it.

"Mom, what is going? What are you and Dad doing?"

Just as Rebecca was going to answer her, they hear the door open, and slam shut causing them to jump. A voice rings loudly, echoing through the whole house.

"Damian, we are in the kitchen. Keep your voice down."

Damian walks into the kitchen, seeing the laptop on the counter.

"What have you two done?!"

Chapter 11

It has been two years since the shadow figure has been working on James; however, now it seems to not be alone. A multitude of others have come within James, as he opens himself up to more. It waits patiently to pick the right moment to act. It knows that while picking with James has been entertaining, the real prize is Madison. She is his assignment, and it will do everything it takes to damage her. The stage is almost set. Her mother has become best friends with the bottle and has totally disregarded her daughter, the perfect storm for what the shadow figure desires. Madison comes in from playing with the girl next door, hearing her mom and James argue again. She goes into her room and falls onto the bed, putting a pillow over her ear to block out the screaming. She hears the cursing and a loud thump on the other side of her wall. She screams, as tears fall down her face. She whispers to herself *"I wish I was not here anymore."* With the shadow figure in the doorway, it smiles saying that this will be the day. It gathers the rest of the spirits in the home, instructing them on what to do next.

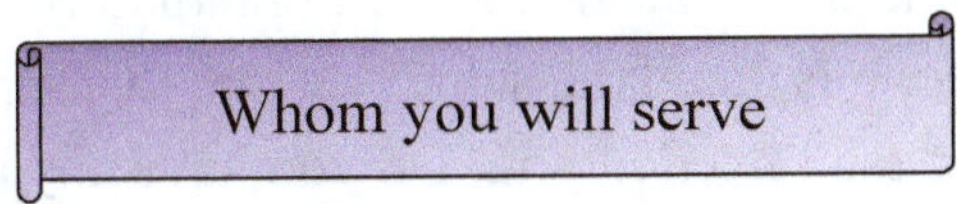

"What did we do? How about you? What the heck have you been doing Damian?"

"I will not have this discussion with you, while Lily is here. The nanny will be here to pick up William and take him to our penthouse in Manhattan."

"No Dad, stop deflecting and tell us what is going? Are you in some type of cult? Is that why when I needed you the most, you were nowhere to be found?"

"Lily, this is a complicated situation that your mother and now you have gotten yourselves into."

Rebecca stops him before he can say another word. With tears in her face, she realizes that she was right this whole time. Everything that has happened over the last two years begins to start making sense to her now. They hear the door open and close. The nanny announces herself entering the home. She comes into the kitchen, greeting Rebecca, Damian, and Lilith. Damian tells her to go upstairs and take William. With a look of sheer confusion, she follows Damian's instructions and takes William away. Lilith begins to worry about her brother, as she wonders if she can even trust her father anymore. Rebecca, still wanting an answer, interrogates Damian.

"So, what did we just watch Damian?"

"There are things at work…things that I did not share with you for your protection. Rebecca, what you did has endangered not just your life, but Lily's as well. How could you be so careless?"

Bewildered, Rebecca lashes out at Damian. Lilith calms her down and tries to rationally get some answers, but tension that is building starts to draw tears in her eyes.

"Dad, I looked at that video and immediately got chills and from what I see, it is dated the same day that I was trying to reach out to you because I needed you. Do you have any idea what has been going on these last two years?? Everything from the scratch marks that I got in our old home to laying in our living room and feeling like I could not move, speak, or do anything. The only thing that I saved me was saying Jesus. I looked for you dad! I needed you and what were you doing? You were joining some cult. I have been getting attacked by something for the last two years and you steadily deny what has been going on."

"Lily come on! You cannot blame me if you watched some horror movies, got scared and started having nightmares. You are a teenager; therefore, you should maybe know what you can and cannot take."

"How does being a teenager have anything to do with being attacked by demons at night? Help me understand that."

"You were dreaming that is all."

"…Wow, you are more delusional than Mom was."

"Excuse me?"

Before Lilith could say something, Rebecca stops her.

"Damian, this family has been tearing apart at the seams. What has been going on and what did I see?"

The more her and Lilith questions him, the more infuriated Damian becomes.

"Listen! I will not sit here and be questioned by a child and most certainly not by you! Lily, did your Mom tell you that she was once a part of the same thing as I was?"

Lilith looks at her Mom, confused.

"Ooh how interesting! Yes, she was with us. Your mother, however, could not cut it. She ended up going to some silly church to pray to a god that either does not exist or does not care. I am leaning more on the latter rather than the former. Look around you, you have what you have because of me! As we speak, the air you two are breathing right now is because of me. I do what I do for you and the sheer disrespect I am getting right now is incredible. Lily, you want to know the truth, right? Well…"

Before he could say another word, Rebecca slaps Damian.

"How dare you! I gave up everything for you! My family, my friends, everyone and this is how you treat me and your daughter? The man I once loved, would have never done this or put his children in danger. What happened to you?"

"Please! We both know who you really loved, and it was not me. Your family made you marry me."

"No Damian, I did love you, but this…this cannot be love."

"If I did not love you, I would not be trying to save your life now. Just give me back that file and all will be fixed."

With tears falling down her face, Lilith is broken by the implosion of her family. The total disdain it seems her father has for them breaks her heart. Rebecca turns to Lilith and tells her the truth about what they have done.

"Yes, Lily. I was with him in that cult, but I chose not to go as far as your father clearly has because of that night when we were in the study. Do you remember that night?"

With tears in her eyes, Lilth says, "Yes."

Rebecca takes her finger, wiping the tears from her eyes. Rebecca cups her face, looking into her eyes.

"When I saw those scratch marks on your leg, I did not want to believe what we were doing was going to have an adverse effect on you. Honestly, yes, I had my desires that I wanted fulfilled. I wanted love. I had a husband, a family and all the material things I could have wanted, but I still did not feel loved. I did whatever it took to fill that void. They told me that this void could be filled by them. I dipped my toe in the waters a little; however, your father is right. I never meant to put you at risk. My actions put you and your brother at risk, and I am terribly sorry for that. If I could go back and change my mistakes, I would. I should have believed you the first time you came to me."

"It's okay mom. I understand. Dad, I saw your occult books in the study that night when you saw me and mom eating ice cream in the kitchen that night you had someone over. I knew all this time, but I expected honesty and for you to protect me, Dad."

Rebecca looks at Damian. She wonders at what point did she

lose her family. She feels like she barely knows William and Lilith seems damaged, mentally.

"Damian, I need you to be honest with me. Is Lily in danger because I have this video?"

"Yes. Some very powerful people are not happy about this. People that you and I know."

"You mean Lucius, right?"

"Yes. However, I can make this right, if you can just give me that file and we destroy that computer."

With tears in her eyes, Rebecca shakes her head. Lilith lashes out in anger at Damian.

"How could you do something that would potentially hurt mom and me? People need to know what is really going on. I saw really famous people in that video that would shock the world."

"Your mom did this the moment she took that video from my office and if you send this video out, you die, your mom dies, your brother dies, and they will make sure everyone just chalks this up to just another conspiracy theory, not to mention that your deaths will be set to just be another crime against a rich family. Don't be stupid, Lily!"

"Mom! You cannot really be trusting Dad right now! He was going to allow us both to be killed. That is why he sent William away, so that we can take the fall for this."

Rebecca hands him the flash drive and tells Lilith to stop it. She wipes her tears.

"If you get this back to Lucius, then everything will be okay?"

"Yes…Yes it will. However, I must take it to him myself."

"Go…Lily and I will be okay here. Just make sure our daughter will be safe."

"I would not have to do this if it was not for you, Rebecca. This is on you."

Damian opens the door and is almost pushed back in by all the wind and rain pouring down. He slams the door. Rebecca goes over to Lilith crying, as she regrets ever bringing Lilith into this.

Wiping her eyes, she looks at Lilith.

"Go upstairs and pack up your things. Only take the things you need: clothes, wallet, everything that has your name on it. Pack it up and meet me in the garage."

Choose ye this day…

"The time is right!" the shadow figure says. It feels it has planned traps through the years and James has foolishly triggered every single one of them. With Madison in its sight, the shadow figure looks to strike. The shadow figure follows James around, as he is leaving yet another club. As the shadow figures see James, he can see the petri dish of spirits that are within him. Every woman he encounters at one of these clubs just makes him attached to another. The shadow figure salivates at the thought of what is about to come next. The suffering that is about to be brought on. It already took care of Maria and now it is time to take out its main target: Madison.

James stumbles, as he tries to walk down the street. In a drunk stupor, he looks up at the streetlight. The shine from it, blinds him. The shadow figure walks to him, seeing him on the ground, whispers in his ear that he should hurry home and see Maddy. James gets up and takes another step. As he walks, he falls again. Frustrated, the shadow figure yells for him to get up. Just when it is about to approach him, several large, winged figures appear before him with their swords drawn. The light from them shines so bright that he begins to cause the shadow figure insatiable pain. It backs up quickly, to see that other demonic spirits have come to its aid. The shadow figure panics as the battle begins. It realizes that its mission is in serious jeopardy. While the spirit that controls that territory has sent help, they will still lose. The shadow figure decides to make its escape from the battle while it can. James sits on the curb, drunk and crying. He thinks to himself how much he is hurting and how much he hates his life. Sitting under a streetlight, he looks up again. The light shines bright, and he sees a man walk up to him.

"Sir, do you need help?"

Slurring his words, James says "You cannot help me. I…I…I'm ju…ju…just fine."

James tries to get up but falls back to the ground. The man helps him up to his feet and says to him that he is too drunk and needs some help. James tries to fight with the man, but peacefully, the man just explains that he is only there to help him.

"I…I don't ne…need yo judgment. Just want to go ho…ho…home."

"Do you really need to go home? I do not think that would be cool bro."

The man looks over at a bench nearby and asks him if he would like to go take a seat and chat with him. James looks at him, not really understanding why this man wants to talk to him. With one of James' arms around him, the man walks James over to the bench, where they both take a seat.

"So, James, what were you doing out here so late at night man? That ain't safe. I found you crying and sitting on the curb."

"I don't need you judging me! I got a lot of crap going on and the last thing I need is to be talking to some weirdo stranger that I am questioning if he is part of my imagination or not."

"Man, listen I am real, so real in fact that I would be the first one to tell you that walking down this block at night, drunk, is insane! Where did you come from?"

"Ju…Just down the street at that…"

James struggles to finish any sentence he has. His head seems to sway back and forth.

"You just came from that strip club, didn't you?"

Looking at the man, James says, "H...Ho...How you......know?"

"Because bro, you smell like it."

James throws up over the side of the bench. The man hands him a napkin from his back pocket to wipe his mouth.

"Listen James, that is not a place for you. You should not be going to a place like that, man. You could have died here, and no one would have seen you until the morning. Nothing good is in that club."

James looks at him and laughs.

"Clearly you have not seen what I have seen in there. Because if you did, you would know there were a lot of great things in that club."

"Bro, it seems like it is, but the only thing you are going to get from that place is pain and regret."

"I already got regret, so whatever!"

"Dude, is that why you are drinking?"

"Hey, I don't need you to be my freaking therapist! You don't know me!"

"Yo, I did not mean to offend, Bro. However, I know that you are hurting and that if you want it to go away, this ain't the way."

"Man, yo...you a J...J...Je...Jesus freak ain't you? Listen I don't want any! Ain't no god ever loved me and if there is one, he would have helped me when..."

Suddenly, James starts tearing up. The man puts his hand on James' shoulder.

"Listen, Jesus is very real and though you are crazy drunk right now. He does love you very much. Don't go home like this man. It won't be a good look for you or Madison."

Just when James hears Madison's name and is about to ask how the man knows Madison, he looks up to see the man that was sitting on the bench with him is gone.

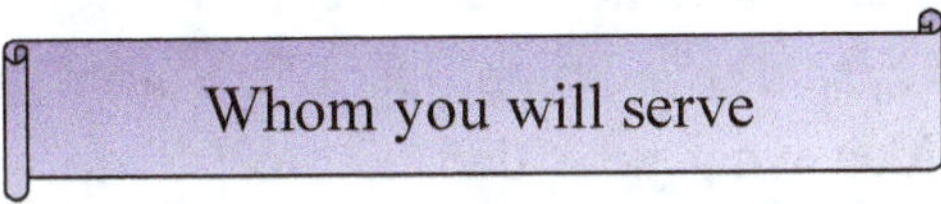

As Lilith is packing her things, she wonders what her mom is planning to do. Would she really do the unthinkable and leave her dad? If she did, what about William? He had been a pain in the neck at times, but she would not want to abandon her brother. She looks over the things in her suitcase, making sure she got the main things she wanted.

Seeing a picture of them all on her dresser, she grabs it. She drags this huge suitcase full of clothes and personal items downstairs, putting it in the car. However, she notices that she does not see anything else in the backseat. "Maybe her things are in the trunk." She thought. She gets in and the wind and rain from this storm makes it sound like something is being thrown into the garage. The roar of thunder causes Lilith to jump, as Rebecca gets in the car.

"Do you have the things I said for you to get?"

"Yes mom. Where are we going? Are your things here too?"

"I will explain everything to you soon."

The garage door opens, Rebecca speeds out. As she is driving, Lilith looks over at Rebecca. She cannot shake this feeling of heartbreak. The look in her mother's eyes, the regret, the despair. It makes her want to cry. As they drive, she is not familiar with the surroundings. It begins raining harder and she cannot tell where they are.

"You know I love you, right Lily? I only wanted the best for you and William. I thought I was going to protect you by my actions. However, it would seem that I was wrong."

"Mom, I am not angry with you anymore. I know what you did and that you thought you were doing the right thing. This is Dad's fault!"

"Lily, no matter what, you have to love your father and respect him. He is a flawed man, just like I am a flawed woman. You have no idea what your dad had to put up with. He needs help, just like the rest of us."

"Mom…You are scaring me. Is everything okay?"

"Yes, it will be."

As they continue to talk, it seems to make the drive time pass faster. Rebecca tells Lilith about how excited her and her dad were when they found out they were having Lilith. This nice story seemed to be the small ray of light in the dark storm that is raging around them. They finally reach their destination, after an hour and a half of driving through the rush of wind and rain. They arrive at a private airstrip where there appears to be this black private jet waiting in a hanger.

"Lily, listen to me closely because what I am about to say to you is very important."

"Mom, you can tell me later once we are on the plane. I figured we were going to leave. I just did not see your stuff, so I was wondering at first what…"

Rebecca stops her, smiling with a tear falling down her face.

"We are not going anywhere. You are leaving."

"What?!...No…No…Mom, no! We are getting on that plane together. Bill is probably waiting for us there anyway."

"No, he is not on that plane. It will just be you going."

Seeing the seriousness on Rebecca's face, Lilith begins to weep.

"No Mom! Please! You just gotta come with me. We can get away from all this and Dad, then have someone get Bill and meet us. Mom! Please don't do this!"

"No, I cannot come, Lily."

Lilith, weeping, tries to convince Rebecca; however, Rebecca suddenly yells at Lilith. Lilith backs down and silently cries.

"Listen we don't have a lot of time. If you do not go on that plane and leave, you will die tonight."

"But Dad promised…"

"Your Dad was lying. Trust me, his poker face is terrible. What I did, is going to attract some powerful and dangerous people to me. I cannot allow my little girl to be hurt for my actions. The guy that your dad and I were talking about, will not forgive so easily. You must disappear Lily"

"Why can't we both disappear?"

"Because honestly, I am not sure if my plan will work. However, it is your best shot at survival. They really want me, not you. If you keep your head down, below their radar, you will be fine."

"I do not understand. Who are these people? What are you all a part of anyway?"

Rebecca hands her a flash drive, putting it into her jacket pocket.

"I do not know much, but they are called the Light Bearers and they control just about every form of media, currency, and business in the world. They killed your grandfather because of what he did that exposed them."

"Are you saying you and Dad were part of some secret society?"

Rebecca turns the car off and gets out. Lilith follows, as they both make their way to the plane. With a heavy heart, Rebecca kisses Lilith on the head knowing that she will never see her daughter again.

"Mom…don't leave me."

"It will be okay. Where the plane is taking you, there will be a friend of mine to take you to family that you will be staying with. Your family will just be meeting you in a certain location. You have your passport and wallet, right?"

"Yes Mom…"

"Good, good…I closed all your accounts. Credit cards, debit cards, savings accounts all dissolved. You will be getting a new name and identity. Everything will appear to be legal. You cannot tell anyone who you really are. Only your family and my friend will." Please Lily, whatever you do, keep out of trouble. Lucius finds you and he will kill you. Do you understand me?"

"Yes…"

The pilot goes to Rebecca, telling her they must go, while the airways are clear of this bad storm. If the storm comes back, they will be grounded until dawn. She check with the pilot to make sure everything is in place at their destination so that there won't be any problems.

With his thick Russian accent, the pilot says "Everything is all set at our destination. We should have no problems with security when she arrives."

"Lily, you have money in multiple offshore accounts so you will be well taken care of. You should not want for nothing. I love you so much Lily."

Barely able to contain themselves, they embrace and Rebecca nods to the pilot to take her onto the plane. Lilith cries, begging for her mom to come with her. Not looking back, Rebecca drives off. As she is driving, she activates the Bluetooth in her car.

She says, "Call Samuel, mobile."

Chapter 12

Finally making his way home, James comes in. Still not understanding what he saw, he is left wondering if the guy was just a delusion or if he was real. Leaving the bedroom, the shadow figure sees that James is in the home. It narrowly escaped the confrontation with the angels. It realizes that it must act now and quickly. It tells the other spirits to be ready to act. James walks into the living, barely making it to the couch. As he sits in the dark, the spirit that is attached to him from the club begins to whisper and plant images in his mind. Not understanding why his head is hurting so much, he goes to the kitchen to grab some water and ice. As he stands over the sink, it seems that the whispers begin to become more alluring as if they are trying to entice him.

"Who are you?" James says.

No one answers. James begins to believe that maybe all of this is in his mind. He grabs himself a shot of whiskey, but still these images and thoughts take siege in his mind.

As the shadow figure watches, it knows that soon it will be showtime. It instructs the other spirits in the apartment to go to Madison's mother. They begin their work with her, while it and the spirit work with James. Both begin to plant thoughts into James, as he begins to entertain each thought that they sow into his mind. As one thought comes after another, he almost seems like a man possessed as he is beginning to want to act on them. Accompanying these thoughts and images, are feelings of anger, hate, and lust. The explosion of this stimuli is the exact cocktail of things the shadow figure knew James would need, not to mention his insatiable lust for alcohol and most recently, drugs.

The stage is set, the players are in place, and the shadow figure enacts its plan now. Seemingly in a delirious state, James walks over to Madison's room. The shadow figure can barely contain himself. James, opening the door, walks in. What happens next plays out exactly as the shadow figure knew it would, given the opportunity. This vile act gives the shadow figure the opportunity to open a door in Madison, allowing spirits into her that will change her life forever.

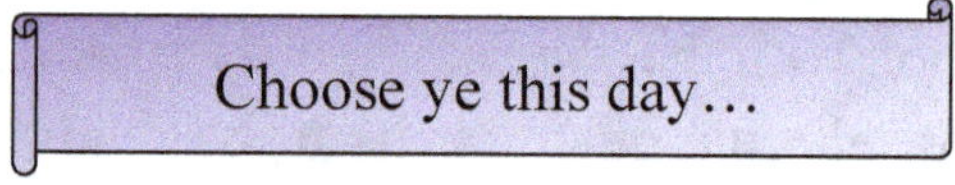

As the phone rings, Rebecca begins to wonder if this is a good idea to call him. She has not heard from him in years. She did not even know if this was still his number. It felt wrong and desperate, but she is a very desperate woman now. She stops at a traffic light. A car pulls next to her, causing her to jump. Thinking that it could be someone that Lucius sent, she speeds through the red light. Just as she is about to hang up, someone picks up the phone.

Waking up, Sam says, "Hello?"

"He…Hey Samuel."

"Um…who is this?"

"You might not remember me, but it's Rebecca."

Shocked, Sam looks at the phone wondering if this is real or if he is dreaming.

"Becca? Is it really you?"

Rolling over and half asleep, Lola says, "Who are you talking to at this hour? Tell them to go to…" Before she can finish her sentence, she goes back to sleep.

"Yes Samuel…It's me."

Careful not to wake Lola or Elias for that matter, Sam walks out the bedroom and goes onto the patio. He lights a couple of torches, taking a seat.

"Wow…I really don't know what to say. How did you even get my number?"

Rebecca chuckles, "You never changed your number, hun."

"I hated when you called me that."

"I know…but you will always be that to me."

"My wife and son are asleep, so I had to go outside. I have not heard from you since we were in…College maybe?"

"…Yeah I know. I am really sorry with how I left things with us. Things were weird, but I should have kept in touch with you. I wanted to. I kept saying that I would call but it never felt like the right time. I did not know you were married. Maybe I should not have called."

"No…No. It is fine. Though it did hurt, I get it. If you wanted to, then why didn't you?"

"Honestly, I don't know. I had responsibilities and my own crap."

Just hearing Sam talk to her, warms Rebecca's heart.

"Sam, I am so sorry for what I did to you."

"What do you mean?"

"I'm sorry for abandoning us, for leaving you high and dry like I did. Sam…I chased after something that took me to some places, I regret going. You loved me and I allowed what my parents desired to top what I wanted."

"I forgave you a long time ago Becca. We make choices when we are young that, when we look back on them, are pretty stupid. I don't harbor any negative feelings towards you."

Sam voicing this causes Rebecca to tear up. Trying to stay focused driving back home, she wipes her eyes.

"Thank you, Samuel. I regret not telling you how much I loved you and how much I…"

"Becca, is everything okay with things between you and Damian?"

"No…No they aren't. I made some choices, some really bad ones that I have to pay for. However, I just wanted to hear your voice. You always knew how to ease my mind if I was panicking or just was in a bad place. I don't know how you would do it honestly."

"Well honestly, I don't know either. Sometimes, you would tell me stuff and then somehow, the words would just come to my mind. I know now that it was Jesus that was doing that."

"Well, I'm glad that Jesus would do that for you and…"

Rebecca weeping a little, "And I could use some of that right now."

"Would you like for me to pray for you?"

"…Yes please."

Sam, feeling his heart break a little, begins to pray.

"Father, I thank you. Thank you for allowing myself and Becca to reconnect after all these years, after all the heartbreak and pain. Jesus, I thank you for your kindness and your love. I ask you to give Becca peace, in the name of Jesus. Your Word says that you would keep us in perfect peace as our minds are stayed on you because we trust in you. I speak peace to her in the name of Jesus. I ask Jesus that she would experience your love and that she would have hope in you."

The tears of Rebecca seem to be ones that have been stored up for a very long time. Sam continues to pray, but in another language. She breaks down and sobs.

"Give her hope in you, in Jesus name amen!"

"Thank you. Samuel…I always will love you."

"…Becca, I…I love you, but not in that way…not anymore. I have Lola."

Upon saying these words, he found his heart in conflict with his morality.

"I know…I should not have said that. I am really sorry, super inappropriate."

"Becca, it's…"

Sam takes a deep breath.

"Becca, you have no need to apologize. Let's just forget it."

"Samuel, I need something from you. This request means everything to me. However, I cannot tell you any details besides what I am about to say to you, and I need you to not ask me any questions."

"What can I do Becca?"

"Do you still have your connections at the airport through your mom?"

"Um…I think some of my mother's friends are still there."

"Do you think they would let you get to the private hanger?"

"Um…why would I ever go to the hanger?"

"Yes or no, Sam? I don't have time for overthinking!"

"Yes, but I do not understand why you need me to get to the hanger."

"Something very…"

Rebecca pulls up to the house, seeing that everything still looks the same. She sits in the car, dreading what is to come next. She wipes the tears from her eyes. She looks out the rear-view mirror, not seeing that she was followed.

"Something very precious to me is going to be there in about an hour or so. I need you to be there to get it and make sure it goes to the next destination. This is very important. You cannot tell anyone about it or where it is going next. I am going to send you a picture now of who will be picking it up next. Give it to them and them only. Please protect it at all costs, I am begging you!"

"Sure…but what am I getting and why aren't you here to do it?"

"What did I just say about asking questions?"

Putting his head down, he agrees to help Rebecca.

"Thank you, Samuel. I…I have to go now."

"Becca, you do not sound okay. Do I need to try and contact Damian or something? God loves you Becca and you are not alone. I am here for you."

"I know. Don't worry about me. Take care of your family and that wife of yours Samuel. You are a lucky man. Goodbye Samuel."

"See you around, Becca."

As Sam hangs up the phone, tears begin to fall down his face. He can feel his heart break as she hangs up. It was as if he was really saying goodbye to her. He gets up, putting on a hoodie and shoes, to leave out to the airstrip. Not knowing what to expect, he gets to the car and begins to intercede for Rebecca.

Rebecca looks at the house, dreading what might be waiting for her on the other side of the front door. She walks to the door and slowly unlocks it. She opens to see the house, quiet as ever. Rebecca looks around checking to see if someone is there, thinking she might have caught someone walking into a room upstairs from the corner of her eye. Slowly, she walks up to the second floor. She grabs a vase to use as a weapon, creeping over to Lilith's old room. She goes in and sees nothing. *"Maybe I am just being paranoid"* She thinks to herself. As she walks out the room, she hears what sounds like footsteps running down the stairs. Quickly, she opens the door to see nobody there. Each step she takes down the stairs brings her further dread. The more sounds she hears here, the more she realizes that Lilith was not making anything up. Something was in their home and it was not welcoming at all. The presence that she felt gave her chills. She runs to the kitchen to pick up the phone to call 911. As someone gets on the line, a shot is heard from behind her. The pain that she feels in her back starts off excruciating but slowly numbs. As she tries to claw out of the kitchen, she hears another bang. This causes her back to hurt even more. She tries to turn around to see their faces, but the pain hurts too bad. She hears two sets of footsteps. While one does not move, the other starts destroying the kitchen.

"Remember to make it look like a staged break-in." the gunman says.

She looks at the phone to hear that the 911 dispatcher is still on the line, asking for her name. Rebecca tries

to speak, but the pain causes her not to be able to say a word. She just grunts and makes loud noises near the speaker of the phone.

"Grab that phone before she gets to it!"

Putting it to his ear, the second gunman hangs up the phone. He tells his partner that she was with a 911 dispatcher and that the police will probably be here at any moment.

"Quickly destroy everything, take a few jewelry items too. We cannot make this look like nothing else than a robbery gone wrong. After you are done, you know what to do."

As they are stealing and destroying her home, Rebecca cannot help, but in her last moments, hope that Lilith is safe and think about William. She thinks how she will never see either of them grow up.

"Jesus, I know you have no right to listen to me at all, but please watch over my children. Keep them safe and protect Lily," Rebecca whispers, as she slowly bleeds out.

The guys come from their bedrooms. Rebecca notices smoke coming into the kitchen, realizing they set the house on fire to destroy evidence of them being there. There is no doubt in her mind now that this is Lucius' doing. She grabs one of them by the pants' leg as they are leaving.

She says "Tell Lucius I will…"

Before she could finish, the guy shoots her again, killing her.

"What are you doing?!?! Let's go! We have proof that she is

dead. Let's get our money and go!"

The gunmen quickly speed off, as the house burns to the ground. As they are leaving, one of the men makes a phone call. Though their adrenaline is pumping, the driver tries to blend into traffic to not draw attention to themselves. The phone picks up and one of the gunmen tells the person on the phone that the job was done.

"Are you sure? I do not need any more screw-ups like at that hospital in Detroit two years ago."

"Yes Mr. Lucius. It is done."

Lucius, with a smile on his face, says to him, "So the girl and her mother are dead right?"

There is a silence on the phone, as the two guys look at each other. Lucius begins shouting over the phone to them.

"I paid you very well to kill the woman and her daughter. So where is the girl?"

"Only the woman was there. There was no girl even in the house."

Enraged, Lucius begins to berate them and explain to them how the job is incomplete then.

"Sir, if I may, the house was burned to the ground and we went into the daughter's room to rummage through it so it can still work in the favor of everyone."

"I need to find that girl. I will only pay you half for a half-done job. However, you find the girl, Lilith, and you will receive everything else."

Lucius hangs up, looking at another member of their organization in the room with him.

"So, was it taken care of?"

"Damian's daughter is still out there. However, we will track her down. Don't worry."

"You said that last time about his Father and look at how that turned out. This is a mess and you need to clean it up. And what about Damian?"

"Damian is fine. He knows what he needs to do. Rebecca is gone and out of our hair. She was not even committed anyway."

"Yes, but their daughter knows what she knows now right?"

"Rebecca was well connected. If she wants her daughter to drop off the earth, she could make that happen. But being a teenager, she is going to make a mistake and once she does, we find and kill her."

Looking at his phone, he tells the other member that Damian got it done and our stuff is gone.

"You better hope so because my dirt is not the only thing that is on that file. All of us could be at risk of being exposed like how we hired some witches to kidnap a child for us."

"Mind your place!"

"'Mind my place'? I am only in this place because of you! You started all of us down this road by you taking Damian under your wing."

Lucius takes a sip of his bourbon.

"Stop worrying and keep your eye on the prize. Everything will work out as it always have. The hospital debacle was an anomaly."

"Just remember, the court of public opinion can be a little hostile to people that try to harm children after all."

"Even if we never find her, who is gonna believe some wacked out teen saying, 'oh the illuminati is real and I have proof.'?"

"This is true."

As this member is leaving, they look back at Lucius.

"Does our deal stand?"

"Yes."

Whom you will serve

Sam finally arrives at the airport. He goes inside, wondering how he would even know what he is looking for. Seeing someone working the counter, he goes to the young man and asks him about where private jets would land.

"Seeing as they are private, I cannot tell you that, sir," the man says.

"Listen, I am trying to get something that is landing here right now for a friend. Now please, help me!"

The guy nods, walking away from the desk. Sam stands at the desk for a couple minutes, wondering if this guy is really helping him or not. He looks over to see several TSA agents walking up to him. Sighing, Sam realizes this is not going to be as easy as he thought it was going to be.

"Sir, we are going to need you to come with us?"

"Why? I have not done anything wrong. I am just trying to get something for a friend. Please…"

"Sir! Please don't make this harder on you than it has to. You can either come with us willingly or cuffed. The choice is yours."

Seeing one of them put their hand on their gun, Sam puts his hands up and willingly goes with them. *"This is some bull! Jesus, I am just trying to help Becca. Please get me out of this!"* Sam thinks to himself. As they take him to this holding room, a couple of them begin to question him while the others run his name on the no-fly list. As they are questioning him, Sam stays quiet as he does not know what to say or who to trust. Rebecca seemed adamant about this being secret and that some very dangerous people could be after it too. This entire situation seemed crazy to him. Just as he starts praying, he hears the door open and a voice say, "Sammy??" He looks up to see this man, seemingly older with a salt and pepper beard. He does not recognize him, but he tells the other agents to give him the room.

"Sammy? You remember me? I was your mother's friend Terrance. We were high school buddies. I met you when you were a tiny fella!

Whatcha doing in these parts? I hear you be causing a scene and that you are being suspicious. From the description, I thought it was you, but I was not sure."

Sam looks at the guy for a quick second and realizes that it is his mom's old high school friend that would come around, just a little older than he remembered. It seemed as if Jesus made a way of escape for him. Sam explains to Terrance why he was even there in the first place.

"You gotta see how that might seem a little weird, Sammy?"

"Yes, but I am running short on time. I must grab this as soon as possible. My friend…she can't be here to get it. It was on a private jet."

"Well private charters land on this private strip on the other side of the airport."

"Can you get me there?"

"Sure can, Sammy! Hey, how is the old girl doing anyway? She doesn't call or text anymore."

"Mom…she passed away some time ago."

"Oh, my…I'm sorry son. Your mother was a good friend. She helped me through a difficult period of my life. If it was not for her prayers, I would not have this job now and be 30 years clean."

This brings a slight smile to Sam's face.

"Let's get your friend's stuff."

Terrance takes Sam out of holding, vouching for him. Having to take the long way around, they travel to the other side of the airport. After several long walks, they finally arrive there.

"There are several private hangers. Do you know which one it is in?"

"Umm…no."

"Do you know anything about the jet?"

"Umm…nope. Don't know that either."

"So…How did you expect to find this in the first place?"

Still confused and not knowing what to do, a thought comes into Sam's head that says, "Go to hangar three."

"I don't know why but something tells me we should go to hangar three."

"What? Boy, you ain't makin no sense."

Sam runs to hanger three with Terrance following him. They get to hangar three, to see that there is a jet that has just landed. The pilot is out refueling when he sees them walking up to the plane. Nervously, he runs into the plane and grabs a gun. Terrance pulls his, ordering the man to drop his weapon now. Trying to deescalate the situation, Sam tries to talk to the pilot.

"Hey, we don't have to do this."

"Don't take another step! Who are you? How did you know we were here?" The pilot says.

"Put the gun down now! I won't ask again!"

"Stop both of you! Listen Becca…I mean Rebecca told me that something was coming and that I was to pick it up."

"You know Mrs. Huntington?"

"Yes! Now everyone calm down! I just want to get this so I can go home. I'm tired, haven't slept and this is keeping me up longer. So please."

"How can I trust you?"

Terrance says, "If you don't put that gun down, you can trust that I will make sure this will be the last time you ever fly anything again."

"Terrance, that is not needed. We don't need to alert anyone. Please sir, you can trust me. I would not…"

Pausing for a moment, him and Terrance are shocked to see a girl walk off the plane.

"You must be my mom's friend?" Lilith says.

"Um…what the heck?!" Sam exclaims.

"Sam, you care to explain to me why you are picking up a

teenage girl here?"

"Umm…. honestly, I don't even know why."

Sam begins to feel as if he opened himself up to drama that he does not want to be a part of, but for some reason, it was like Jesus was giving him peace about all this. Sam looks at Lilith, approaching her.

"I do not know what you have gone through, but I am here for you. What's your name?"

"Lily."

"Hi Lily. I am Samuel."

"So, you are the one that got away? She told me stories about you. That she use to call you goo…"

Embarrassed, Sam cuts her off.

"All of this is cute, but if someone does not start explaining some things, everybody here is going in holding until we sort this out."

Sam looks at Terrance, wishing to explain this whole situation, but at the same time wonders if he would believe any part of the story.

"Lily, I spoke to your mom early this morning. She told me to get you and take you to your family."

"You talk to mom?! Is she okay??"

"I…I…"

Hanging his head down, he tries to reassure her that he believes that she is fine. He does not know if he is really doing that for her or himself. He goes to Terrance to explain everything. Lilith grabs her things from the plane. She hugs the pilot, thanking and biding him farewell.

"Sammy, please tell me you are not trafficking her?"

"Trafficking her? No! Please I just want to get this over with. Just let us go and pretend none of this ever happened."

"Pretend none of this happened? Sammy, a little girl stepped off that plane. This changes everything! I have to fill out paperwork and make some calls."

"Please! No! Those calls would put my life in danger!"

"In danger by whom?"

"…my dad."

Shocked Sam says, "What did your dad do? Was he abusing you and your mom?"

"…Not in the conventional sense."

"Listen Terrance, let us go please. I promise we will be out your hair. Let's just go our separate ways."

"Sammy there are cameras everywhere. You cannot hide this."

"Yes, you can. My mom owns the land that the airport is built on. Thereby, she owns the airport."

"Little girl, that means nothing. This is federal stuff. I gotta…"

Terrance stops when he gets some radio chatter. He steps to the side to talk to the person on the other end. As Lilith and Sam continue speaking, he comes back to them.

"Listen I do not know what is going on or who you are lady, but I was just ordered by my superiors to let you all go. I was told she was never here, and this plane never landed. So, I guess you both are free to go."

This whole situation seemed foreign to Sam. More and more, this is starting to feel like some spy movie to him. He takes her things, and they get back into his car. Sam begins to drive. As he makes his way down the freeway, he looks over at Lilith and the total blank look on her face. She seemed so sad, like she just lost her whole world. A tear slowly falls down her face. Sam becomes nervous to even speak to her. He still cannot believe that Rebecca's daughter is in his car.

Wiping her tears, Lilith says, "My mom used to talk about you quite a bit. I see why now."

"Excuse me?"

"I just mean that you are everything she said you were, which is a kind, gentleman."

"Oh, I did not realize that she would talk about me."

"Yeah, it makes me wonder why my mom chose my dad over you. I don't even know you, but you seem like a way better man than he is."

"You should respect your father."

"And it is because of my father that my mom and I are in the mess that we are in!"

"What mess are you both in?"

"I...um... cannot say. By the way, my mom said that my family would meet me at the Brooklyn building downtown and from there, I will be going to Canada and then Europe I guess."

"Europe? That is a lot of work she is going through just to keep you safe. It is almost like she wants you to be lost."

"Yeah, that is the general idea."

So many thoughts are going through Sam's head right now. So many questions he wants to ask; however, he doesn't want to be rude, nor does he want to put Lola and Elias in danger. He continues to drive, and Lilith begins to ask him about the relationship between him and her mom.

"Our relationship was...complicated."

"I have time and I could use something good to take my mind off of this craziness that is my life right now."

"Well, your mom and I...We dreamed of a life together. Your mother was amazing, athletic, and beautiful."

"Wait, mom was athletic?"

"Yes! She was an amazing track star. Like seeing her run was mesmerizing. She won several trophies and stuff in college."

"Wow...mom never told me."

"Your mother was the most graceful runner I had ever seen. Most people thought that she was the most stuck up because of her parents."

"You know, I really did not care for my grandparents."

"I can totally understand that. They were the reason she chose your father over me."

"Wait…what?"

"Me and your mother were from different worlds that just so happened to align occasionally. My father worked for her father. He was a tech for his company. I remember the first time I met her, officially, was at a company Christmas party that your grandfather put on. I saw her from across the room. I spoke to her, not knowing we actually both went to the same school."

"But mom went to a private school, a very expensive one at that. How did…"

"How did they afford it considering I don't look rich?"

"No offense."

"None taken. I only went for two years before I transferred to one in the city. We just kept in contact. We dated. Man, I was head over hills for that woman. She was everything. However, because of my background and unfortunately the color of my skin, they did not want her with me."

"That is disgraceful! How could mom just allow that to just fly? If she loved you and you loved her, she could have just been with you. I just don't understand. My father is a monster."

"Honestly, I do not know the full reason why it happened the way it did, but if it was not for her being with your dad, she would not have you. And I know she loves you so much."

Tears begin to fall down Lilith's face as she laments over her loss.

"Listen, I cannot begin to imagine what you have lost. However, what I can say is that, beyond what happened between your father and mother, God loves you so much."

"You know, I know my mom started going to church and all that, but church didn't save her. So where was God then?"

"He was still there. Just like He is here now and He knows

just how much pain you are in. In fact, God can give an account for every tear that you have cried?"

"What? That does not make sense. Why would a god care about my tears?"

"God cares about your tears because He cares about you and loves you. He does not like seeing His creation broken and in tears. When I lost my mother to Cancer, I thought similarly. It was not until I had an understanding that death was not His desire for His creation, but life. Life is what God wants for us all and that is what your mother wanted for you. That is why she sent you away and stayed behind. That is why He can give an account because He loves you and that is just how much He cares."

Just as Sam finished talking, they arrived at the building where the meet was taking place. Seemingly arriving early, he sits with Lilith as she weeps in her hands. As he hugs her, silently praying for her, he begins to see why God ordered his steps to be here for Rebecca's daughter. This was a moment where she really needed to have an encounter with God and in this moment, he had made himself a willing vessel to be used by Him. He begins to speak to Lilith the words God gives him to say,

"God loves you Lily. He loves you so much and though your mother and father are not here for you, God says that He is always here for you. He knows about every tear that is falling, about every tear you cried silently in your sleep. He loves you and is here for you always."

As he says these words, Lilith just breaks even more. Sam, still holding her, begins to shed tears as well. Several moments later, Sam hears a car pull up. He looks out and asks her if they are her ride. Wiping her tears, she looks out; however, she cannot tell due to the rain. They both get out and cautiously approach the car. A man and woman get out of this small car, with long bright yellow raincoats.

The woman, speaking with a thick French accent, asks "Are

you um…I don't know how you say it, but goo- ?"

"Yes, it is me." Sam says, trying to save himself from embarrassment.

Lilith looks out, not really recognizing the woman. The woman explains to Lilith that it had been a very long time since they had seen each other, but she was her cousin. The man shakes Sam's hand saying,

"Thank you for saving my cousin and bringing her here. Without your willingness to do this, Lily might not have made it to us."

"No problem at all."

The woman grabs Lilith's things and helps her into the car, while Sam and the man speak.

"Have you heard anything from Rebecca?"

"No…and that is what concerns me."

Appearing saddened, the man says, "So I guess my worst fears have been realized."

"I feared the same thing, but a part of me did not want to accept it. When she hung up the phone from me, I just got this overwhelming feeling that I would not speak to her again."

"Yeah…my cousin allowed Damian to get her into some things that she began to not want parts of anymore. I had always hoped she would eventually give her life to Jesus, but hey…like Jesus would not force Himself on anyone, I cannot force Jesus onto her, even if she is my cousin. All I can do is pray."

"Yeah, that is all you can do. Hey, I never thought any of her family were saved."

Laughing, the man says, "Well, our family is very complicated. Most of our family either worship a false god, don't believe in Jesus, or don't care to know Jesus; however, with Jesus, there is always a remnant. And after all, someone has to stand in the gap for my family."

"Amen! What's your name by the way?"

"My name is Mickal."

Mickal and Sam shake hands. Just as they are bidding each other farewell, Lilith runs up to Sam, giving him a hug.

"I do not know what happened in that car but thank you. I...uh......really appreciate it."

"That was Jesus, not me. It will get better, with time."

Just as she is walking away, Sam calls out to Lilith.

"Yeah, Sam?"

"Try Jesus. You can try everything else, but I promise you this: Jesus is everything you will ever need."

Seven Years Later…

Chapter 13

Opening his eyes, Elias looks around in a state of panic. Feeling the cold touch of the concrete on his back, he sits up. Looking around, he calls out to his mom and dad. However, he hears nothing but the haunting howl of the wind. He sits, wondering how he even got to this place. Frightened and cautious, he walks around and realizes that he is in some sort of prison.

"Hello, is someone here?" Elias says.

Hearing no response, he decides to traverse deeper into the prison. As he walks past every empty cell, he sees words written on the walls. He cannot quite make out what it says. His curiosity says to go see what is being said on the wall, but the fear that is slowly creeping over him says to run. Elias begins to hear these voices cry out. They are faint, almost having this ghastly feeling to it. He calls out again, yet nothing but these same voices call out. This feeling of dread comes over Elias, almost paralyzing him where he stands. He closes his eyes, saying to himself, *"This isn't real...This isn't real!"* He repeats this to himself multiple times until he feels someone behind him. He turns to look behind him to see nothing there.

From one cell block to another, Elias seemingly can find no one in this abandoned prison. Crying, he screams out for help as loud as he can. Suddenly, he hears the voices he heard earlier. However, this time, they sound a lot closer than they did before. He quickly runs down the hall. He stops at a dead-end, with only a choice of left or right. Panicking, he turns left and runs calling out to the voices. He hears himself getting closer and closer to the source of the voices. *"Maybe it is Mom and Dad,"* Elias thinks to himself. As he passes each cellblock, it seems as if the appearance of each cell worsens. He stops to look around and sees that the prison has completely changed. He walks downstairs to the first level. As he walks past each cell, they all seem broken and old. The bars look to be rusted and dilapidated. Elias notices that there are no words written on the walls of these cells. Just as Elias was approaching one of the cells, he hears a scream again, but this time it was clear and sounded like it was right next to him. Elias steps over just a few cells and sees a girl in the fetal position within the cell. The walls of the cell appear to have writing on them, as if the person on the ground has scribbled on the wall using blood.

In big red letters, the word 'perversion' is written. He goes up to the cell door to try and get the person's attention, to try and see if he can help her; however, he hears another voice. He looks over and sees another cell with 'fear' written as if the person that wrote it was insane, with someone inside frozen in a state of pure terror, with their cell door open. More and more voices begin to become noticeable. He goes back to the person in the first cell he saw. He pulls on the bars, trying to talk to them.

"Hey, my name is Elias. Help me please! I don't want to be here."

The figure in the cell does nothing. He hears a loud bang. It startles him and he realizes that it came from the same area. He goes further down to find the sound. He discovers that it is a guy in this cell, yet he cannot make out his face. The guy seems to be very angry. He looks up and sees 'wrath' written using similar bloody letters. Elias tries to make out the other words, failing to do so. He tries to talk to each person in a cell. He even tries to free some of them, but it ends in failure. He looks at the end of the cellblock to see this large, looming figure. Its shadow is darker than any shadow Elias has seen. The voice he hears coming from the figure creates this heaviness in his chest. Elias, scared, tries to take a step back; however, with every step he takes, it comes closer. The voices from the cells become silent. The figure tells him that it knows he is afraid and that he will soon be in one of those cells.

"I want my mom and dad."

Taking another step, the figure says "They aren't here, but you will be. You will be just like the rest of them." The feeling of fear overtakes Elias. Crying, he screams for his Dad and Mom. The figure rushes towards him to grab him.

Choose ye this day…

Bruce, waking up from what seemed like a sleepless night, gets up to see about Isabella. He goes to her room, seeing her sleep peacefully. He is mesmerized by the sheer beauty of his daughter. It often catches him by surprise because it seemed not that long ago that she was just a little baby in his arms crying, yet now she can make her own bowl of cereal and can even do a little cooking. While this moment is one that brings him much joy, he only wishes that Candice and Isabella could have a better relationship.

It has been over three years since he has seen Candice and Diana. He tries to go and see them, but it seems her mother is always making excuses as to why coming there at that moment would be a bad time. Though he talks to Candice sometimes using video chat, he feels that he is missing key moments of his daughter's life. She is already in high school and she just seems to be growing up so fast, while he is getting older.

"Babe, where are you?" Alexandra says.

Going back into his bedroom, he goes over to kiss her.

"I was just checking on Bella."

"You always stalk her in her room, while she sleeps. Are you still having that dream again?"

"No."

"Bruce, you must be honest with me. I cannot help you if you hide things."

Kissing her, he assures her that he is fine and takes her request for breakfast.

"Omelet du fromage" Alexandra says smiling.

"Now you know my French is rusty."

"Omelet with cheese babe…omelet with cheese."

Isabella runs into their room, jumping on Bruce's neck. She kisses him on the cheek, saying "I want pancakes!!"

Saluting, he says, "Yes ma'am!"

Whom you will serve

Screaming, Elias wakes up. His scream causes his sister, Faith, to wake up crying.

Sam and Lola wake up due to the kids.

"Crap! This is the tenth time this month he woke up out of his sleep screaming."

"I know Lola…What do you expect me to do? I have tried talking to him multiple times, but I do understand what is going on."

Irritated, Lola gets up, mumbling, to check on Faith. Sam lays there and begins to pray for Elias, before getting up to check on him. Walking over to Elias's room, he sees him crying in bed. He sits beside him, hugging him. As he holds him, praying for his mind, he begins to pray in the spirit. He looks at Elias, letting him know that everything would be okay. Sam asks him what the dream was about. Elias begins to tell him, struggling to hold back the tears. Elias tells his dad about it with such a description that it begins to make Sam wonder for a brief second if his son had visited this place. Sam explains to Elias that it was only a dream, that none of it was real. Elias asks him to check his room to make sure the monster in his dreams was not there. In hopes of reassuring Elias, he walks to his closet, opening the door to show him there is nothing there. He checks under his bed, showing him that nothing is there. Sam kisses his forehead and tells him to get some rest. Leaving the room, Sam hears a still, small voice that tells him to anoint the entrance of his room. Sam stops for a moment. Unsure of what he heard; he just shuts Elias' door. Walking back to bed, he sees Lola rocking Faith back to sleep. He plops down onto the bed, with Lola coming in moments later.

"Did you get Elias back into bed, Sam?"

"Yea…He was scared. I don't understand how his dreams are so vivid. The way he described it, the touch, the feel of the things in the dream, you would almost think that this boy has been in a prison before."

Lola turns to face Sam.

"We have to pray because I do not know how much longer I can take waking up at dawn because of his nightmares. We might even need to fast."

"Uh…I am not sure. I mean maybe it's what he's watching."

"Sam, what do you think he watches that could possibly be causing nightmares like this? I mean we try to make sure we don't watch anything scary."

"Lola, I don't know. I just know this has made me late for work more times than I care to count. Between him and our daughter crying, I am beat!"

"And I'm not?!"

Sam sighs, placing his hand on hers, but she pulls away.

"That is not what I am saying. I'm………I'm sorry Lola. I'm just tired and trying to understand what's happening to our son.

He's being chased by demons in his sleep, barely sleeping sometimes. The last dream he had was him standing in a pool of his family's blood. That's creepy."

"Wait…. when did he have that one?"

"This was like a month ago."

"And you just thought that you should just now mention that to me?"

"I really thought I did. It was during my Canada trip."

"Oh right, the trip where you refused to tell me why you went or where you were going to Canada. That Canada trip, right?"

"Please Lola, don't start with me about this. That was three whole years ago when that happened. You gotta let that go babe."

"Oh sure. I will let it go, when you tell me the truth."

"I cannot tell you and you know why."

Lola, angrily, mumbles something in Spanish.

"Sam, you don't even know what actually happened. You just ran on the word of some woman…"

"She was a friend, Lola"

"Oh, excuse me, a 'friend' that asked you to do something and you just did it."

Irritated, Sam sits up and says, "Seriously?!"

"Yes, seriously Sam! You left the house like a thief in the night, and I didn't see you until dawn. I called all around looking for you. Marlinda was worried that whoever was after Elias, when he was born, had somehow got to you. I was just shocked that you didn't even tell me."

"I had to leave at that moment."

"And that makes it right?!"

"I did not say that. However, let's address the real problem."

"Excuse me?!"

"Yes, the real problem, which is that for all this time you have held on to this and you think that I am cheating."

"I never said that."

"You don't have to. You've stopped trusting me and become very suspicious of every move I make."

"Can you blame me??"

"Yes……Yes, I can because if I told you that I could not explain it at the moment, but I will in time. You should trust that. You should trust me. You have been feeling like this ever since you had Faith."

"Feeling what, Sam?!"

"Feeling insecure, the same way you felt when we were younger."

Upset, Lola turns away from Sam, with tears falling down her face.

"One of the qualities that I adore most about you is your loyalty…and it is one of the qualities about you that I hate the most."

Choose ye this day…

Making breakfast for his ladies, Bruce's mind begins to wonder. He thinks about what has been happening to his family over the last few years. It breaks his heart to know that his two girls aren't as close as he would desire them to be. Alexandra walks into the kitchen, tapping him on the shoulder, seemingly breaking him out of his trance. She hugs him and compliments him on the amazing smells coming from the kitchen. Isabella soon follows behind her mother.

"Are you ladies ready for breakfast?"

"Yes sir!" says Alexandra and Isabella, saluting their dad.

As they all prepare to eat, Bruce's phone rings. He looks down to see that it is Diana calling. He looks up at Alexandra and Isabella.

"Who is it Bruce?"

"It's Diana."

"You haven't heard from her for how long?"

"It's been over a year, but it's always drama with her and we're all having such a good time."

Placing her hand on his, she lets him know that it is okay for him to answer. He walks away, answering his phone. Alexandra cuts Isabella pancakes, pouring the warm maple syrup over them. Alexandra's heart just melts every time she sees Isabella's smile. She just simply wishes things were different with their whole family. She can hear Bruce raise his voice to Candice's mom, arguing with her about seeing Candace. She cannot imagine how he must feel, not being able to see his own daughter. The lies, the deception, and hate are creating a rift that she prays does not hinder the relationship between Isabella and Candice; however, she fears that it is already there and getting worse.

"Mommy?"

"Yes, dear?"

"Is Daddy angry with the person on the phone?"

"Um… well ma amour, your dad just really wants things to be better with you two and wants to see Candice because he misses her."

"Why can't Daddy see Candice?"

"Sometimes, adults can be dumb."

Alexandra tells Isabella to stay at the table while she goes and see what is going on with Daddy. As she goes into the room, she sees Bruce visibly furious and in tears. He hangs up, throwing his phone at the wall, startling Alexandra.

"Bruce, what is wrong?"

"I just found out Candice is in the hospital."

In tears, he tells her about the phone conversation.

"I'm so sorry."

"Alex, she won't let me see my daughter and is spreading lies about me to her. This ain't right!"

"I know baby…Do you want to pray?"

As Alexandra begins to pray for Bruce, Isabella comes in, hearing them pray. Bruce, opening his eyes, sees that Isabella has grabbed his hand. Once Alexandra is done praying, Isabella hugs her Dad, saying "It's okay Daddy. You don't have to cry."

Whom you will serve

Alone with Faith, Lola sits up in bed and thinks about Sam's words. She never thought that he would bring up her past. It hurts for her to think that Sam really sees her as this woman that is still insecure and weak. This is something that she had gotten over, and it is wrong for him to bring it up. Lola gets up, gets dressed, and gets Faith ready for a little trip. As she is getting Faith ready to leave, she hears her phone ring and sees that Marlinda is calling her. An eternity seem to past since since she and Marlinda really sat and talked.

"Hey Miss…I mean Mrs. Marlinda."

"Oh yeah get that right, it's Mrs. now. I's married now!"

"How can I help you?"

"I was just about to see if you wanted to have lunch or something."

"You know, I have not been out the house in a while now. I think I will take you up on that offer. I just get to pick the place this time. Last time, you took us to that awful restaurant on fifth."

"Hey, now! In my defense, I didn't realize it was gonna be that terrible."

Laughing, Lola says, "And that is why I'm picking this time. I will send you the address."

Marlinda agrees to meet her. Lola feels like this is something she needs because maternity leave has not been too kind to her this time around. It feels as if the walls of their place are closing in on her. She packs Faith's diaper bag and loads Faith up into the car.

On his way to work, Sam ponders on what was said before he got up to leave. He did not mean to hurt her, but he just cannot help but to feel like he has been under a microscope since that night seven years ago. The more he thinks about it, the more it irritates him. As he is driving on the freeway, he begins to feel the pull on his heart. Sam cannot quite explain it. Suddenly, he hears a voice say something. He cannot quite make it out, but it gives him pause. Thoughts begin to plague his mind about Lily, about where she is and if she is even safe. He has not seen her since his last trip to see her three years ago. He has not received so much as a phone call or email from her. He takes out his phone to reach out to her, to try and give her a call. Just as he is about to call her, he hears this voice again. However, this voice is a bit clearer and very distinct. It is so clear that it scares him a little.

The voice says "Samuel, tell Lola the truth."

Chapter 14

Multiple people walk into the boardroom, preparing for the meeting. The tension in the air is thick, as this is not normal due to them just having one. As each board member sits in their seat, they whisper and murmur about what could possibly be the cause of this. Stock prices have taken a little dive lately, but it was not anything that would be out of the ordinary. Some even begin to get nervous as things have been changing around the company, especially with leadership. As all are seated, they wait anxiously to see who called this meeting. The minutes turn to hours, as they wait. Just as one member was preparing to leave, the room doors open, and they are shocked to see who called the meeting.

Choose ye this day…

Packing their things to prepare to leave for the airport, Alexandra looks at Bruce and asks if he is sure he is ready for this encounter with Candice.

"I gotta be ready. Diana is so irresponsible! She allowed her to just do whatever and now she is in the hospital. This woman only calls me when there is something I gotta fix!"

"Mi Amour, I know you are upset. However, being angry will not fix the situation. Right now, Candice needs you and you have to bridge the gap in our families. I don't want Isabella growing up not knowing her sister, like I did."

"I know baby. Well, we will see if that is possible when we

get there."

Alexandra hugs him, assuring him that everything will be okay. Bruce goes into Isabella's room, helping her get ready.

"Daddy, is Candice okay?"

"Bella, she will be okay. I'm sure of it. We just gotta see her first."

"Yaay! I miss my sister"

Bruce carries out their bags, while Alexandra straps Isabella into the car.

"Daddy?"

"Yes, Bella?"

"Can we pray for my sister, now?"

Bruce laughs and says, "Sure."

"God, please let my sis be okay. Let her not be sick anymore and be happy and smiling. In Jesus name, Amen!"

Whom you will serve

"Ladies and Gentlemen, Hello. Hope everyone is doing well this evening."

One of the board members speaks up, saying "Damian! What are we doing here and why is your secretary here on official board business?"

Tiffany looks at Damian with a smirk.

"Well before we get to that I have a couple of announcements to make."

"Where is Lucius? You have no authority to make or call any board meeting without him being here. You are just a regular member, like the rest of us."

Damian looks at Tiffany, smiling.

"I'm glad you brought that up because that's one of the things that's about to change."

Damian looks at the clock, seeing that it has just struck 6pm. He claps his hands together, making his first announcement.

"As of right now, I now have controlling interest in the company. You now work for me."

The board members are shocked and outraged. Many of them begin shouting and cursing him. "Impossible!" shouts one of the members. "You would have had to take all of our shares without us knowing or buying us out," Says another member.

"You are exactly right. And if you would look at the folder in front of you, you will see that all of you here are at a crossroads. As you all open your folder, you will see documentation that proves, lock, stock and barrel, that you are all guilty of insider trading. And as egregious as those charges are, for some of you, you can continue to flip through those pages and it gets worse. However, there is a lifeboat there, waiting to save you. Your lifeboat comes in the form of another document that is in there that requires your signature. This document you would sign would be giving me a significant number of your shares to me, which would then give me controlling interest in this company and cause all of you to work for me. I mean for some of you, this is as good as it's going to get, especially with the dirt I uncovered on some of you."

The room falls silent, as they are all shocked at how Damian amassed so much knowledge about them. One of the older members slams his hands on the table, standing up.

"How dare you threaten me child?! I was here when you were just a twinkle in the eye of your father! This…this documentation, this "evidence", is just a fabrication. None of this is real. You're just trying to bully us all and I will not stand for it!"

Before Damian can reply to him, Tiffany stops him.

"Listen, if you really believe this is all a farce, you are free to walk out that door, out this building and find out. However, I can promise you this: If you or any of you

for that matter leave this room, our deal is off the table and we will take everything! We will leave you with absolutely nothing, your children will have nothing, wives will have nothing. Those fancy excursions some of you like to take, gone! We will see to it that you all will never see daylight or know the sweet comforts that you all are so used to ever again……oh and if any of you think about coming after Damian, me, or William, let's just say I would strongly reconsider those lines of thought."

All the board members look at each other, wondering what to do. The entire room watches as one of the members sign their name, giving away some of their shares. Many of them try to tell him not to do it, even warning him that this is not right. He closes the folder, getting up to give it to Damian. As he hands it off to Damian, he says to him, smiling, "You will always have a vote of confidence from me and Starzl group, plus I'd rather be at the devil's right hand than in his path."

"Thank you, Darren, for your loyalty. It will be rewarded very soon. You have my word on that," Damian says.

Shocked, many of them wonder what they had on Darren that was so incriminating that he was so willing to sell off his shares to them so quickly. As Damian and Tiffany look around at them, Damian tells them that his offer has a very immediate expiration date . One by one, they watch as each person on the board sign their names on the dotted line. Another one of the members begins to speak up about Damian's father and Lucius.

"What does Lucius have to say about all this?! I don't think he would be pleased with you two, essentially stealing his company. What do you think he's going to do to the two of you when he discovers your treachery?"

As Tiffany goes around the room, collecting their folders, she says, "Oh don't you worry your pretty, little head about that. That matter is officially above your paygrade now."

"Now that this little matter is out of the way, we now get to announcement number two. As of now, Tiffany will be our new Chief Financial Officer. You all will now answer to me and her now."

"This…This is ridiculous! Just because you had sex with your secretary, does not mean that she gets a seat at this table. She just slept her way to the top, like so many others before her. I will not tolerate having to take orders from a lowly secretary, let alone a woman that is a harlot!"

As the older member says this, they all remain quiet seemingly in solidarity. Damian slowly walks over to the older member. He places his hand on his left shoulder, frightening the man at first. He smiles.

"George, my friend, one thing my father always respected is your honesty. I remember he would rely on that honesty and respect from you. You were his 'go to' guy."

As Damian continues to talk, George begins to feel weird. He cannot place it, but it is almost as if he cannot move the left side of his body. He starts feeling this sharp, stabbing in his chest. He tries to move his left arm, but nothing happens. He tries to speak, but he realizes his words are beginning to slur a little. He begins to think to himself that maybe he is having a stroke or a heart attack of some kind. He falls down to his knees, still unable to move or speak. He finally collapses onto the ground.

Horrified, the board rushes to his side, as Damian walks back to the front of the room. They ask George if he is okay but get no response.

They go to check his pulse, but Damian stops them, saying, "I do not think you need to worry about George anymore. So, does anyone else object to these changes?"

Choose ye this day…

Bruce goes to pick up their luggage, while waiting for Alexandra to pull around with the rental. Thoughts of regret begin to rush his mind, wondering if maybe all of this is his fault. He begins to think maybe him being away caused Candice to act out and end up where she is now. Trying to ignore these thoughts, he grabs their luggage and begins loading it up into the car. As the cool Memphis air goes across his face, it brings him feelings of nostalgia. He reminisces about when Candice's mom first picked him up from this airport after being deployed. It was in this very airport that she told him that they were going to have a baby. That moment seems so far now that it almost feels like a distant memory. He gets in and they make their way to the hospital. As the car drives off, Bruce looks out the side view mirror, noticing something odd staring off at them in the distance.

Whom you will serve

Following her GPS to the location she gave to Marlinda, she sees that it is the new brunch spot that she heard about on the news. She takes Faith out of her car seat, walking in to see Marlinda is already on her second cup of coffee.

"Oh my… Marlinda! I'm so sorry if I am late! I just had to get Faith together and stuff and I did not realize…"

"Child please! You are right on time. Did you even check your watch?"

"Um……no. I just looked at your coffee cups and thought that I was late."

"No, I just love their coffee. I mean, have you even had one from here? It is amazing! Best coffee in the city."

"I am more of an iced coffee or espresso type of gal."

The two of them laugh, as Lola straps Faith into the

highchair. "Oh, and how is my second God-baby doing?"

Marlinda says, tickling Faith. Faith smiles from ear to ear.

"She is good, when she isn't screaming on the top of her lungs at night because of Elias."

"Why is Elias causing her to cry at night? Is he messing with her?"

Lola quickly shifts the subject, by asking her about married life. Right when Marlinda is going to answer, the waiter comes over to take their orders.

"Oh sir, can you please bring my daughter a fruit cup and a small cup of water please?"

"Sure ma'am."

She thanks him and continues with her conversation with Marlinda, asking her about things with her husband.

"Girl, Lewis is fine. He is always trying to stay busy, working on different stuff. If you didn't know him, you would think that man is Superman. Always trying to fix people's problems. His kids are just lovely."

"Didn't some of your family move up here too?"

"Child, yes and they are a headache and a half! Always sumthn goin on with them."

"I can totally get that, but I know how excited you were a few years ago when you found out they were coming. It is your nieces and nephews, right?"

"Child, yes! They got more kids then I can count. Seems like they were multiplying like rabbits back home. Every time I talk to them, seem like somebody else havin' a baby."

Lola laughs, reminding her that God gave her exactly what she asked for. They both laugh, as they are continuing to talk. The waiter comes back, asking for their food orders. They place their orders and wait for the food to come. Moments later, their food arrives, and Lola's eyes almost glaze over at how delicious her food looks.

She can smell the fresh maple syrup that is slowly falling down her berry stuffed French toast and her bacon appears as if it was cooked to perfection. She looks up at Marlinda, seeing this succulent T-Bone steak with scrambled eggs and cubed potatoes.

"Um…really Marlinda?"

"What? I came hungry. Steak and eggs is a southern breakfast, anyway."

"Sure, it is."

Marlinda prays for their food. As they eat, Jesus begins to speak to Marlinda, about Lola and urges her to talk to her about her family. As Jesus is speaking to her, she just looks at her and Faith. She smiles and asks her about Sam.

"We are fine…"

Marlinda looks at her, staring.

"What?"

"Here is the thing, you are not a very good liar. So, I can discern that are lying."

Defensively, Lola says, "No I am not." She stops eating to help Faith with her food.

"So, what you are saying is that the Holy Ghost is lying?"

Irritated, Lola reassures her that everything is fine. Marlinda tells her to stop feeding Faith for a second and to look at her. Lola turns, looking Marlinda in the eyes. Marlinda takes her by the hand.

"Baby, Jesus cannot help you when you are lying to yourself. I suspected something was wrong when I looked at you. It was almost like a spirit of heaviness was on you or something. I just could not place it. Jesus just confirmed it for me, as we were praying for our food. Now, tell me what is wrong."

As Marlinda says these words, it is as if a levee breaks in Lola. Tears begin to fall down her face. She puts her head down, crying.

"It is okay baby. That is why we are here, to help one another.

Remember, we are many members of the same body. So, when something is wrong with a finger, the rest of the fingers need to band together to help out. However, you cannot get help by lying to yourself and trying to fool Jesus. The only person you makin' a fool of is you."

"I know. I just had to be tough all my life and it is hard sometimes to let people in when something is wrong with me. I just want and try to keep it all in."

"And how is that going for you so far?"

"Real cute Mrs. Marlinda" Lola says, drying her eyes. Seeing her cry, makes Faith get a little upset. She takes Faith into her arms, reassuring her that mommy was okay. She rocks her in her arms a little, as Faith begins to quiet down.

"See, even the baby knew something was wrong. Now don't the Word of God tell us to cast our cares on Him?"

"Yes but…"

"There are no buts with Christ. It is just His Word and the promises in it."

"I know."

"So, what is going on?"

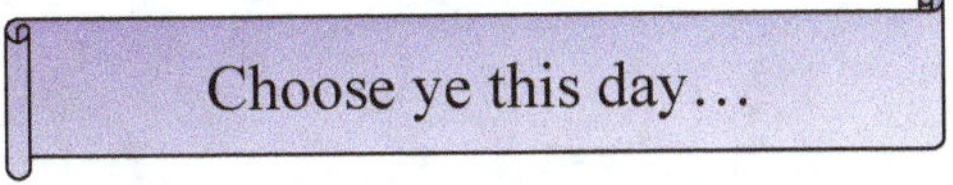

As the last of the board members leave, Damian shakes a few hands. He assures them that these changes will be best for business. Tiffany collects all the folders, placing them on the table. The final member leaves, with Damian shutting the door right behind them.

"Well, that could have gone over much worse than it did. And to think, only one of them had to die for this to work."

"Yeah, well…George would have been a problem anyway. He was old-fashioned and would never have gone with what we are about to do."

Tiffany approaches Damian, putting her arms around his neck.

"How long do you think it is going to take before Lucius finds out what we've done?"

"If I know him, like I think I do, he probably already knows by now. It's just a matter of figuring out what his next move will be. You got George's body moved quick."

"I used to have to clean up messes for Lucius, so I just made a call to his cleanup guy.

As they kiss, Tiffany looks at him smiling.

"I cannot believe it is our sixth anniversary already. The time has gone by so quickly."

"Yes, nevertheless, I cannot imagine anyone else by my side. You were there even in the worst of times."

"I know and trust me; you will get your revenge. I promise you that."

"So, phase two?"

"Yes Mr. Huntington. We are in phase two. Just remember, if you aim for the king, don't miss!"

Chapter 15

Laying on the clean, cold bed, Candice's mind begins to wonder. Thoughts of how things could have gotten this bad. All of this seems to be like a bad dream. One moment she is singing in front of people, the next moment she is waking up in a hospital bed. She tries to think back to figure out what happened, but it is all a blur. Diana walks into her room, with tears of joy in her eyes. She rushes over to her bed, embracing her.

"Mom, I am okay," Candice says, struggling.

"No! You are far from okay. Do you know what happened?"

"Um…No. I cannot seem to remember what happened. I remember singing in front of people, things started to get hazy and next thing I know I am waking up in this bed."

"You lost consciousness, while singing. You must have hit your head hard. Let me see if I can find your doctor. They were running some tests on you. I will be back."

"Okay, Mom."

Candice tries to sit herself up, but she begins to get an excruciating headache that stops her in her tracks. She turns over on her side to rest. Just as she closes her eyes, she hears a knock on the door. Candice looks up to see her father, stepmother, and Isabella standing in the doorway.

Whom you will serve

"It is complicated. I don't even know how to describe it,

which is so freaking frustrating. You know, the worst part about this is that I truly believe Sam is a good man."

Confused, Marlinda asks her to explain.

"I think Sam is cheating on me…"

Pausing from eating, Marlinda bursts into laughter.

"Excuse you! You think this is funny? You asked me to tell you how I feel, and you laugh?"

Lola, feeling offended and angry, prepares to pack up her and Faith's things.

"Girl, sit your butt down! You not going anywhere."

"You just laughed at me after telling me to open up. I'm straight on this."

"That is the problem with your generation. You are all emotion without common sense. However, let's entertain this line of thought: What evidence do you have to suggest that Sam…your Sam, the same Sam that did everything he could to make sure Elias was safe at that hospital, the same Sam that stuck by you after people talked about you and dogged you in the church, is cheating on you?"

"Since you want to be such a smart aleck about it, I will tell you. Sam has been extremely secretive these past few years. He has been taking random trips to Canada by himself, saying that he was handling business there, but he could not go into it. He would always say 'when everything settles, I will explain. I promise.' It has been years since he's been saying this now. I would then ask him about it and after a while, he started getting annoyed by me asking about it. There was even a situation that happened in New York. We talked about and do you think he even considered me and how I have felt since? No! All he has thought about was himself. What he did in New York hurts."

"To be fair, nothing even happened. He was burning a candle at both ends and almost got burned. You still ain't forgive him for that??"

"Yes I did!"

"Are you sure? Because it does not sound like you have. You cannot say you forgive him and then in a passive aggressive manner, remind him of it."

"It isn't even just that. This all started after a secret phone call he got seven years ago. This whole thing has been so hurtful. You say the same Sam that stuck by me after people talked about me and dogged me? How about after all the times I stuck by him when he was broken?"

As tears slowly begin to fall down Lola's face and she continues to vent, Marlinda can see the brokenness that is within Lola.

"Sam was a broken little boy that was so insecure and timid that he couldn't even look people in the eye and ran from confrontation.

Sam did not even know who he was, as a person.

How about after all that Sam put me through, I stayed with him! Even with him entertaining other women in front of me, I stayed with him...I frea—"

Without finishing, Lola breaks. The dam that held back everything she had been feeling for years has finally broken. Marlinda gets up from her side of the booth, going to Lola's side. She embraces Lola, quietly praying for her. Lola then begins sobbing. As their waiter comes over to check on them, he asks Marlinda if everything was okay.

"Yes, just someone needed a good cry that's all," Marlinda says quietly.

The waiter nods, understanding and says that he will leave them be.

"I am so sorry I laughed at you Lola, please forgive me. I had no idea, and I did not take this as seriously as I should have."

Not responding to her, Lola just sobs.

"You do not have to talk, just listen to me. This is not just coming from Sam. This is a brokenness that stems from a long time ago, your feelings of abandonment. I do not know much about your past, but you gotta deal with your abandonment issues, Dear. If you don't, they gon destroy your marriage. Rather if it was your mother or father, you gotta let that mess go. Jesus can heal that, but if you do not let it go and give it to him, it will kill you, Sam, and your children. No matter who might abandon you, I can tell you Jesus will never abandon you. He said He will never leave you nor forsake you. That is a promise. Sam and you gotta talk dear. I do not believe Sam is cheating on you, but secrets will destroy your marriage. Don't allow the devil to plant seeds in your mind. You gotta cast those thoughts down."

Sobbing, Lola asks, "What about me makes people want to leave me?"

"Oh baby, there is nothing that you did that made people want to leave you. They left because they did not see your value and that's their loss. Some people do not know that coal can become diamonds. People turned away from Jesus, not knowing that He was everything that they were hoping for."

"Th…this just hurts so bad. I am trying to be the best wife I can be. I know I have had two kids and everyth—"

Marlinda stops her and reassures her of her beauty.

"Thanks, Marlinda. I really appreciate it. People have left me all my life and I feel like Sam is doing the same, after everything. I just cannot believe he would do this to me."

Marlinda wipes her tears, gently picking up her face and looking into her caramel-colored eyes.

"Listen to me, that devil is really trying to do a number to yo head. You are beautiful and loved. You are a gorgeous girl and don't let that devil tell you differently! Sam isn't unhappy with you and he ain't cheatin on you. Jesus loves you so much, but you gotta let go of the past. He might have struggled with being insecure, but you still struggle with it. This abandonment issue has developed into an insecurity issue. My sweet girl, you are so loved."

Marlinda hears this still, small voice that tells her to tell Lola that she is so loved. As she tells her this over and over, the cracks in the dam Lola created around her heart burst as she breaks down again.

"Jesus, she needs you. Heal every broken place in Jesus name. Every place of disappointment Jesus, let her know that you will never disappoint. Uproot every insecurity in Jesus name and I cancel every lying word that the devil has spoken over her in Jesus name. You are beautiful, you are Jesus' priceless ruby. You are so loved Lola…you are so loved Lola. Jesus said you gotta love yourself first sweetie. Jesus will not abandon you. He is a good, good Father, perfect in all His ways."

As Marlinda prays and speaks what Jesus wants to tell her, tears begin to fall down her face. It is as if she can feel Lola being freed from her insecurities as she prays. For the first time, she starts to feel what Lola has kept pinned up for years. This dam Lola created has kept so many people at arm's length, even Jesus. Marlinda can feel the breaking of Lola. Marlinda just continues to say what Jesus tells her, further breaking Lola. Faith begins to start crying, sensing something is not right with her mother. Marlinda grabs Faith, praying and expressing Jesus' love for her, as well.

Choose ye this day…

"Hey Candice, can we come in?"

Looking down, Candice nods. Bruce rushes into the room, hugging Candice tightly. He kisses her on the forehead. Isabella looks up at her, smiling.

"I'm happy you are okay."

"Thanks, I guess."

"Candice, what happened to you? Your mother did not tell me anything over the phone."

"I'm fine Dad. It was nothing."

As Bruce continues to talk to Candice, Diana walks into the room. Her presence in the room draws the attention of everyone. Diana's eye turns to Isabella and Alexandra. Seeing Bruce with them gives her a feeling of disgust. Not addressing them, she looks at Candice and tells her that the doctor is coming soon to talk to them about the test results. Bruce tries to talk to Diana, to figure out what happened. Diana, completely ignoring him, addresses Candice.

"I'm glad you woke up dear. How are you feeling?"

Frustrated, Candice says "I'm fine."

"Diana, I was talking to you. What happened to our daughter?"

"Oh, I'm surprised you actually came. When I told you she was singing, you didn't seem to care to come then."

"Diana why are you lying?! You didn't say anything to me about her singing?"

"You are suc—"

Just as Diana and Bruce start arguing, the doctor comes into the room. "Excuse me. If there is a problem, you need to take it outside my patient's room."

Before Bruce or Diana could say anything, Alexandra speaks up.

"We uh…apologize for the disturbance."

"You are okay," The doctor says.

Alexandra reaches her hand out, introducing herself, Isabella, and Bruce. Bruce asks the doctor about Candice and her condition. As he looks at her, she begins to fill up with regret and guilt. He even begins to wonder if what is happening could be somehow his fault for leaving her mother.

"Well, we did some blood work and a few other neurological tests because she hit her head. So, we want to make sure that her head is fine. We did find some things that are alarming. It seems her body is deficient of key vitamins and proteins."

The doctor looks at Candice, noticing that she put her head down. She goes on to list the different things her body was lacking. Bruce felt his heart begin to break as it seems like his little girl was falling apart in front of him. He goes to touch her hand and she pulls away from him. The look on her face, brings tears to his eyes.

"What does all that mean doctor?" Bruce asks.

The doctor looks back at Candice and begins to speak to her. "Listen Candice, I can tell them what I found. However, if you want to tell them, I can give you a minute and come back.

With everyone looking at her, Candice says nothing. She just has a blank stare at the white wall on the right of her.

"Based on what I am seeing, it would suggest to me that she was purging and has been for quite some time. Also, there are trace amounts of drugs and other laxatives in her. It would explain why she dropped on stage. She was dehydrated and isn't really retaining anything vital to her body. These are all the signs that a person that is suffering from Bulimia would show. Furthermore, I discovered her underactive thyroid. This would further explain the fatigue and weakness. Currently, I am working with another doctor to see if we can figure this thyroid situation out."

As the doctor looks at their faces, she can see the mixture of emotions that they are feeling. She tries to reassure them that everything will be okay and to remind them that she is alive so that is a good thing, considering everything she is going through, but she can tell she is only getting through Alexandra. She places her hand on the foot of Candice, telling her that everything will be okay, and she will help her. Before she leaves, Bruce stops the doctor.

"So, what are the next steps? What can I do?"

Being honest with him, the doctor explains to him that Candice really needs them right now. With the underactive thyroid and her bulimia, she could have died. So, she expresses to him that Candice needs the mental support from both of her parents right now, instead of them arguing right in front of her. She places her hand on his shoulder and tells him not to blame himself and she will be back with the other test results. As the doctor leaves, she closes the door behind her. Bruce watches the door close, and notices out the corner of his eye, the same odd figure staring. Quickly, Bruce turns to see what it was but misses it again. Under his breath, Bruce prays. Meanwhile, Diana begins to interrogate Candice about her purging and where she has been getting drugs from. Candice, still looking at the wall, says nothing to her.

Bruce tries to get Diana to stop, but she snaps at Bruce, calling him a derogatory name and saying not to talk to her. She begins to go on about this being his fault and that he abandoned his daughter for someone new.

Alexandra steps in and kindly asks to speak to her privately. Diana, being irate, tells Alexandra that they have nothing to talk about. As Isabella sees all this, she softly tries to get everyone to stop because it is making her sister upset. As Diana continues to raise her voice, this causes the nurses to alert security.

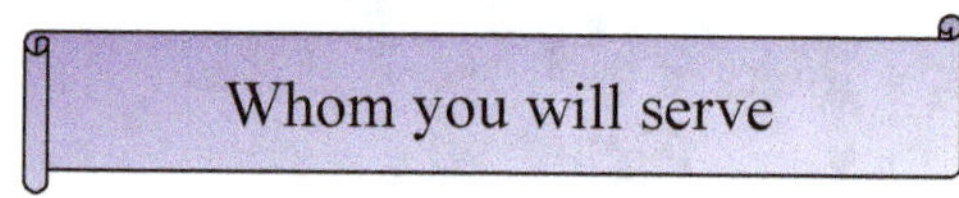

A car pulls into the driveway. The surrounding lights reflect off the cleanliness of the black paint job. The quiet hum of the engine is turned off and a young man gets out of the car. As he comes in, he takes out his wireless earbuds to the quiet solitude of the mansion he lives in. He calls out to see if anyone is around. As his voice carries throughout the place, he hears nothing but silence greeting him in return. He drops his bag at the door and begins walking around. Room by room, he sees how each one seems undisturbed. He walks into the kitchen, seeing several pots and pans on the stove with food in them.

He lifts one of them to just be hit by the delicious aroma from within. He gets a smell of the fresh herbs that were used in the making of this dish, from Rosemary to Parsley. He looks around to see if there is a utensil that is near to try this delectable dish but comes up with nothing. Just as he is about to dig for one, a woman greets him.

"Excuse me sir, I can serve you at the table if you would like."

"That would not be necessary. I am just getting a taste of it."

"Are you sure? Because I wou—."

Before she could finish, the young man interrupts her.

"I just said that would not be necessary…jeez. If I tell you, it is fine, then it is fine. Where were you when I called out for anyone? You did not answer me."

Nervously, she says "I…I'm sorry sir. I was just on the other side of the house and did not hear your voice. I only came into the kitchen because I wanted to finish dinner for everyone."

In a dismissive tone, the young man instructs the woman to grab his things that are by the door and take them to his room. She nods and walks away.

He goes to try the dish using a spoon from the drawer. He feels the rush of each flavor as the gumbo touches his tongue. It is like a culinary firework show, sending a rush of different sensations to his palette. He is amazed every time she makes this gumbo. It is like a different experience each time. As the woman walks back into the kitchen, she asks the young man if he likes the dish.

"It is good, I guess. Did you get my things?"

"Yes, sir. If you want to have dinner before your parents get here, I can make a place setting for you in the dining room."

"Sure. My father should be home soon."

The young man goes to sit at the table. As he looks around, he feels the loneliness of the dinner table. This loneliness deepens and with every moment, it makes him angry. The woman presents gumbo to him, but he gets up, telling her to bring it to his room.

"Are you sure? I'm sure they will be home soon."

"Yes! Just do it!"

Appearing saddened, the woman says, "Will that be all Mr. William?" Saying nothing, William leaves the dining room and heads up the spiral stairs.

> Choose ye this day…

As security comes, they ask the nurses what is going on. The nurses direct the guards to Candice's room. As they get closer to the room, all that can be heard is Diana's voice. The arguing that is coming from the room begins to alert and disturb other patients and their visitors. As they enter, they try to diffuse the situation. One of them goes to Diana, trying to calm her down; however, Diana tells the guard to get out. The guard stresses to her that they will remove her from the hospital and call the police if they need to. Ignoring him, Diana berates Bruce about him being the cause of Candice's sickness.

"If it was not for you leaving us for this chick, your daughter would not be in the situation. How could you do this to her?!"

"Diana, you need to cal—"

Shouting at him and putting her finger in his face, Diana says, "Don't you freakin tell me to calm down. You, that chick and that bas—"

Before she could finish, Alexandra steps in between Bruce and Diana saying, "We need to talk, now!"

Diana continues to shout at them. Having had enough of everything and with tears in her eyes, Candice screams, "Stop it! I want everyone to get out!"

Diana tries to smooth it over, but Candice ignores her and begins to cry. One of the security guards walks Bruce and Diana out her room, while the other one speaks to Alexandra right outside the door. She apologizes for the mess they have caused. She turns to Isabella sitting in the chair, instructing her to stay there while the grown-ups talk around the corner. Isabella nods her head. Alexandra looks over at Diana and Bruce talking in the middle of the hall. Never has she been this upset, ashamed, and disappointed in Bruce. She begins to wonder how to approach what she is about to say. As she is walking towards them, she begins to feel a slight headache. It is almost as if someone or something is stabbing her in the head. The pain slowly intensifies as she gets closer to

Diana. Before she walks over to them, she prays under her breath for her healing and protection from any demonic attacks. Alexandra goes over to them, demanding to talk to them now in the waiting area beside them.

"What are you two thinking?!"

"Excuse you? I don't need you tell me ho—" Diana, with boldness, interrupts her.

"Save it! Candice…your daughter is in there, literally starving herself to death and you want to argue about who your ex-husband, emphasis on ex, is with now? You need to grow up. Candice could have died Diana. You can hate me, disrespect me all you like, but what you won't do is ever disrespect my daughter…ever! Bruce, I am so disappointed with you for allowing this debacle to continue. You know I do not like to be embarrassed, but you are better than this Bruce. This is not the type of man that you are. We need to come up with a way so that we all can co-exist in peace. We don't have to do it for us, but for our children. Diana, whether you like it or not, Isabella is her sister. There is nothing you can do to change that. So, what is the solution?"

Diana and Bruce look at Alexandra, not really knowing what to do.

While in the room, Isabella looks concerned for Candice. She does not want to see her grief. As Candice continues to stare at the wall in silence, Isabella goes over to try to hold her hand. As she grabs her hand gently, Candice yanks her hand away.

"I'm sorry! I did not know you were sleepy. I just wanted to make sure you are okay."

Angrily, Candice says "Don't touch me!"

This frightened Isabella, making her sad. Isabella asks her what she did wrong, and Candice begins to snap on her, unleashing her wrath on her little sister.

"You existing is what you did wrong. I hate everything about you. You took my father away from me. I care nothing about you and you mean absolutely nothing to me. You are ugly and worthless. I mean look at you, you used to call me 'sissy' like we are some kind of family. You are not my sister because I did not ask for you. I hate you and your mother…and my father.

I wish you were dead and if it were up to me, I would do everything I could to make sure my wish came true!"

Just as Alexandra, Diana, and Bruce come back into Candice's room, they see Isabella sitting in the visitor's chair sobbing. Alexandra rushes to her, asking what is wrong. Isabella says nothing but just continues to cry.

"What did you do Candice?"

Candice says nothing to him. Bruce, visibly angry, pushes the issue. Diana then stops him and asks for a moment outside the room.

"Listen Bruce, that wife of yours wants a solution then fine. I want you and your new family to leave. Take your wife and child and never come back here again. You know I could easily take you to court for alimony and child support, making your life and new wife very miserable. You leave here, never showing your face here again and having no contact with Candice and I won't take you to court."

"You cannot do this Diana."

"Decide Bruce or I will decide for you."

"I want to see my daughter."

"Well, consider this the last time."

"No…No I won't accept this."

"Well, these are my conditions. Take it or leave it. Oh, and if you tell Candice of this, the deal is off."

"…Fine"

Alexandra looks at him in disbelief, shocked that he would even agree to such terms. She tries to advocate for him and yet is shut down by Bruce.

Walking back into the room, Bruce consults Isabella and tells Alexandra that they are leaving.

"I love you Candice and I always will. No matter what anyone says to you, know that you are daddy's little girl."

Under her breath and in tears, she says, "You say that but clearly I was so easily replaced."

As they gather their things and walk away, out the corner of Bruce's eye, he sees a shadow figure within Candice's room.

Chapter 16

As Lola gathers herself, she hugs Marlinda and Faith, gripping them tightly. She expresses her thanks to Marlinda for praying and being with her. She brushes it off, telling her that it is not an issue. It warms her heart, knowing that Marlinda is there for her.

"Marlinda, I really don't know what I would do without you being in my life."

"Girl, yes you do! You would be just fine because you got Jesus and with Jesus, everything is alright. I won't be here foreva, but Jesus will be. So, you would be alright."

Laughing, Lola says "I guess so. What do I do about Sam?"

Sipping her coffee, Marlinda explains to her what she should do, but tells her that she should be aware to use wisdom as well because she does not want to cause anymore conflict or give the devil more ammunition to use on them. Lola messages Sam and prepares to leave with Faith.

"Let me take Faith and pick up Elias from school. You go relax, spend some time in the presence of Christ with prayer and some good ole worship music before you talk to yo husband. You will want to be in the right head space."

"Thanks, you are a godsend."

"Baby, I just want y'all to succeed."

Lola pays for their food and leaves with a plan to save her marriage.

Leaving work, Sam sees a message from Lola. Just seeing her name right now fills him with dread. He does not know what she is about to say in it, but it cannot be good. Over the last several years, he has felt like he was torn between two truths. While he knows hiding things from Lola is wrong and will do nothing good for their marriage, he cannot sit and pretend that breaking Rebecca's dying wish would not break his heart and make him feel as if he betrayed her. The conflict within makes him feel like he is going to break in two. He feels like he

has just been going through the motions of his life for the past three years at least. Reluctantly, he opens the message to read it:

Hola Papi, I know we started on the wrong foot this morning and we cannot take that back, but we can fix it. We can fix it by talking about how and where we went wrong. I do not want things to end the way they did. So, when you get home, I would like to talk to you. I am so sorry for blowing up on you. Te quiero, Cariño.

Taking a heavy sigh, Sam gets into the car preparing to take this journey home. As he is driving, so many thoughts go through his mind. He wonders what changed with her. With all the problems they have been having lately, what will come out of this conversation they will have and if things will get better with them. While on the freeway, he finds himself stuck in traffic. He hears this still, small voice that says again *"Tell her the truth."* Still not really recognizing the voice, he pays no attention to it. Again, the voice says, *"Tell her the truth."* He is sure that he hears this voice but does not recognize it, but at this moment, he decides to speak back.

"What am I supposed to tell her? Oh, by the way, I have been protecting my ex's daughter for someone or something that has been trying to kill her?"

Sam hears nothing back.

"Typical. Why am I not surprised by this development? All I am trying to do is the right thing and all I do is catch a case for it. I am so over her mess for the past five or so years. All it has lately been is problem after problem and I do not think I can take anymore of this."

Suddenly he hears the voice again "Sam, tell her the truth."

He begins to become frustrated and says, "And what will the truth get me?"

The voice then says, *"If you do not tell her the truth, your marriage will be destroyed."*

Whom you will serve

Looking into the mirror, a young woman barely recognizes herself. When most people see her, they see a gorgeous, young blonde woman with long legs and a

pretty face. No one bothers to see her beyond what they, physically, see. When she stares at the mirror, the only things that goes through her mind are the scars of her broken past. Slowly, she moves her fingers across her face and feels where different bones in her face have been broken. Those memories begin to turnover in her mind, like the coming tide washing over a beach. As she touches every part of her face, terrible memories of her past come into her mind. It is as if her life has been one bad, sick and twisted show. Despite all that happened to her, she came out to be a beautiful looking woman, but ironically, it is that beauty that she hates most of all. In a fit of rage, she hits herself and punches the mirror. This only leaves her feeling more pain. Tears begin to fall down her face, as she is tormented by all these memories. Behind her, the shadow figure sees her. It laughs at her misfortune. It, along with the rest of the demonic spirits within her, begin to put all these strange thoughts and images into her mind. Thoughts that are trying to tempt her to harm herself. Covering her ears, she tells them to shut up and she runs out of the bathroom. She goes to pick up her phone and she sees that she has got a text that is asking if she wants to go to a party. She sends her reply and goes to get dressed.

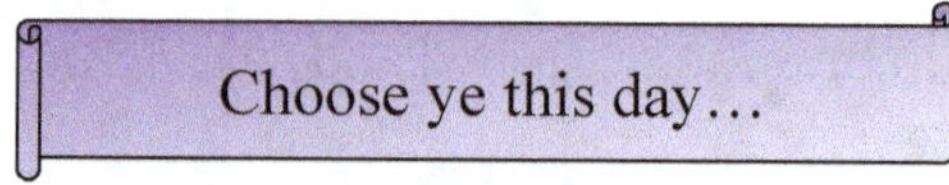

As William is listening to his music in his room, he hears a buzzing from his phone. He looks to see one of his friends on the basketball team ask him about a party and if he is down to go. Checking the time, he wonders how pissed his Dad would be if he went out on a school night to party. Just as he is going to tell his friend he is planning on passing, his friend sends him a message: Bro, before you wanna pass us up. We gonna have some fine girls and some fire drinks my dude. We about to win this championship tomorrow so let's get some early celebrating in now, plus I am gonna need my wingman. So, you in or out??.... please say in!

William looks at the phone and replies to him: You had me at hot women. Text me the location and I will be there. William gets up, putting on his coat to leave. As he is getting ready to go downstairs, he hears a door open and close. He rolls his eyes, opening his bedroom door. He looks over the rail to see his Dad and Stepmother walking in. Their laugh and kiss disgusts William. As he walks down the stairs, he tells them to get a room.

"Oh, you think you are so funny, William. How was school today?

"Great."

Just before William could get out the door, Damian stops him.

"Woah, where do you think you going at this hour?"

"Um…a bunch of the guys are getting together before our game tomorrow. You know, last min strategies and stuff. You and Mom are coming to the game, right?"

Damian and Tiffany look at each for a second.

"I mean if you can't, it's whatever."

Tiffany takes him by the hand and assures him that they will do everything they can to make it, but there are some things they must take care of. Knowing that this likely means they will not be there; he just shakes his head in agreement. Tiffany kisses him on the forehead and tells him to make sure he is back home before midnight.

"Okay."

Damian gives him a stern look and says, "Seriously, I am not joking with you. Your car better be in that driveway by midnight."

"Yes sir."

William closes the door behind him. Tiffany looks out from behind the curtain, watching him drive off. She walks over to Damian, giving him a kiss.

"What was that for?"

"Oh, you are about to find out sir."

Just as they go in for another kiss, their housekeeper walks in on them.

"Oh, excuse me Mr. and Mrs. Huntington, I just wanted to tell you that dinner is ready. Is there anything you would like for me to do before I leave for the evening?"

"No that will be all, Cynthia," Damian says.

"It smells delicious."

"Thank you, Mrs. Huntington. I hope it will be to your liking."

As Cynthia walks out the door, Tiffany pushes it close. She walks up to Damian, saying "Now, where were we?"

Whom you will serve

As she looks through her closet, she can find nothing that screams how she is feeling. Just as she is about to give up, she sees the perfect outfit. She quickly gets dressed and runs out the door. A voice yells at her on the other side of the door, asking her where she thinks she is going. Ignoring it, she makes her way out and into her friend's car.

"Hey girl! You ready?"

"As long as you and I can pre-game before we get there."

Her friend opens her bag, showing her the liquor she brought. "Oh, that's it?"

"Um, excuse you! You know I take care of my girl."

Her friend pulls out a small baggie with some pills in it. She takes the bag from her friend, taking one of the pills.

"Madison girl, I see you!"

"I'm always up for a good time. Let's go. There better be some hot guys here too because I did not put this outfit on for nothing."

The shadow figure looks at them with sheer bliss in its eyes, as it sees all the different spirits attached to them, specifically his charge Madison. It wonders what damage it and all the other spirits can do to her tonight. Writhing with pure excitement, it tags along with them. Her friend shifts into drive, speeding off.

Choose ye this day…

Sam pulls up to his house. Sitting there, he contemplates all the choices that led to this moment. Part of him feels that maybe this is really his fault, and he should not have lied to Lola about what happened that night; on the other hand, if it would have been Lola that asked him to do something like this for her and it was

Rebecca in this position, he would make the same choice. He

is yet haunted by the word that he heard spoken that if the truth is not revealed, it will be the end of his marriage. This all seemed to spin out of control so quickly. He looks at the door, wondering what is going to happen next. He goes in, seeing Lola. He looks at her, asking her about her day. She tells him that her day was okay. Before, Sam could say anything else, Lola stops him.

"Sam, stop. I see you are already thinking about what to say and that mind of yours is working overtime right now to say the right thing. However, I need to get this off my chest first."

"I kn—"

"Sam, since we first met, I always thought you were a great guy. I would look at you and I could tell that you were great. Since the first time you saw me and I you, I truly believe that we knew then that we loved each other, and I knew, or should I say thought it would be us versus everyone. However, somewhere along the way, you left me, Cariño. You left me hanging."

"What do you mean 'I left you hanging'?"

"You did. I got pregnant and it was supposed to be me and you. We said it was us versus everyone and you let people, the same people in our church, talk and do me real dirty and you let that crap ride. That's how you left me hanging."

Sam puts his hands over his face, using his palm and fingers to rub his eyes and nose.

"Oh my God Lola, you seriously still on this?! I had your back and I defended you."

"Where Sam? Where? Because every time I turned around, you were cheesin' in the face of the same people I knew were talking about me. So, help me understand Sam."

"That is not true."

"Why would I lie, Sam?"

Sighing, Sam says, "I don't know Lola. How about the fact that you haven't truly trusted me as much as you think or say that you do?"

"I did trust you."

"Oh bull! If you really trusted me, you would trust that I would have your back. Trust that I would never hang out with anybody that would disrespect my girlfriend, the mother of my child. The problem is you."

"Excuse me?"

"The problem is you. You've never gotten over your issues and that each time you assume something that is not true because of your own fears Lola. The real issue is that you refuse to acknowledge your scars, your pain. You try to have this tough exterior and put on this persona around others, when in the dark, you're hurting."

"Sam, you can't even acknowledge how I feel. You completely steamroll my feelings, which is why we're where we are now."

"No, we're where we are now because of your fears. Fear, that I will leave you like your dad left your mom."

Mumbling in spanish, Lola says, "Don't you dare bring my father into this…period!"

"See? The sheer mentioning of him brings up this anger in you and you never have healed from that. I am not your father, Lola. You keep putting me in the same box as him and I'm tired of it."

"Can you blame me? You're supposed to hold me down. You're supposed to be the one that covers me, the one I can rely on. But what do I see? First, you allow people to talk about me behind my back and then you smile in those snakes' faces and break bread with them. Next, you're taking mysterious trips to see someone, some woman. And Sam, if you lie or act like it isn't a woman, we're gonna fight."

Sam says nothing to deny it.

"See, I knew it! And you don't see how that would hurt me?" Lola says, tearing up.

"I'm over this, Lola. I'm tired of you blaming me for your past when it's YOURS to fix."

"The past?! You want to bring up the past, I see."

"Yes, the past…Your past! This inability you have to just be honest with me, let alone yourself."

"You want to talk about the past and honesty, let's talk about it! What about New York huh?"

Sam glares at her from the corner of his eye.

"Nothing to say I see?"

Angrily, Sam walks up to her.

"We talked about what happened in New York and I won't go back over that again. If you want to have that conversation, then you can have it with yourself, and I will leave."

"And you wonder where my mistrust in you comes from??"

Sam begins to head for the door.

"Here you go running again, like a niño pequeño."

"I am not running. Unlike you, I'd rather walk away from you than hurt you with my words."

"Wow, you actually want to care now. You only waited seven years to start. I guess it's better late than never."

"Wow! Petty much, Lola?"

"Petty? Petty? Petty is being able to keep it 100 with me but choosing to hide like a coward. Petty is allowing your wife to have all these thoughts in her mind about not being a good wife or good enough for you anymore after having two freakin kids. Petty is running and avoiding this conversation because you're too insecure to actually be an honorable man of God for once in your life instead of a weak, pathetic, and selfish excuse of a man."

"Wow, Lola. I guess I see what you really think of me after all these years. You have no idea how I've been feeling these past several years.

All I've done, keeping a roof over our heads, being the head of—"

"The head of what? Because if you're about to say the head of this house, you playin yourself."

William pulls up to his friend's house, where he can already hear the festivities beginning. As he walks in, his friend spots him through the crowd.

"Aye, Bill! What's up bro."

"Hey, I see you did not disappoint with the hot girls."

"Dude, listen my parents are away, and it is time to play!"

Laughing at his corniness, William says, "Jamie you gotta promise me you will never say that again or you will never get laid."

As William surveys the room, he cannot help but to attract the attention of the people there. He is one of the most popular boys, if not the most popular boy, of the school. Everyone, both teacher and student, knows William. Students know him for being the best basketball player in the entire school, while the teachers know him by his family. Huntington is a household name amongst social circles in New York. Even the parents of the kids here tell their kids that William and his family are of the utmost importance. As he walks through the crowd, his mere presence grabs their attention. This creates a kind of groupie effect, where all the guys wish they were William so that they can get girls and the girls want the attention of William. He can feel the attention and admiration he is receiving, feeding into the huge ego he already has. A young woman approaches him with a green skirt and short, tight matching blouse. William can tell she is trying everything she can to make him see her. As she slowly walks over to him, he becomes slightly interested in what she is presenting.

"Hi William. My name is Cecelia," she says, gently moving her hair behind her ear.

"What's up Cecelia. You look…incredible."

Cecelia giggles, saying thank you and asks him for a drink.

"So, how does it feel to have all eyes on you?"

"Well, what can I say? It is just something about me that the girls love. The guys aren't really my problem."

Jamie looks over seeing who William is talking to. He goes over and tells William that he needs a sidebar.

"Bro, you know that is ole boy girl, right?"

Placing his hand on Jamie's shoulder, William says, "Dressed like that? Looks like she's about to be my girl tonight."

"Oh shoot. Bro do yo thang! I got something I'm working on right now."

William looks over seeing who Jamie was talking about.

"Oh okay. Well Jamie, looks like your hands are about to be full."

"Facts, Bro!"

William walks back over to Cecelia, apologizing to her. She accepts and says, "But for the rest of the night, I hope you are all mine." As they both take a walk to the dance floor, William looks at the door, seeing this beautiful blonde girl and her best friend walk in.

Choose ye this day…

Madison and her friend, Kate, walk into the party. They see all the guys there, from football players and basketball players to the guys on the swim team. Kate looks over at Madison. They lock eyes, laughing.

"Madison girl, was this not worth it? I mean I don't see not one guy here that isn't at least an 8 or better."

Madison points to one person all the way in the back, laughing.

"Girl, he don't count!"

They start giggling when they are greeted at the door by this tall guy with dreadlocks and a deep raspy voice. He gives them both drinks and asks them how they hear about the party.

"Oh, I started this week and my girl here is starting tomorrow," Kate says.

"Welcome ladies, we got food, we got drinks. So, if y'all need anything, hit me up."

"How can I hit you up, if I don't know your name."

"Isiah. My name is Isiah," he says, smiling.

Isiah's smile instantly draws the attention of Kate. His smile mesmerizes her. Kate tells Madison that she thinks she found her prince charming. Madison laughs at her.

"Girl, no. Did you see him? My goodness! I'm about to go take him up on that offer. Madison, you coming or naw?"

Though Kate is talking to her, Madison's mind is distracted by the sight of this tall, fit guy with this letterman jacket dancing with this girl.

Whom you will serve

Seeing this blonde girl, William feels this other-worldly pull towards her. Just as the DJ changes over the song, William tells Cecelia that he needs to go check on his friend and he will be back. Cecelia tells him that it is fine. She needs to find her friends anyway. William looks through the crowd to see that the blonde girl is gone. He fights through the people dancing to try and find her. He looks around but does not see her anywhere. He runs into Jamie and asks him about the blonde girl.

"Bro seriously?! There are like 80 blonde girls here. You can just have your choice."

"That is not what I meant. This girl was different."

"Uh huh…Listen, I do not know, but what I do know is that I am about to be a little tied up for the moment. So, if you would excuse me sir."

Jamie runs off to talk to another girl at this party. William frantically searches the party to try to find this beautiful girl that has caught his eye. He looks over at the bar to find two young ladies talking to a guy. William walks over, cautiously, to see if this is the girl he has been searching for. Closer he gets, he realizes that the guy with the girls is Isiah, but neither of the girls is the one he is looking for.

"What up, Isiah."

"Aye, William! What's happening bro? You ready to be MVP again for the 20th time this year?"

"What can I say, I'm just that good."

"Yeah man, as modest as ever."

"Ladies, I didn't mean to intrude."

"No, you are fine…as long as we can all get a pic," one of the girls said.

Isiah and William agree to a selfie with the girls. They take the picture and one of them slips Isiah her number, as they walk away. William complements Isiah on his catch. He asks him about his mystery blonde.

"Oh, I thought you were gonna hook up with Cecelia? I saw y'all over there dancing real close. You know she taken right?"

"Yes, I do and clearly she don't care so why should I? And man! The girl I saw was hot bro! I'm trying to see what's up with her. She was blonde, long legs."

"Oh, I think I know who you were talking about! Bro, her and her friend look like they came in already partying hard, but she was fine though."

"So, you seen her?"

Isiah smiles and points straight ahead.

"Yep…that's her."

William grabs two drinks, heading over there towards her and her friend. As he gets in clear view of her, he really takes in how beautiful she really is. Her long blonde hair seems to gently touch her red and black sheer shirt with her black tight leggings. Her flawless figure is almost hypnotic to the eye. It is something about her that gives him this insatiable desire to have her. He goes to them and introduces himself.

Choose ye this day…

The shadow figure sees the different spirits in operation in the room. It is amazed at the ignorance of these kids. Spiritually, they have no idea of the doors that they are opening by their choices tonight. Every sip, every moment of reveling opens a door for a different spirit. It sees the manipulation, the twisting of their young minds. For some of them, the spirits are embodying the individual.

"Ignorance is definitely good for business," it says.

The other spirits see the shadow figure walking about. It keeps an eye on Madison, while it has fun with its other victims. It finds it so easy to plant thoughts of anger into a number of these kids, as they are all either drunk or high. It looks to see several spirits associated with lust and perversion attached to different individuals. This party is a cesspool of sin and death and it loves it like a pig loves the filth of a pigpen.

A spirit of lust operating in Madison, brings attention to the boy that spotted her.

"You know who that is, right?"

"Yes…that is VIP, thanks to the actions of his father. He

revels in that spirit of pride. I like, I like!"

"What's the plan?"

"Let's see how this plays out. This is a win-win for us; however, we have the potential here to really have something good on our hands."

"Will Jim be okay with us working with the boy?"

"So, from my understanding, there are huge plans for this boy. I mean these plans go all the way to the top."

"You mean?"

"Yes."

"His father has already cursed their bloodline multiple times over due to the vows and actions he has taken. From my understanding, the ones that are with him are the big guys. Jim will want to know about this interaction but just let this play out and we go from there."

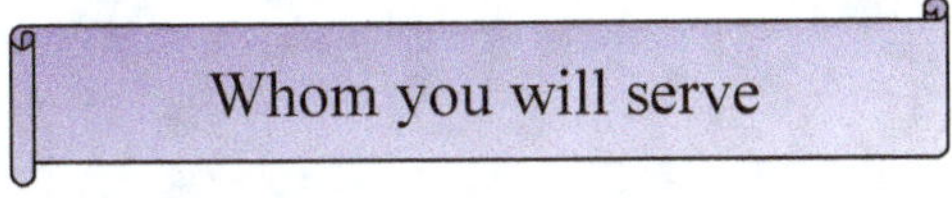

"Excuse me ladies, let me introduce myself, my name is Bill."

Madison looks at him, feeling this indescribable attraction she has to him. Playing coy, she greets William. She sees his cockiness but cannot control how she is feeling. It is as if she feels like a sort of gravitational pull is between them. William reaches his hand out towards her. As Madison goes to shake his hand, William kisses her hand. Madison's heart flutters as his lips come up from her hand. Kate notices the subtlety in William's actions. She tells Madison that she is going to give her some alone time and if she needs her, she knows what to do. Madison, totally enamored by William, ignores Kate.

"I...I'm Madison," she says bashfully.

"You from here?"

"No, I'm from Poughkeepsie, originally. As of now, I live a ways from here. However, when I heard there was a party, I thought I could grace you all with my presence."

"Oh, your presence was definitely noticed."

Madison smirks, blushing. She says to him, "Oh you noticed? So, you been stalking me since I got here?"

William gets a little closer to her, saying, "And if I was...?"

Hearing her favorite song come on, Madison takes a drink from William's hand. Quickly, she drinks it and takes William's hand as they go to the dance floor.

Chapter 17

Sam looks at Lola, feeling so angry with her. It is as if he does not even recognize his wife. Sam can feel his frustration with Lola building and building. He tries to stop himself from saying what is currently on his mind now because he knows that it would totally crush her. Before saying anything to her, he takes a deep breath.

"Lola, you have no idea what I lost. You stand there acting like you know truly what is going on, but per your M.O., you are ignorant to what is truly happening."

"Then explain it to me please! Explain to me why my husband is hiding things from me, who this woman is you are continuously talking to and why should I ever trust you after what you have done?"

Sam says nothing to her.

"Nothing. You have nothing to say to me right now? Sam, I am so disappointed in you."

"Lola, I am not cheating on you."

"Then what is it?! Why am I losing my husband?"

"You're not losing me."

"I am, whether you see it or not, I am. I can feel your distance Sam. What is happening? I wanted our kids to be in a stable home, not a divided one. Where did we go wrong Sam?"

Looking down, Sam can feel Lola's heart shattering to pieces. He pulls out his phone. He goes through his text messages and shows it to Lola.

"It isn't what you think it is. Here, this is who I have been seeing and talking to."

Bracing herself, Lola looks at the phone and sees the name *Lily*. She reads through the messages, looking at him intermittently.

"So, her name is *Lily*?"

With tears in her eyes, she throws the phone back at Sam. She storms into their room, preparing to pack her things to leave.

"Lola, where are you going?"

Lola says nothing. Sam hears her throwing clothes and other things into the suitcase. Sam walks into their room. He asks her where she is going, but she says nothing.

"Lola, what are you doing?"

She looks at him in tears, saying "I am leaving you Sam."

"What?! What do you mean?"

"What part of 'I am leaving you' don't you understand?"

"Wait, tell me why though."

Slamming the clothes that she was carrying from the closet into the suitcase, she says, "What do you mean why?"

"I just showed you the truth. You read the messages."

"Sam, Darling…You are still lying to me and I didn't want to believe it was a woman, but it is. I'm leaving because you're still copping out and not being honest. Whatever you're doing, I'm removing myself and the kids from it."

"No! I am telling you the truth. I've been going to see Lily, but we aren't cheating."

"Then what is it?! What will it take for you to tell me the truth Sam? See the real problem is you're lying."

"Lola, I am not lying to you. You can call her if you want."

"That right there, is the dumbest thing you've said in this. Which is another reason why I'm leaving."

As Sam watches her continue to pack, he remembers the words that were uttered to him while he was driving. The prophetic word, warning him that he is going to lose his marriage unless the truth is revealed.

"Lola, stop please…"

Lola looks at him, crying. She sees this yet feels nothing for him and his tears. It breaks her heart to see what has become of them.

"Lola, I am not cheating with her. She is or was at the time a teenager. Do you remember me telling you about Rebecca?"

"Wait, this is teenager? Sam, you need to explain yourself and fast! No, I do not remember. Who the heck is Rebecca? Refresh my memory."

"Rebecca is my ex-girlfriend, that's who called late that night."

Lola stops, looking at Sam. She fears that the situation is about to become devastatingly worse. She begins to connect the dots and fear the worse. The thought that comes to her mind about who Lily is makes her feel like her knees are about to buckle. Before she could ask the question, she put her back against the wall.

"Sam…Is Lily yo—"

"No, Lola. She is not my daughter."

Lola takes a deep sigh of relief, but she cannot understand what happened. She asks him to explain.

"Lily is Rebecca's daughter."

"Why did your ex feel that it was okay to call a married man late at night and why did you feel it was okay for you to not tell me about this call?"

"I…I cannot answer those questions because I don't know."

Furious with him, Lola asks, "What happened?"

"This might not be what you want to hear, but even I don't fully know. If I had to guess, I would assume that she called me because she trusted me when she felt she could not trust anyone else in the world."

"So, Rebecca, trusted you? Were you in contact with her

prior to her calling that night?"

"What? Lola, no! What is your problem? At this point, you just want to discover that I'm cheating. I am not your father Lola!"

"I didn't say yo—"

Sam yells at her, "You didn't have to!"

"Why are you yelling at me?"

"Because you are just looking for any sign of cheating so you can leave just like your father cheated on your mother! If you want to leave, that is fine. You don't need to search this hard for an excuse."

"I do not want to leave but see it from my end. This looks horrible."

"You want the truth? I'm trying to tell you, but you keep acting as if you're waiting for this mystery ball to drop that's never going to drop."

Lola sits silently on the bed, pondering on the words of Marlinda earlier that day. She had never seen how damaging the stuff with her father really was.

"Rebecca called me. I was just as shocked as you are hearing this."

Sam sits next to Lola, further explaining what happened that night.

"She called me, and I knew something wasn't right and it wasn't because she actually called me. Her voice, her…tone was off. I've known her for years and this did not sound like the Rebecca I knew. So, we talked, and she asked me for a simple favor, or so I thought it was a simple favor. She couldn't give me the details. She just needed an answer. And I said yes."

"I don't get it Sam. What was this favor?"

"She needed me to get something from the airport for her, something of great value. I asked Rebecca what it was, but she said she couldn't tell me, for running the risk of someone finding out."

Lola cups her face into her hands, taking a deep sigh. She says, "So I am guessing Lily was this thing she wanted you to get?"

"Yes."

"This…whole thing sounds crazy, Sam. This sounds like something from a movie. You have to see how this sounds insane? Is this why you stayed in New York for so long awhile back?"

"Also, yes. I was using work as an outlet to grieve her death. It affected me a lot more than I thought."

"You could have just come to me, Sam."

"Right, go to my wife and explain to her about how the death of my ex has completely wrecked me, That is a conversation I would have enjoyed having."

"You think in hindsight, this conversation was better?"

"No, babe. Lola, this is the truth. So, I said yes. She said I couldn't tell anyone because she didn't want to endanger you or Elias."

"However, she felt like it was okay to put your life in danger. Sam, you cannot see how this doesn't sound right? This makes no sense. What happened to her?

"Lola, I don't know."

Lola wipes her eyes, asking him "Sam, why did you feel that you had to agree to this? And why did you feel you had to hide this from me?"

"Lola, I…"

"Sam, you hid this from me for seven whole years. Did you not trust me with this?"

"Lola, I did not know what was happening. I mean for goodness sake; I went into this blind. I just trusted Rebecca and went with what she said."

"Sam, you spoke to your ex. She asked you for a favor and

you had no clue what it was about, but with no questions, you said yes. And you had no problem keeping this from your wife. In what world is that okay?"

"I never said it was okay, but if the roles were revers—"

"You would have a problem with me keeping this from you."

"No Lola, if you were my ex and you asked something of me like this, I would have trusted you to do the right thing, even if it was uncomfortable for me."

"I'm sorry, but I guess you are better than me because that is a huge leap of faith."

"It isn't when I know I can trust you. You asked me to make you a promise and I would be keeping it."

"At the expense of your marriage?"

Sam pauses before he answers, wondering if his answer would make or break them. He stands up, walking to the doorway of their bedroom.

"You were willing to sacrifice our marriage for this girl and your ex. That hurts Sam."

"Lola, you have no idea what I've lost and have dealt with. You see me just keeping a secret and while you were focusing on that, I had to mourn the death of my friend and the loss of another. So, while you sit there with your self-righteous attitude,

I had to deal with the fact that the first time I talked to my friend for years was also my last time. When I hung up that phone, I knew that would be the last time we would ever speak. I have loss more than you know."

"Self-righteous? Don't you dare try to be the victim here!"

"And you say I refuse to acknowledge how you feel, but here you are doing the exact same thing."

Lola sits, looking down. She looks at Sam. She can't help to feel angry with the choice that he made, but as she looks at him, she begins to see the brokenness inside of him. Seeing Sam sad always breaks her heart. She walks over to stand next to him, taking him by the hand.

"Sam, I need you to be honest with me. Did you have feelings for her still?"

"Lola, I—"

"Sam, just be honest with me."

"You are still making this about you."

"I'm trying to understand what made you play hero for your ex. If there was some part of you that still had feelings for her, I just want to know."

"Lola, enough. You want to know? Fine! No, I do not have feelings for Rebecca, but yes, I still cared about her and our history. She was my friend. While you are so focused on her, you have yet to mention the girl that lost her mother. You never asked me about her, but you care so much about Rebecca that you refuse to see the real victim in this, which is a girl that lost her mother because of the actions of her father."

Lola takes a deep breath and apologizes to him for not understanding. It did not change how upset and hurt she was by him keeping all this from her, but never really considered how things were from his perspective. As she apologizes, she feels as if a wall breaks in Sam and he breaks down sobbing. They slide down the wall, collapsing to the floor holding each other. Lola comforts Sam, telling him to let it out. While he is crying, she begins to pray in the spirit.

As she speaks, he can feel the weight of everything he has been feeling for the past seven years being lifted. It is like he is experiencing freedom from all the doubt, anger, and grief inside of him. Crying, Sam says to her "I am so sorry Lola." She continues to pray and begins to cry also. Lola stops and just holds Sam. She thinks to herself how she finally feels connected with her husband again after feeling like she did not really know him or that he changed. She kisses him on the cheek, singing to him in Spanish how much she adores him.

"Thank you, Lola." Sam says, drying his eyes.

"You are always welcome. Sam, we are a team. I've spent seven plus years holding so much against you, both far past and most recent present. And I don't want to do that anymore mi amor."

"I know Lola…"

"For the past seven years, we haven't been a team and we've allowed the devil to get a foothold in our marriage because we were slipping. However, no more.

Next time you want to play hero, you might want to loop in your wife. No, you better loop in your wife."

As she says this, she playfully gives him a punch in the arm. Playing off that it hurts, he rubs his bicep.

"Sam, you are right. I need to heal from my past trauma with my father. I will find someone to talk to."

"Lola, wait. I didn't mean to make you feel li—"

"No, Sam. I need to. Yes, I am going to pray and talk with Jesus about it, but I also need to discuss it with a professional. I cannot just keep unloading on Marlinda and hurting you with accusations. Because of the hurt between us and the healing we need to do, it just cannot be you. I hope you understand that."

"No, I get it."

"So, are we in agreement: Me and you do things and operate from now on as a team?"

"Yes babe."

Lola stands up and goes into the closet, continuing to pack up her clothes. Sam sits there confused because he thought they had solved their problem. She comes out the closet, grabbing a second suitcase.

"Well, how about you take me to meet Lily? And we figure out what the heck is going on. I mean after all, even Superman needs Lois' help occasionally."

Sam kisses Lola. He says to her, as he goes in to grab some

of his things.

"Naw babe, you're definitely more of a Selina type."

"Wait, who the heck is Selina?" Lola says, confused.

Chapter 18

As William dances with Madison, it is as if time itself has stopped and it is just them on the floor. It is the first time William has ever felt anything like this. Something in him is drawn to her, instinctively. Looking into her eyes, he is smitten by her. As they dance, he can tell she is drunk. He looks over seeing Cecelia looking at them, staring holes into them both. He sees his friend Jamie looking at him, giving him the thumbs up. As the song ends, Madison turns to look William in his eyes. She can feel the same intense connection with William. Considering everything with her, she never thought she would ever feel this with someone. She has this insatiable hunger for him. She tells him that she could use another drink.

"You party hard, huh?"

Slurring her words, Madison says, "Baby, it's the only way to party. So, you gonna get me this drink or do I have to get it myself."

As William watches Madison walk past him to the bar, he follows her as if something is pulling him to her like a magnet.

He gets Madison and himself another drink. He sees Jamie calling him.

"Madison, my friend is calling me. Let me see what he wants."

Kissing him on the cheek, she tells him to come back. William goes over to Jamie, asking him what he wants.

"Bro, who is she?! You betta make sure you get her number. I would watch her though man. Remember we need you sober for tomorrow.”

“Her name is Madison. Man, I don’t know…I feel like I am drawn or something. It is weird. I look into her eyes, and it is like, I am speechless and don’t worry, I haven’t even been drinking like that.”

As they continue their conversation, they hear commotion at the bar.

As they finish packing, Sam asks Lola if she asked Marlinda if she could watch Faith and Elias. Lola tells him to make sure he contacts Lily, as there will be a major time difference between them and her. Sam calls Lily to let her know what was happening.

“Hello, Sam?”

“Hi, Lily. Um, we need to talk.”

“Sam…” Lilith says, crying.

“Lily, what’s wrong? What happened?”

“They are gone, Sam.”

“Who is gone, Lily??”

Lola comes into their room. Sam signals to give him a minute. Sam tries to calm Lilith down, but she just becomes more frantic and afraid.

“I knew my dad would find me.”

“Lily, stop. Calm down and talk to me. What happened?”

“My cousins Sam…Mickal and his wife are dead,” Lilith says, crying.

Jamie and William run over to the bar to see Madison arguing with some guy. Jamie becomes slightly nervous, telling William that they must be careful not to get the cops called on them.

"Bill, my parents will kill me if things are not kosher when they get back here."

William goes over to try to diffuse the situation between them. He goes over to Madison, asking her what the problem was. She explains to him that the guy just tried to grab her, and she punched him. William looks over to see that the guy that grabbed her was Cecelia's boyfriend. William tries to get everyone to calm down, but the situation just begins to escalate even more. Cecelia walks over, trying to figure out what was happening.

"Bill, what is going on and why is my boyfriend's lip bleeding?"

Drunk and angry, Madison says, "Tell your idiot boyfriend to keep his dirty hands to himself."

"Excuse me? Who is this trailer trash?"

Kate rushes to Madison's aid, as Cecelia gets in Madison's face. Kate pushes Cecelia back. Cecelia's boyfriend, enraged and embarrassed, tries to get to Madison; however, William steps in front of him.

"Dude, let it go. Don't embarrass yourself more than you already have."

"Bill, I will only say this once: Move!"

"No."

"Why you defending her? She clearly shouldn't be here. I mean, look at her! She needs to learn some manners and trust me, I can teach her some."

"Just walk away. I think a busted lip is enough."

Jamie gets word that the police have been called due to the loud music and the noise.

"Yo, I need all of you to let this go. The police are on their way," Jamie says to all of them.

"Not until this trailer trash apologizes to my boyfriend."

"You call me trailer trash again and your lip will look like your man's."

Just as Cecelia's boyfriend is about to push through William, he punches him to the ground and a large fight ensues.

Choose ye this day…

In shock, Sam gives Lilith his condolences. He asks her what happened to them. "I am sure it was my father that did it."

"Lily, I am so sorry for your loss. I really am, but you cannot expect me to believe that your father did this."

"No, I'm not saying that it was really him, but the guy my dad works for."

"Who are you talking about?"

"Sam, they died in a house fire. It's the same way that they said my mother died."

"I thought your mother's death was due to a gas leak in the house? That is the story that was told to me."

"From my father, right? And you actually believed him?"

"Listen, are you still in Canada?"

"For now, I am. I will be leaving soon. I'm scared he is going to find me."

"Lily, stay put. I'm going to get a red eye and come see you. It will be okay."

Taking a deep breath, Lilith agrees and hangs up. Sam looks over at Lola, explaining to her everything that just happened. Lola does not know what to think about the whole thing. She explains to Sam that all this sounds crazy and Lilith sounds like she is a nut.

"No Lola. She is not crazy. She is just a little girl that lost her mother, brother, and now the two people that were supposed to take care of her and keep her safe."

"What doesn't make sense to me is if it was a house fire, why is she so sure that it was murder?"

"It was reported that Rebecca died the same way."

"And that makes sense to you?"

"Nothing about any of this makes sense. I just want to help her and get back to having a normal life."

"I hear you on that one."

"My concern is that she is freaking out and it will cause her to operate in fear, always looking over her shoulder."

Lola grabs her bags, telling him that she found a flight that is leaving in four hours. They take their bags, preparing to go see the girl who has lost everything.

Whom you will serve

As the large fight breaks out, the police arrive on the scene and pull up to the front of the house. Jamie yells out to everyone "The cops are here!" Madison, looking at Kate, tells her that she cannot get arrested. She and Kate sneak out the back, while the cops come in to try to bring order to the place. As they are breaking up the fights, they begin to handcuff everyone and call for backup. Kate and Madison get into the car. She catches the eyes of William, as he is cuffed, while they drive off. The police go around, taking statements.

William and Cecelia's boyfriend continue to yell at each other. The police arrest and take a few of the kids in for being drunk and disorderly, including William. As those arrested get into different police cars, William see one of the cops step to the side to make a call on his radio.

Damian takes a walk through the halls of the upper floor of

his house. He looks over to see that William still has not come home yet. He becomes annoyed, as it seems he has been acting out more and more lately. He had just chalked it up to his hormones and just being a teen; however, he will not allow William to screw up his plans. He goes to look at his phone to see that he has a message from Lucius.

"Crap!"

He goes into the bedroom, waking up Tiffany.

"Babe, what is it?"

"It's Lucius. He just sent me a message."

"It's probably nothing." Tiffany says, being half asleep. She tells him to check it and see what it says. Damian opens the text and as he reads it, he becomes enraged.

"Crap! That boy is going to ruin everything!"

"What happened?"

"William just got arrested."

Waking up, Tiffany asks him to repeat what he just said.

"Tiffany, are you deaf? I just said he got arrested."

"I am sorry. I am just over here trying to sleep, and you are yelling. Wait, what time is it?

"It's going on 5 a.m."

Jumping up, Tiffany says "Crap! Damian, we gotta get there before some moron with a phone leaks the news that our son has been arrested and his face is plastered all over the tv."

"Agreed. You stay in bed and if I need something, I will give you a call."

Damian replies to Lucius, telling him thanks for the heads up. Anger boils up in him that someone that he views as an enemy had to let him know about the trouble in his own house. He gets in the car, heading to the police station.

> Choose ye this day…

Madison sits in the car, in a total daze. It seems like she is having an out of body experience. She has been feeling the effect of the drugs and alcohol that she had taken. She thinks to herself that she might have overdone it tonight.

Kate looks over at her, telling Madison not to throw up in her car. Madison, barely able to form words properly, says to her "I…I got it."

"Okay girl. If you need me to pull over, I can."

"I'm fine."

Madison looks up at all the streetlights they drive past. The shine from them begins to hurt her eyes. She hears Kate talking, but it sounds very muffled. With every pothole that they are hitting, it makes Madison more nauseous. As they stop at a traffic light, Madison rolls the window down to try and get some fresh air. The cool air hits her face, bringing some comfort. This is until she gets a whiff of sewage. Madison yells for Kate to pull over. Quickly, she pulls to the side. Madison flings the door open to throw up onto the sidewalk. Kate gently pushes her hair back, holding it in her hand.

"Girl, are you okay?"

Madison does not answer but continues to throw up.

"You were going a little too hard tonight. I know you usually party a lot, but to take all those pills and drink so much. You gotta calm down a bit. Is everything okay?"

Madison sits back into her seat, wiping her mouth. She thanks Kate for holding her hair.

"Listen, I do not need you to check on me. I'm fine."

"You sure because if you ever need to talk, I—"

Madison then yells at Kate, saying "Stop it! Our friendship is fine just how it is. I do not need you prying or trying to be close to me. Just stop it! Not like you ever cared anyway."

"What? You trippin!"

Madison stumbles out the car, yelling at Kate. She yells at

her and says that she will walk home.

"Are you crazy? You could hurt yourself. And you are my bestie, Madison. I had yo back tonight even though it was all your fault!"

"He should have never touched me. I do not like people touching me."

"Just get in the car, Maddy."

Slowly tears began cascading down her face, Madison says, "Not like you ever cared. You suck! You hurt me and still hurt me all the time. I hate you!"

Kate gets out of the car, holding Madison. She tells her that it is okay and that she will not hurt her. Kate helps Madison into the car. As she is getting in, Kate could not help but notice the bruise marks on and around her knee and inner thigh.

Whom you will serve

Lola and Sam board the plane, getting ready to see Lilith. Sam cannot help but to wonder if Lilith is making all this up and they just died in an accident.

However, a part of him does find it odd that both situations are so closely connected and that the circumstances are the same. Lola gets off the phone with Marlinda.

"So how mad was Marlinda for us dropping off two kids on her suddenly?"

"She was not mad at all. She was so happy to see Elias and Faith. They adore their Madrina."

"That isn't surprising. She loves those kids."

They hear the pilot make the announcement that they are about to take off shortly. Sam looks out the window, checking out the view. Lola places her hand on top of his, asking him about his thoughts.

"I don't know Lola. I think I'm just concerned about Lily. I'm worried that she is being paranoid, and, in her paranoia, she is gonna drive herself mad."

"You cannot add that kind of pressure onto yourself. She isn't your daughter. Our kids are here. Plus, she is practically grown and can make her own choices."

"Lola, it's not the same. You haven't heard her story. This is not a child that is just being a bratty rich girl with first world problems. If what she says is true, then she could be in trouble. You don't know what her father is capable of."

"And you do?"

Just as Sam was about to answer, the flight attendant delivers the takeoff instructions over the speakers.

"Okay. All I am saying is, let's go into this using wisdom. Whatever action Jesus wants us to take, we will do it. We need to be level-headed about this and not just go flying in like some superhero. We ain't got no powers babe. Let's pray about what we should do and go from there. We're looking at least a six-hour plane ride. So put the cape back in the bag superman until we get a plan."

Laughing and giving her a kiss, Sam says, "Sounds like a plan."

They pray and as they finally take off, Lola snuggles under Sam. She says to him, as she falls asleep, "You always have to be the hero, Cariño."

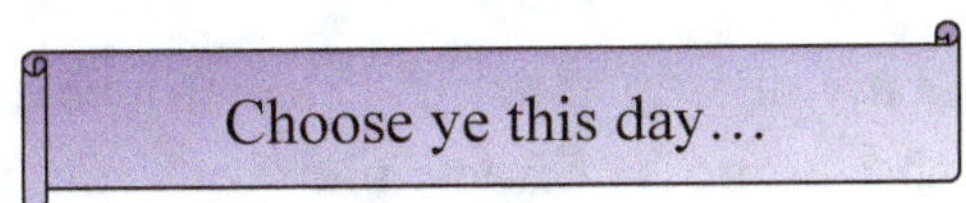

Damian arrives at the police station. As it is only hours before sunrise, he grabs a pair of shades to conceal his identity. He goes past each desk, disgusted that he must even be in such a wretched place. He looks around, seeing the common criminal. He tries to make sure none of these commoners touch him, as he feels that he is above all the people there. He goes to the front desk, asking for the police captain. The officer tries to explain to Damian that William has not arrived just yet and that he has to wait, but Damian does not want to wait. He demands him to get him on the phone now. He tells him that their sergeant is there and that he will get him.

"Thanks," Damian says in a condescending tone.

Damian sees the sergeant come to greet him. Not wasting time on small talk, he tells the sergeant that they need to talk privately. The sergeant invites him into their break room. They go in, closing the door behind them.

"How may I help you sir?"

"From my understanding, you have my son in lock up. You need to release him now."

The sergeant looks at him and she laughs. She explains to him that there is a process and that is not it.

"And I wasn't asking. I'm telling you to release him."

"And who are you?"

"My name is Mr. Huntington. My son's name is William Huntington. You are going to release him. The last thing I, I mean we, need is for it to leak out this God forsaken place.

"Excuse me? We don't have an—"

"Please! You do. All you need to know is that if any media outlet discovers that he is or was here, I'm going to sue the crap out of everyone here."

"From what my officers told me, he destroyed a young man's face and he wants to press charges, plus your son has a warrant. So, he will be here."

"Give me a sec."

Damian pulls out his phone, sending a text message. He sends the message and tells the sergeant that she should be receiving a call soon. She looks at him, curiously. She tells him that it does not matter who he texted; they cannot make this go away. She feels her phone go off. She looks at it and tells Damian that she will be back. Damian watches her go out and smirks.

Whom you will serve

Kate pulls up to where Madison lives. Kate asks if she needs help getting upstairs.

Madison reassures her that she is fine, though she is stumbling out of the car.

"Girl, be careful! Are you gonna even get up and sober up in time for school today?"

"Crap! I probably should have slowed down,"

Kate says laughing "You think?"

Both girls laugh, as they realize how stupid this night has been. Madison hugs Kate, thanking her for being there.

"Girl! I love you. I always got your back."

Madison, still trying to sober up, gives her a thumbs up and tries to walk to the front door. Out of concern, Kate calls out to Madison.

"Yes Kate! Go home before you get me caught and I get in trouble."

"You know if you ever need to talk about some stuff, I am here."

Madison pauses and says, "Girl yes! Is there something you need to get off your chest?"

Kate wonders if she should bring up the bruises and marks, but she just tells her to get up on time so they can be there for their first day. Madison waves at her, as Kate drives off. As Madison goes up the stairs, heading home, she hears a voice call her name.

Chapter 19

Damian looks through the glass, seeing the sergeant arguing with the person on the phone. It is made clear to him the kind of power he has truly amassed over the past seven years. By just sending one text message, it has moved mountains for him. He worked hard these last several years to have this kind of power, to have these connections. What he did in the conference room was nothing compared to what he is currently capable of. The information he had about so many people and the skeletons in their closets were colossal. This is the power he desired for so long and now, the only thing that stands in his way was Lucius. Damian goes over in his mind how crushing it was to find that his wife and daughter had been killed by someone he considered to be a mentor and friend, even though he suspects this same man is the one that ended his father's life. Lucius had destroyed his life and he swore that he would make him pay.

He and Tiffany started by taking away the power he had in the company and while Lucius is still very powerful in their group, both in his influence and in his occult practices, he has been as an old lion in the savanna just resting on his laurels of the past. It is time for new leadership and he and Tiffany will make sure that their goals are fully met, without the deadweight that Lucius has become.

Damian sees the sergeant walking back towards him. She stops to say something to one of her fellow officers. Damian can see that the text was very persuasive. With his arrogant smirk, Damian can barely contain himself. As she comes in, she slams the door.

"Who are you?"

In arrogance, Damian says, "Oh whatever do you mean? I told you my name. Is that too hard for you too?"

"I just got off the phone with my captain and the freaking police commissioner, both of which were terrified of you."

"Well, what can I say? The best weapon one can have is fear. Fear is power, control, and when used correctly, is a great motivator."

"I got a direct order from the commissioner to cease all investigations and to drop the charges against your son. And yes, any bodycam footage of your son will be wiped as well."

Angrily, Damian says to her, "Good! If I see one media truck outside, you will understand why they are afraid of me."

"I'm not afraid of some entitled brat with a silver spoon in his mouth, who thinks that he can just wave his money and do whatever he wants."

"The only reason you are barely able to afford your husband's chemo and your home is because of me. God giveth and most certainly, God can take away…if you tempt me."

She is left in shock, as there is no way he could have possibly known that she was struggling to pay for her husband's hospital bills.

As Damian makes his way back out, he sees some officers wrapping up William's processing. The sergeant follows behind him, letting Damian know that everything will be as if William was never there. William can see the disappointment on Damian's face. He looks at Damian and says, "Back or front?"

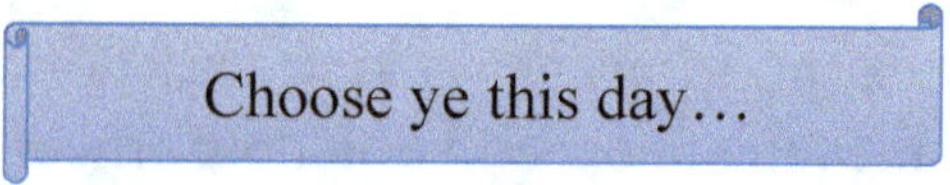

Opening his eyes, Elias sees himself in an unfamiliar area.

He looks around to see what is happening, but he just sees several buildings around him and it would appear as if he woke up in the middle of a street or pathway. Some of them appear to look like houses with gates. He is startled by loud metal clashing and what sounds like people either arguing or fighting. He wants to run out to see what is happening, but a part of him is afraid of what he would find. Fear has him in its cold, dark grasp, but suddenly he remembers what his mom and dad said about fear. He remembers that they told him that there was no love in fear and that God never wants his children to be afraid. So, they helped him remember a scripture about fear. He tries to remember exactly what it says, but it is hard. However, he gives it a try anyway.

"God's Spirit has made me strong. It is loving and is not fear."

As he says this, he starts feeling a little better and begins to be able to move. He repeats these words until he can freely move. He sees that not only can he move but he can make out the voices that are yelling. He sees a main street in front of him. As he sees it, he begins to run towards it. The closer he gets, the clearer the voices become. He sees something hit the ground. This thing hits the ground so hard that it causes the earth beneath his feet to shake a little. He flinches, wondering what the heck he saw. He gets to the street and is shocked by what he sees transpiring.

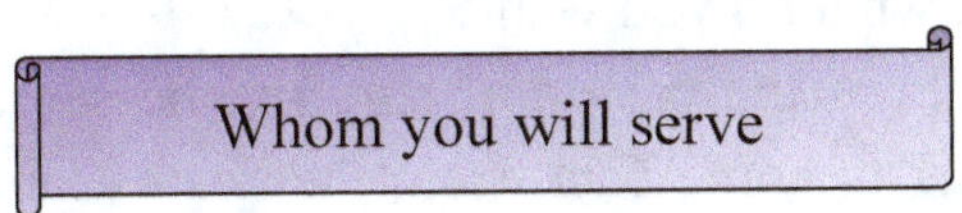

As Damian and William walk to the back, the sun slowly begins to rise. Damian's wrath starts to spew out.

"William, have you lost your mind?!"

William says nothing to him, infuriating Damian more.

"Boy! You hear me speaking to you. Do you have any idea what it took for me to clear this whole thing up?"

Irritated, William says, "Oh, I'm sure you are about to tell me."

"What's your problem? I had to hear from Lucius that you were in jail. Do you have any idea what this could've done to me…to us, as a family?"

"Oh, so now we're a family?"

"Excuse me?"

"Come on father! We haven't been a family since mom and Lily died in that house fire. I mean for God's sake; you married your secretary just one year after they died!"

Walking up to William, Damian says, "You be very careful about the next words coming out that ungrateful mouth of yours."

"I find it kind of funny how you come here to get me, but when I mentioned my basketball game, my stepmother was the only one that said she would be there. Do you even know that I play basketball?"

"Of course, I do. I cannot be at every game."

"Dad, you haven't been to any of my games! It has always been Tiffany."

"William, there are things happening right now that I cannot get into, especially in public, but it will all be made clear soon. And when the time is right, I want you by our side, together."

"And what if I don't want that?"

"William, what do you want?"

William opens the car door. Angrily, he says, "I want my mom and sister to come back from the dead! Can you do that? Huh? Oh yeah that's right, you can't! So, there is not a single, freaking thing you can do for me!

Choose ye this day…

Elias looks to see many angels and demons at war with each

other in the air. As their weapons clash, it creates a sound that is piercing. He goes to a crater to see where the demon fell. There seem to be so many that he cannot count them all. The chaos of the scene causes him to run for cover. He sees the large wings of the angels and is captivated by their beauty, while frightened by their sheer size and scale compared to him. Looking out across the field he sees someone being harassed by one of the demons.

"Stop! Leave them alone!" Elias yells.

He runs towards them, throwing anything he seems to get his hands on at the demon. However, it ignores Elias. Just as Elias is about to get close to it and the people, an angel comes to help. It says something to the people and points them in the right direction. The angel sees Elias and flies towards him. Elias, being scared, shrinks back away from it. The presence of the angel gives Elias this feeling of reassurance that it is okay and that he will be saved.

Elias finds himself in an alleyway with other people around him, adults and kids. They all appear to be terrified and covering their eyes. The sword clashing becomes louder and closer. While everyone else is shielding their eyes, Elias finds himself fixated on what he is seeing. This fierce battle in the air seems like something out of one of his dad's comics or a movie. He is wondering if all this is a dream or if this is truly real.

"Where is my mom and dad?" Elias asks.

Someone answers him, saying "Stay behind this gate and do not move. Everything will be okay."

The longer the fight progresses, the more intense it is. Elias looks behind him to see some people praying, while others are frozen in fear. As one demon hits the ground hard, Elias sees it and for some reason, he does not fear this thing. It tries to go towards the gate, but an angel stands in between where the demon landed and the gate, attacking it. Elias looking up, begins approaching the gate. The people behind him beg him not to approach it, but something seems to draw him to the conflict he sees.

The intensity of the fight shakes the very ground they stand on. He sees a few demons break off from fighting the angels, flying over to attack the people and Elias. Full of courage, Elias sees a stray sword beside him. He picks it up and without fear, rushes towards the demons bearing his sword and preparing to battle. Just as he is about to clash with the demons, he wakes up with his heart racing.

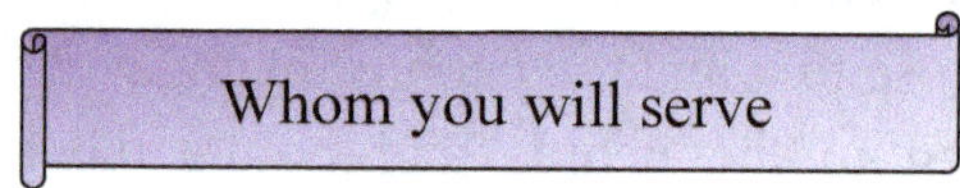

William slams the door shut. Damian, confused and angry, gets in. He tells William that he understands his pain. Damian looks over at him, seeing his black eye.

"What was this fight even about? I hope you repaid him for giving you a black eye."

"Oh, you care now? If you must know, yes, I did. I broke his freaking face. And it was about a girl I met."

They continue the conversation, as Damian drives off.

"So, all this was over a girl?"

"No…well, yes. The guy on the football team thought I was hitting on his girl, which I was, but she approached me so obviously she didn't care. Later on that night, he approached the girl that I was dancing with. He put his hands on her and she busted his lip. I stepped in and when he tried to go for her again, I hit him."

"Well, at least you made sure he knows not to place his hands on you again." William stays silent.

Damian looks over and says, "William, you were destined for greatness. Don't let petty things like this screw up your future. So, what is her name?"

"Her name is Madison."

"Hmph, that is a nice name. Does she run in our circles?"

"What do you mean?"

"You know what I mean…"

"See here is the thing dad, I didn't ask her if her family's net worth matches ours nor did I ask her about the neighborhood she lives in. All I know is that her name is Madison."

"Just be wise William. I cannot afford you screwing up."

"And you continue to make everything about you."

As they pull up to their home, he slams the car into park.

"Let me explain something to you: You ungrateful, little boy. What I have done and am currently doing has been all for you. I've done some really unseemly things to get to where I am now, and I refuse to let anyo—"

"See here you go making everything about you again! I didn't need you to come to my rescue. I could've handled it on my own."

"Don't ever interrupt me. If you could've handled it, I wouldn't have heard it from someone else that you were there. You were about to get charged with assaulting that boy. It was I that cleared that up and helped you. So, know your place boy. Here is what you're going to do. It's time for you to get ready for school. You're going to go upstairs, get your stuff together and get there on time. Are we clear?"

William says nothing to him.

"Are…We…Clear?"

"Yes."

"Yes…?"

"Yes sir."

They both get out of the car. As they are walking in, Tiffany, in a panic, greets them both. She asks them about everything that went on and if there are some things she needs to do on her end. Damian assures her that everything is good and that they cleared up the issue. He also, indirectly, makes it known to William that he is currently on punishment. William's bedroom door slams shut.

"What is going on with him?"

"That boy almost ruined everything. I had to call in my favor with the police commissioner."

"Seriously? What did he do?"

"He got into a fight and broke a boy's face."

"Woah…How did you make this go away?"

"Well, our police commissioner has certain skeletons that if outed, would end his career. And that is the best-case scenario. Also, I assured him that when it is time for reelection, that our company will make a very generous contribution to his campaign."

"Why would he do something so silly?"

Irritated, Damian explains to Tiffany about Madison.

"This boy," Tiffany says, sighing. She goes on to say, "I will talk to him. You are needed elsewhere."

"What do you mean?"

"Apparently, there are some senators that want to meet with you. They are interested in working with us on a few ventures. I think this will be beneficial if we want to take control from Lucius. Do you think we should let William in on what is going on?"

"No. He cannot know what really happened to his mother and sister. If he did, he would never forgive me. He brought it up today."

"Brought up what?"

"The circumstances of Rebecca and Lily's deaths."

Tiffany goes over to Damian, comforting him. She explains to him that it might be better for him to explain everything, as it might bring William some much-needed closure. Just as Damian was going to say something to her, William comes down, getting ready to leave for school. Damian expresses to him that he is to come straight home from school.

"You are aware that's not gonna happen because of my championship game tonight, right?"

Damian says nothing, as he had totally forgotten about his son's game. Tiffany interjects, reassuring him that she will be there. This places a slight smile on William's face as he leaves for school.

"Damian, after all of this, you gotta make this up to William. If you don't, we're gonna lose him and we want to bring him into the fold. Get dressed so we can head in and you can meet those senators."

"Are they up for reelection or something?"

"No. Lucius placed them in contact with you. It's that time again for us to select who we'll place in position to become president next year when everyone is campaigning."

"Right. That makes sense. What would I ever do without you, Tiffany?" "Probably forget that you will be running late if you don't leave out the house in the next hour."

Damian kisses her and quickly rushes to get ready.

Choose ye this day…

Madison goes into the apartment and from the living room, she can see the sun rising. Quickly and quietly, she goes to the bathroom to splash herself with water so that she can try to sober up. She thinks to herself how this is her first day at a new school. She does not want people to see this poor girl from Poughkeepsie, but to see her as more. She hears the voice call out to her again. She turns her head, thinking that she got caught sneaking back in. The hairs on her neck quickly stand up, as she knows that it would be trouble if it was found out that she was out last night.

She does not want to go to school with fresh bruises. She goes back into her room, quickly changing into her school clothes. She sees a text from Kate, letting her know that she is on the way to pick her up for school.

"Crap!"

Madison quickly freshens up, when this very quiet, eerie voice says, "Maddie." She turns around, seeing nothing. A part of her starts becoming scared, but she ignores it when she hears James stumbling into the bathroom. Trying to avoid him, she sneaks past him to go into her mother's room just to see if she would say goodbye to her. Madison peeks her head in, just to see her mother out cold on her bed from a night of drinking and drugs. She runs out the door, hearing James on the other side , yelling. She runs downstairs to go out the door, to see Kate waiting for her.

"Hey girl! You look like crap!"

"I feel like crap. I did not get any sleep and I feel like I look horrible. On a scale from horrifying to fine, how do I look?"

"Eh…You look like you could use a pick-me-up. Wanna go get some coffee?"

"That sounds amazing. I hate wearing these uniforms."

"This is a preppy school, Maddie. This is what we gotta wear. Plus, I think it makes you look cute."

"Oh, shut up and drive."

The two girls laugh, driving off. As they are leaving, the shadow figure watches them from Madison's living room window. It sees them and smiles as it plans to make Madison's life much worse.

Whom you will serve

Micah walks around his room, gathering different things. He becomes frustrated, as he feels he is forgetting something.

"Micah, hurry up before you are late for your first day in this American high school."

"I know Father, but I'm forgetting something."

"Make sure your sister is ready too. I'm going to drop you both off."

"Aiya! Are you ready?" Micah says, yelling down the hallway.

"Yes! Stop yelling Micah." Aiya says, annoyed.

He looks around, realizing what he is forgetting. He goes over to his drawer, underneath his clothes and sees his small Bible. He puts it in his bag and goes get a look at himself in the mirror. He barely recognizes himself in this tie and shirt with this blazer. He hopes that he will be able to catch up since he is coming to this new school in the middle of the school year. He goes to the car, seeing his father and his sister waiting patiently for him. His dad smiles, hugging him.

"Your mother would be so pleased with you. May her soul rest in peace."

"Thanks, Abba."

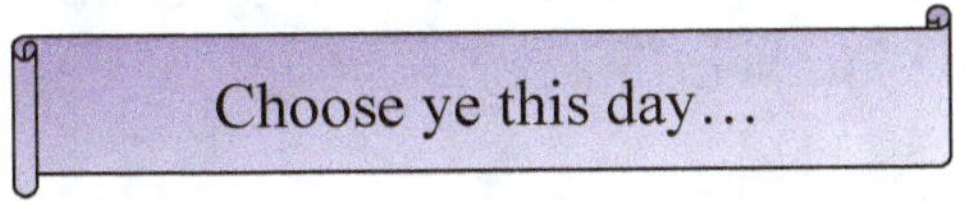

William arrives at school, and he can tell that everyone is looking at him, especially the football team. It is like this
fight made him even cmore popular. Everyone is a fan now. This feeling fed William's arrogance. It makes him even more boastful than normal. All the girls are staring at him and apart from the football team, the guys want in his sphere of influence even more now. While William is at his locker getting his things for his first class, Jamie comes to him asking about what

happened when the police took him.

"Yeah, I just got off."

"Wait, nothing happened? Like you got off free?"

"Yep."

"Bro, you are lucky. I don't know what your parents did, but they must've pulled all the strings."

"Yeah, I guess you can say that. My dad seems to know everybody."

"Dude, you got the attention of everyone at the school. And the football team ain't too happy with you right now. You broke the face of their star player."

Just as Jamie says this, some of the football team walk past them. They give William a glaring stare as they walk past.

Annoyed, William says to them, "Can I help you? If you have a problem, don't whisper about it. Come deal with it."

When he says this, the team stops and walks back towards William and Jamie. The rest of the basketball team rush over, coming to their aid. Just when a big fight is about to begin, the principal and other faculty members get in between them. The principal threatens to suspend every player involved. This settles everyone down and disperses the crowd. Jamie and William get their things for class, rushing off as they realize that they are about to be late for their first period.

Whom you will serve

Micah and his father arrive at the school. Micah takes a deep breath and his father places his hand on his shoulder. He tells him that everything will be okay and to remember that Allah is watching over him. Micah, saying nothing, just shakes his head. He gets out of the car and waves goodbye to his father.

Micah, standing on the steps, begins to pray.

"Father, I thank you for this day. Thank you for your grace and being a loving Father to me, Aiya, and Abba. Please keep them and protect them. I pray that I have a good day and be someone that my mother would be proud of. In Jesus' name, Amen."

He goes to the office, telling them that he is there to get his schedule. He looks at his schedule, realizing that he is about to be late for his first class. He runs over to the classroom, knocking on the door.

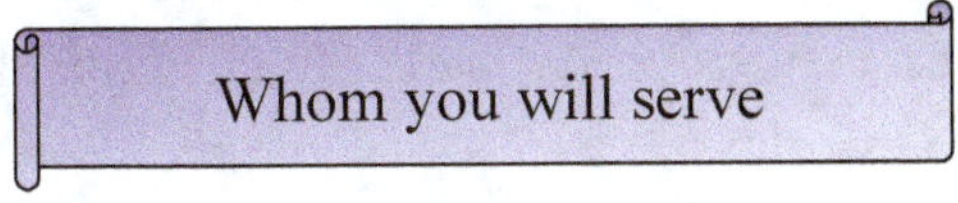

Kate and Madison pull up to the school. They look at the clock and see that they are late. Quickly, they run into the building and hope they do not get detention on their first day at this new school.

"You got your schedule, Kate?"

"Wait, we could've had our schedule already?"

"Did you not check your school email?"

"Um, no! Dang it! I gotta go to the office today. I guess I will see you at lunch later girl?"

"Yep."

Madison darts down the hall heading to her first class.

As William and Jamie sit there, they hear a knock on the door. He sees a young man, about average height with short hair. He is wearing these thin glasses and gives off real nerd vibes. William and Jamie snicker, poking fun at him. The teacher looks at his information and is very impressed by what he sees. He then makes his introduction to the class.

"If I can have your attention, please. We have a new student in our class, and it seems that he has skipped a whole grade, as he has had exemplary grades and astounding test scores. I would like to introduce you to Micah Assaf. Would you like to say something to the class?"

Nervous, Micah says, "Thank you and I look forward to working with you all." The class looks at him and says nothing. William looks at him and stares at him as

he gets to his seat. Just as the teacher is about to continue with the lesson, there is another knock at the door.

Choose ye this day…

She knocks at the door and uses the glass as a mirror to make sure she looks her best. The door opens and the teacher greets her. She expresses her apology for being late. She goes to explain that this is her first class.

"Wow, this seems to be the day for new students I see. I guess since you are new, I am going to take it easy on you. I see you are also an exceptional student."

As she thanks the teacher for the compliment, she looks out to the class, and she sees William among the students. She puts her head down, trying to stop him from seeing her blush. Her heart flutters as they catch each other's eye. So, she makes her introduction to the class.

"Um, Hi. My name is Madison Queen and yeah…this is awkward."

She takes her seat right in between Micah and William. While her body is drawn to the familiarity of William, it is something unexplainable about the warmness of Micah that draws her soul to want to be near him. It is as though she is sitting between two opposing forces.

Chapter 20

A loud voice comes over the speaker, alerting the passengers to see that they have arrived in Winnipeg. Sam and Lola wake up, rested and ready to go on this journey. Sam grabs their bags, while Lola takes her purse. She tells him about how amazing her nap was and how great it felt to sleep for once without a child's cry making you jump out of your sleep. While she is saying this, Sam cannot help but think about Lily and what she said. Is it possible that someone could be targeting her and her family? This all seems too weird to be ignored. As they are walking to get a rental car, Lola takes Sam by the hand. She can sense his mind racing with different kinds of thoughts. She lets him know that everything will be okay and that she is with him no matter what they must face. Sam gives her a smile and asks the person at the counter for their car. The person at the counter notifies them that their car is right outside. With bags and luggage inside, they make their way to see Lilith and to finally get some answers.

Whom you will serve

For more than seven years, the shadow figure has wreaked havoc on Madison's household. Between the abuse, drug use, and alcohol, they have made its job very easy. For a lot of the damage that was done, it had to do little to no work.

"It is amazing how much humans talk and the things they would do to each other with their words. The things James,

Madison, and her Mom have said to each other practically did all of my work for me. They have no clue how powerful their words are. It is pathetic."

As it walks about the apartment with the other demonic spirits, it receives word that Jim needs it to report to him. The shadow figure meets with Jim in a nearby alley.

"Do you have anything to report to me?"

"Yes. I have been following her and the spirits that you sent reside within her and they are doing a number on that girl, I must say."

"From my understanding, you encountered someone of great importance to our kingdom?"

"Oh, the boy? Yes. That boy has some serious issues. He is ruled by his over abundant pride and daddy issues."

"That boy is very special to us and we plan on using him. Doing anything to disrupt those plans would have very serious consequences for anyone who screws this up."

"It would seem they are drawn to each other. I could push them even closer…"

"Proceed with caution. Be strategic. Meanwhile, your next assignment is to destroy Madison's family and torment her mind to the point where she is broken."

"It will be done."

As the shadow figure leaves, it plots with the other spirits on how to finally put the nail in Madison's coffin.

Choose ye this day…

It has been a while since Candice was in the hospital. As she is in school, she began to prepare for the time of her day she dreaded the most: lunch. She is becoming self-conscious of what she eats, as she hates her weight. She goes to her locker, opening it up to look at herself in the mirror.

A voice says to her, "You are ugly and fat. Nobody could ever love you, most certainly a guy and you should take those pills in your bag."

Just as she is about to reach for the pills, her friend comes to her asking if she wants to sneak out for lunch. Quickly wiping her tears, she agrees and skips school to get lunch. She is talking to Candice about all the things that are happening, about them graduation and prom, but Candice is wrapped in her own thoughts. Her friend taps her and asks if she is okay.

"Yeah, I'm fine. Just thinking."

"What are you thinking about? Who taking you to prom?"

"Eh, no. I'm probably not going."

"Why girl? Any guy would be lucky to have you as their prom date."

"Ain't no guy trying to ask me out."

"Please, you just thinking that now, but you never know what will happen."

With them eating their food, Candice asks her friend how long they have been friends and if they would be friends if it was not for them being in the same grade. "I'm not sure. However, I'm glad that we are friends. What is going on with you Candice?"

"You remember when I was in the hospital?"

"Yeah, I am glad that you're okay."

"Well, my family found out about my pills and forcing my food back up. I've been taking the pills because I hate the way I look. I've worked so hard to lose weight, but it didn't work."

"Candice, you act like you're overweight."

"I feel like I am."

"I've seen overweight and trust me, you aren't it. So, what if you are a little thick in certain parts of your body? I know some people that love that."

"It's not just that, but I haven't seen nor heard from my father since that day."

"Seriously?!"

Breaking down, Candice shakes her head. Her friend gives her a hug, apologizing for what happened and for Candice having to go through this. As she is holding Candice, Candice begins to have thoughts and images flash in her mind. This is not the first time she has had these thoughts, but it is the first time that she has wanted to act upon these thoughts. In a place of vulnerability and being lost, she looks at her friend and gives into those images and thoughts. As Candice does, she is ignorant of the door that bursts open within her in the spiritual realm.

Whom you will serve

William is shocked to see Madison in his class, let alone in his school. He wants to get her attention but wonders if she even remembers who he is due to her being completely blown out of her mind. He leans in to try and get her attention but is caught by his teacher.

"Mr. Huntington, is there something you would like to say to the class?

Just when William is going to respond, the bell rings for class to end. Everyone gathers their things and

exits the class. Quickly, William gathers his things to get to Madison. He looks up and sees that she is gone. Jamie goes to him, asking him about Madison.

"Dude, did you know that she went to our school?"

"No. She must've just started coming today."

"Hmm, that is odd. This is our last year."

"I know right! But this works for me."

Playfully hitting William, Jamie laughs and says, "Focus on

tonight Bro! We gotta bring the championship home. Our school has had the gold for seven years in a row. It's our time now, Bro!"

"I got you. Now get to class and I will see you soon".

As William heads to his next class, he yearns to see Madison again.

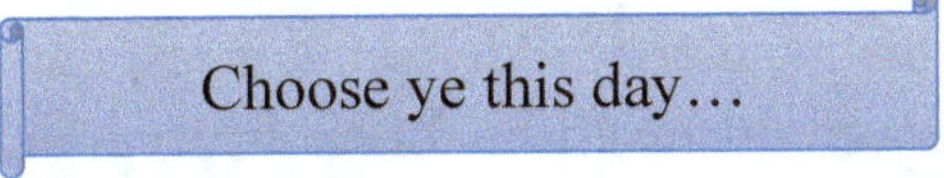

They arrive at the house where Lilith aunt's family lives and see the array of cars at their home. Lola is amazed by the size of the house. It seemed like their front yard would go on for miles. Sam stops the car, looking at Lola.

"Are you ready?"

"Let's finally get some answers Sam."

"Listen, this is a young woman that lost her mother not too long ago and now has lost someone else that was supposed to be there for her. Whatever happened here is still affecting her. So please, Babe, don't be pushy.

"Oh, mi amor, when am I ever pushy?"

Looking at Lola, he says "That cannot be a serious question."

They get out of the car, walking towards her aunt's house. As Lola gets to the house, she begins to discern that the environment of where they are seems unsettling. It is as if she has a migraine and a feeling of sudden heaviness. Beneath her breath, she begins to pray. They walk in and Sam notices that Lola begins praying in the Spirit. He takes her hand, as they go deeper into the house and join her in prayer.

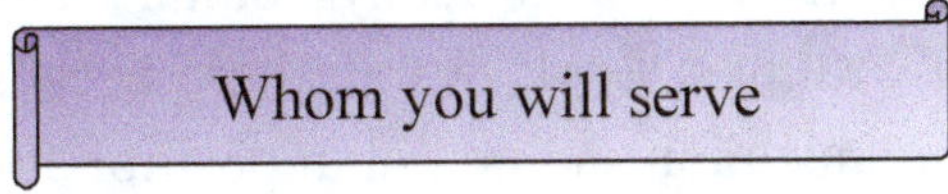

Damian enters the conference room where he is greeted by

the senators waiting for him. The one that is older appears very distraught, while the one that is younger leaps forward to shake Damian's hand.

"Good Morning gentlemen, apologies for being late. Had some early business that needed to be taken care of."

He shakes the hand of the younger senator, while the other does not take his hand. The older senator responds, "It is no big deal at all. We were just waiting for about 30 minutes. So, no big deal.

"Passive aggressiveness…I like that."

"Don't mind him Damian. We haven't met, but my name i—"

"Senator Taylor of Vermont. The youngest Vermont has ever voted for. You consider yourself very conservative, despite your very liberal choices over the last few months. From my understanding, you have some big ideas for this nation.

"Yes, we both do in fact. And from my understanding, Lucius told us that you would be the perfect person to help us achieve these goals. My colleague here, Senator Mark Urkin, would join me on the venture."

"I'm assuming these plans include the oval office, right?"

Mark, speaking up in a condescending tone, says, "I see what Lucius pays you the big bucks for."

Damian begins to become visibly annoyed by Mark's demeanor. Taylor assures him that they mean no harm but wonders why Lucius is not dealing with them himself.

"Lucius is busy with other priorities."

"And we aren't a priority? Listen, I do not like being handled, especially by someone whose daddy couldn't keep his mouth shut about our dealings. Look, we are here because we are the ones that the organization should put in position for presiden—"

Nervously, Taylor apologizes for Urkin's attitude.

"Don't you dare apologize for me again. We have done

everything that was asked of us. Voted on legislation that the organization wanted passed, shook the hands of enemies just to forward our agenda and I…I mean WE need this. We deserve this and I refuse to be denied."

After Urkin's rant, Damian sits there in silence for a moment and laughs.

"What's so funny?"

"What is funny old man is that it can be clearly seen that you are trying desperately to keep a grasp onto the last remaining power that you have in the twilight of your life. It is rather sad. Lucius probably knows how desperate you are, and you are using Taylor, rather riding on his coat tail hoping, praying, that he gets elected so that he selects you as his Vice President for some unknown reason. It cannot be for your wisdom. You haven't made a wise decision since first getting elected."

Pouring himself a drink, Damian says to Taylor, "If I were you, I would ditch Urkin and find you someone that is suitable to stand by your side and not some desperate old man seeking to have some semblance of power."

"I have power Damian. More power than you can imagine. The only reason you are where you are now is because of Lucius. He protects…"

Urkin begins to cough heavily. Taylor rushes to his aide to check on him. Damian looks over at him, continuing his drink.

"See Senator Taylor! He can barely handle the stress of a heated discussion, let alone being Vice President. You deserve better."

Gathering himself, Urkin says "I…I can handle myself! I had power while you were still sleeping in your mother's womb. That is the problem with you all in this new generation: no respect for what was. You are only here because of your father's mistakes, and he had power too or so he thought.

"Are you finished? I have better things to do than entertain you."

"No, we are far from finished."

Senator Urkin storms out of the room. Just as Senator Taylor was about to leave out, Damian stops him and asks him, "Do you want to be President?"

"Um…"

"Yes or no?"

"Yes."

"Side with me and I will see to it that you will be in that Oval Office before 50."

Choose ye this day…

Sam and Lola are amazed by the number of people that are here to support Lilith's family. While these people seem to be perfectly normal, something still feels off to Lola. It was like the atmosphere of the house that they were in was cold, heavy, and overwhelming. Through the sea of people, Sam thinks he has spotted Lilith. They go over to speak to an older man and woman with Lilith.

Sam called her name to make sure it was her. Lilith sees Sam, giving him a big hug. She expresses how happy she is to see him, with tears in her eyes. Wiping her eyes, Sam tells her that it is okay and that they are sorry for her loss.

"Oh hey! Who are these people?"

"Oh sorry. This is Sam. He…He is my old teacher. He just came for moral support."

"Hello, I am Jacob," He says, reaching out to shake Sam's hand.

Reluctant to play along, Sam is slow to take his hand. Lola jumps in to introduce herself.

"Hello, my name is Rosa. You will have to excuse my

husband. We had a long, tiring flight here."

Chuckling, the older woman spoke up, "oh no worries, we are glad you all came to support our family at such a tragic time, especially Lilith. She is very special to us and our family. I am Marybeth, Jacob's wife and Lilith's aunt. If you need anything while you are here, please don't hesitate to ask."

Lilith explains that she will tend to them.

"Very well. Just stay nearby Lilith. We don't want you going too far."

"Yes, Aunt Marybeth."

As they all talk, Lola's migraine intensifies. She tells them that she is going outside for just a second to get some fresh air. Quickly, she rushes out, just to get away from whatever is inside the house. Sam and Lilith follow behind her, wondering what has her rushing out of the house so fast.

"Babe, are you okay?! What is wrong?

"Sam, I don't know what the heck is in that house, but it is not good. I was feeling weird before, but once I got in, I just got this heavy feeling."

"We don't have to go back in there, Lola. Things are definitely off in that house and the people in it. For a second though, I just chucked it up to all those pretentious rich people.

"Seriously Sam?! Lily is right here! That is very rude!"

"Lola, it is fine. Its not like he is wrong…"

Lola scowls at Lilith and continues at talk to Sam.

"This is serious Sam. There is something wrong with that house and I am not going back in."

"Lola, it's okay. Nobody is making you go back in. Being serious, I do think something is off with the people in that house." Sam says, comforting her. Lilith interrupts, telling them that they should leave anyway because they need to talk.

"That is something we can agree on, Lily," Lola says.

As they all get in the car, Jacob and Marybeth watch them

leave.

"Do you believe that is her teacher, Mary?"

"Absolutely not. She told us that she came here for school, which is a definite lie. I think this was Rebecca's doing."

"I'm going to make the call then. I think Lucius would be interested in this development, as it was thought that she died with Rebecca. Should have known my sister would try to find a way out. I'm surprised she stayed in touch with that dark-skinned fella. I suspect he was the one that helped her make it out."

"Of course! Rebecca always had a weakness for these colored people. Mary, tell Lucius what we've discovered and ask how we should proceed and if we should tell Damian."

Whom you will serve

Coming from her third class, Madison runs into Kate and begins to ask her about her first day at this godforsaken school.

"It's okay, I guess. It ain't like our old school, but it's better than the alternative, right?"

"I guess. Do you remember the guy I was dancing with at that party last night?" Kate chuckles, saying, "Which one? You danced with so many."

"Oh, you think you funny, huh?"

"Yeah, I remember. He was fine!"

"Lower your voice Kate," Madison says, smiling. She goes on to explain how William is in her first hour class.

"Uh huh…I think you two were almost destined to hook up."

"Maybe…I just don—"

Just as Madison was going to explain her feelings about him, William came up to them. Madison begins to feel that overwhelming attraction to him. It is like something in her yearns to yoke to something in him. William asks how their first day is going so far in. The reaction William has on Madison astonishes Kate. In all her years of knowing her, she has never seen her so enamored by someone where she is hanging on their every word. It is clear to Kate that she is spellbound by his sheer presence. As Madison and William continue to flirt with each other, Kate picks up the hint and tells Madison that she will see her at lunch.

"Are you enjoying your day here at our exquisite establishment?"

"Umm…I guess. It seems to have the essentials."

"Really now? Stay with me and I can show you really what our school can offer you. It has some colorful personalities."

"Would you be one of those 'colorful' personalities?"

William smiles, saying, "No, I am simply the one everyone wants to be."

"Wow, someone is full of themselves."

"Nah, I am just that guy. I am the lead scorer on the basketball team, straight A student and the top of every class I have been in. So yeah, I am definitely that guy."

In disgust, Madison turns from him and gets ready to walk away.

"Wait, I'm kidding. Not about my accolades, but the other stuff."

As William continues to talk to Madison, a crowd of girls coming down the hallway walk past them. All of them greet William in a flirtatious manner. This causes Madison to side eye William, as she can see how cocky he is.

"You know, you're right. Clearly you are the guy…the guy that all these girls get at."

"No, it isn't like that at all."

Sarcastically, Madison says, "Sure."

As she walks away, William asks her if she will come to his game. He assures her that a fight will not break out this time around. Being enamored by his charm, she says, "My friend Kate is my ride. So, if I can convince her to come, then yes, I will be there. You better not lose."

William looks at her and says, "Baby, I don't ever lose."

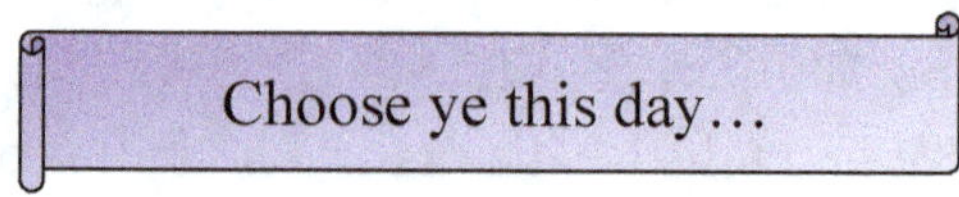

Sitting at his desk, Damian contemplates his plan to destroy Lucius for everything he has done. All those years ago, when he discovered that he killed his father, he wanted to kill him during that ceremony and the only reason he did not was because of Tiffany.

The anger and hatred continue to bubble within him, so much so that he has dreams of how he would kill Lucius. It would seem like ever since that ceremony, he has had this profound sense of wrath in him and it will only be satiated by act of killing Lucius. He told him that Rebecca and Lilith were safe and now his wife and daughter were both dead. His revenge for this transgression further fuels his wrath. He does not just want his life, but he wants to steal everything that Lucius has spent his entire life earning. He wants to embarrass him before all those that look to him, like that feeble old man Senator Mark Urkin. Damian starts to fall deeper and deeper into darker thoughts. He becomes so lost in these thoughts that a knock on his office door by his secretary startles him.

"What!" Damian says, forcefully.

"I…I'm so…sorry sir. I just wanted to let you know that a Mr. Lucius is here to see you an—"

Before Damian's secretary could finish his statement, Lucius walks into his office, telling the secretary to leave. Beaming with confidence, Damian buttons a button on his blazer and walks from behind his desk to sit on the front of it. Lucius walks in, speaking to someone on the phone. He tells the person on the phone to keep track of the situation and report back to him. Damian goes to greet Lucius, but before he can get a word out, Lucius says, "What the heck were you thinking, Damian?!"

Whom you will serve

"I am starving! Would it be possible to talk and eat?"

Lilith points them in the direction of a local diner. She states that they have some really good food and it was the place that her cousins would take her to. After what Lola felt in that house, she becomes very leery of Lilith and what she and her family are spiritually bound to. It starts becoming visible on her face that something is wrong. As they go to get seated, Lilith tells them that she must run to the restroom. As she leaves, Lola asks Sam about this and if they are doing the right thing.

"Of course, Lola. We are helping someone in need."

"Yes, that is great, but this is something else. Everything about this situation seems off Sam. I am feeling the same way now that I felt back when Elias was born. There is something off with her family. It was like we walked into a coven of witches or something, just felt wrong. We can't go back, you know that right?"

"No, I agree…those two were acting strange like they knew something. Man!! I hope I did not blow our cover!"

"That is the least of our problems. I am hoping we even making it out this country. If they are as rich as they looked, we could disappear off the face of the earth and people would be none the wiser."

"Well, there is no turning back now, I guess."

"Cariño, if you say we help this girl, then, as the head of our house and my husband, I got your back."

Sam kisses her hand, as Lilith walks back to their table.

"Sorry about that. Thank you, guys, for coming all the way here. I know that was a long flight."

"It is fine," Lola says.

"We weren't formally introduced but, I am Lily. I didn't want to involve Sam's family. I am really sorry I pulled your husband into this."

"Well, we are one. So, if somebody got a problem with my husband, they got a problem with me. Oh, and I'm happy to meet you. I'm Lola."

Lilith laughs, explaining that she had never seen this type of relationship before. "This is what a marriage, a real marriage looks like. You have the other person's back."

"Yes, so I am sure you all have questions."

Together, Sam and Lola give a resounding "Yes!"

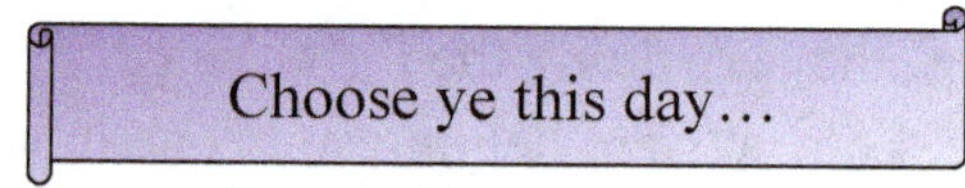

"You know you should probably relax before you pop a blood vessel."

"Don't you dare tell me to calm down. Do you have any idea what you have done, boy?"

"Uh let's see, I told an entitled old man, who knows nothing, to go chill and that he will never be President, while seeing promise in Senator Taylor. Yep, I think that pretty much sums it up."

Seeing that Lucius is visibly angry, Damian goes into further detail about why he did what he did.

"Listen, Urkin is a feeble old man. If we put him in office, he will die under the stress, and we will be at this all over again. My plan is a lot better and for the long term, it will accomplish our goals."

"What goals, Damian?! You went into business for yourself.

I pro—"

"Yeah, yeah, I figured you were the one that made that empty promise."

"You don't get it. We cannot afford to fail now. If that is who the powers that be want in position, then that is what we must do. If we don't, the consequences will be dire."

"No, not we, You. The consequences will be dire for you. That man does not understand what real power is. He is in this to cover up the things he does in the dark, not for real power. And I must say, the deprived things that man partakes in would even make the devil hurl."

"That is not remotely funny. The demons we conjure and get power from are very real. We sold our souls to these things. If we do not comply, we will die."

Getting a drink, Damian says, underneath his breath, "Oh, I am well aware."

"You will fix this. We need this for the good of everyone."

"Um, no I won't be fixing anything, Lucius. His time is done. Senator Taylor will do everything we require. I know it."

"And you are not hearing me, boy! You don't want to go to war with me. Your father did it and failed. What hope do you have?"

As Damian grips his glass tightly, he imagines in his mind all the diverse ways he could kill Lucius right in his office without anyone knowing. As he comes out of his own head, he warns him of his own hubris.

"Hubris? Boy, you dare threaten me?"

"Lucius, I do not make threats. Threats are made by people who are ignorant fools that have no plans for what they will do. Threats are for those afraid to take real action. Threats come from the mouths of the incompetent."

Getting in the face of Lucius, he goes on to say, "I make promises. I have the authority and might to follow through with everything that I would do to you and only the foolish and ignorant would not take me at my word. And you better believe, I have fulfilled almost every promise I have made. So, I will make you a promise here, I promise you Lucius, your time is almost up!"

Something happened at this moment that shook Lucius to his core, something that he never thought would ever happen to him. For the first time in his long life, he was terrified.

Whom you will serve

"Where should I start?" Lilith asks.

Lola looks at Lilith, expressing to her that the best place to start is at the beginning. Lilith begins to explain what happened that night between her, her Mom, and her Dad.

"My mother stole some data from my father because…she and him were in a cult."

"Um, what kind of cult?"

"I am getting to that. There is a lot so can I…"

Lola apologizes and tells her to finish.

"No, I am sorry for being snappy. I got a friend to hack the drive and on it, we saw my dad taking part of some ritual on Halloween. I really don't know what was going on, but it was the same night that something else happened to me."

"What happened to you?" Sam asks.

"I cannot really explain it, but it was like I couldn't move, speak or do anything. I also had instances where I would lay in bed and I would get these scratches on my legs."

"How do you know you didn't scratch yourself?"

"Because human hands cannot be shaped like that."

As she goes on to describe it, Lola begins to get this chill up her spine.

"Geez, what the heck did you get yourself into, Sam?"

"I know my mother would never have wanted you all to be endangered because of me. Lola, you gotta understand, my mother felt like she had no choice."

"Yeah she did, but she just chose Sam. Lily, I have nothing against you or your mom; however, she put Sam in the crosshairs of something that he was not fully informed on it caused friction in our marriage. So yeah, I am slightly salty about that."

"I am sorry."

Sam assures her that he and Lola are fine now and with time, they will be better. Lilith continues to tell her story. Sitting there listening, part of Lola feels that this story is just too outlandish to be true. She knows that the kingdom of darkness is a real thing, that witches are real, especially since one tried to take their son, nine years ago; however, cults and everything else that Lilith says are happening, seems like they are out of some comic book or horror film. Nevertheless, there is also this still, small voice that confirms everything that Lilith is saying. Lola steps away, going to the restroom to freshen up before the food comes out. As she is in the restroom, this voice says to Lola, "Listen to her, Lola."

"Seriously Jesus? I am not trying to argue the point, but this all seems crazy."

"Listen to her, Lola."

As Lola wrestles with this in her spirit, Jesus allows her to have a vision of what happened to Lilith. Seeing what happened left her in total shock. She leaves the bathroom, comes back to the table and apologizes to Lilith. She admits that part of her did not believe her, but she does. Lola begins to explain to her what happened to them at the hospital with Elias.

"Woah, now that sounds crazy."

Laughing, Lola says, "Crazier than saying I caught my dad selling his soul on tape?"

"Good point," Lilith says, giggling.

"Now that Lola is back, continue with your story Lily. Why did your mom leave the cult and what is their name?"

"I don't know if I want to say their name out in the open."

"Don't be afraid, Chica. Just say your peace."

"As my mother started going to church, she became torn, I guess. I am not sure. She said it had to do with what I was experiencing. There became a schism in our family and my mother wanted to protect my brother and me. An—"

"Wait… wait… wait, you mean to tell us you got a brother out there?"

"Yes Lola, I do."

Lola sits back in the booth, taking a deep breath.

"Wait, Sam…Did you know that Lilith had a brother?"

Sam looks down, as he contemplates their previous argument. Just before he could go into his explanation, Lilith cuts him off.

"Lola before you ge—"

Lola tells her to stop talking and looks at Sam. In Spanish, she asks him the question again.

"Lola, listen to me, yes I did know."

Placing her hands over her eyes, she starts murmuring in Spanish.

"I only knew because spoke to Damian. I know I did not tell you and I am sorry, but I had good reason."

"What good reason could you possibly have?"

"Damian threatened to kill you and Elias."

"What?! When did this happen?"

"It happened a few years ago."

"In New York?" Lola said with a sigh.

"…Yes. Damian held a gun to me and threatened to kill me, you and our son if I did not tell him why Rebecca called me. Of course, I did not, but I knew he was not going to pull the trigger."

"Excuse me?! How did you know that Samuel? You could have died! I could have loss you!" Lola yells.

"Lower your voice, Lola."

"Don't tell me to lower my voice, Sam." Lola says in Spanish.

"He was drunk and just wanted to talk. I knew I was going to be fine."

Trying not to freak out, Lola takes deep breath and a sip of water at her table.

"Listen Lola, I am sorry about my father's actions. I—"

"Does he even know you are alive?" Lola says.

"I am pretty sure my dad and brother think I'm dead, right Sam?"

"Yes, I made sure to reenforce the idea that Lilith died and he was to blame for their deaths."

Lola is in total disbelief by this tale that was told at this table and the actions that her husband has taken over the past seven years. It seems far-fetched that something like this would even take place in the real world, let alone to someone she knew.

"I gotta to be honest, I am totally speechless right now."

"Babe, I know this a lot to take in, but it is all real. Damian was a lot of things, but I did not think he was capable of this."

"My father is the cause of all this Lola. I want to bring him and all those people surrounding him down, but the people in this cult are very powerful. They are called Light Bearers."

"On the nose much?"

"What do you mean?"

Sam interjects to explain to Lilith what Lola meant.

"Lucifer means Light bearer or morning star. He was the angel that led a bunch of other angels to get kicked out of heaven."

Lilith pulls out a folder with a bunch of papers in there. She explains to them that her mother had been researching them and trying to figure out just how deep they are entrenched into the world. As she looks out the window, she notices a car that is just sitting there. It is a blue car with slightly tinted windows with two guys in it.

"Sam, how long has that car been there?"

"Um, they've been here for a while. I was trying not to freak you or anyone else out."

"Sam, that is important information! We need to go, now! I'm pretty sure they work for my dad and the guy that killed my mom."

As they rush out to the car and pull off, Sam notices that this blue car follows behind them.

Choose ye this day…

In fear of what will happen next, Lucius scampers out of Damian's office. When the door closes shut, Damian, in a fit of rage, throws his glass at the wall. The shattering of the glass draws the attention of people outside of his office. He calls Tiffany, hoping that she will pick up.

"Hey Babe. What's going on? Please tell me you are heading to William's game."

"No…No, I'm not. We're all meeting tonight, correct?"

Hesitant, Tiffany says, "Yes…"

"Great! Because tonight's the night that Lucius dies."

"Whoa, are you sure you want to do this now? I thought we were going to wait a little long."

"Screw that! He dies tonight!"

"If this is really the night you want to do this, you prepare and make sure everyone is onboard. We only get one shot at this. I will go to his game and make up some excuse as to why you cannot show up and will meet you at the usual place. Damian, you know once you do this, there is no turning back."

Damian hangs up on Tiffany and begins preparing for tonight.

As Tiffany arrives at the school, she knows that William will be disappointed that yet again, his father has flaked on him. As she goes into the gym, she sees that the game has already started. She sits next to this beautiful young lady, who seems to be really into it when he gets the ball. He shoots from three point line and the young lady and her friend jump out of their seats cheering for him. She looks over at her, wondering who this girl is that has taken a liking to her son.

Whom you will serve

Sam goes in and out of traffic, trying to lose this car that Lilith believes to be following them. It seems to be on their tail. As they head off the highway to see if it is really following them, Sam sees the car keep going past them.

"I don't know how, but my dad has to know that I'm alive and is looking for me. I promised my mom I would stay safe. See why I am paranoid now?"

"No, he can't know Lilith. I am sure of it."

"Someone is following us, so clearly you didn't."

Lola tells them both to stay calm and instructs Sam to get them off the street and someplace quiet.

"Lilith, we will get you somewhere safe" Says Lola.

"No place is safe for me Lola!

She looks over at Sam for help.

"Lily, you are safe. Nobody knows where you are. Your dad does not know. Your mom made sure of that."

"No Sam, I'm not. These people can find me anywhere. If they find me, I am dead. I gotta run."

Lola interjects asking her where she would run to and reminds her that the world really is not that big.

"Out of this country for sure!"

"That won't work Lilith. You cannot keep running."

"I have to try, Lola. And I don't want to endanger you, Sam and the kids." Lilith says looking at Lola with tears in her eyes.

Lilith collapses under the weight of her own tears. Lola looks at Lilith and she can see the sheer terror that this whole ordeal has put her through. Lilith has become a bondservant for fear because of her trauma and because of this Lola can finally see it clearly now. With this new vision, a tear falls down Lola's eye as her heart breaks for this broken girl. It seems like all the sound has been drowned out and it is just her and Lilith. As each tear falls down Lola's face, she takes a step to Lilith until she is right in front of her. She bents down and embraces her.

"I know what it is like to be a prisoner of fear. You have been terrorized by nightmares, cults, demons, and everything else."

Lilith cries in her arms. Lola places her hands on Lilith's soft cheeks, looking her in the eyes with a determined look.

"Baby girl, I also know you can be free from that warden called Fear like I am too, if you want to be."

"My mom and my cousins are gone. Sam was all I had. I am afraid…"

"Oh, don't you worry about us. we'll be alright," Lola said wiping her tears. "I know that I had my doubts about your story before and I am sorry about that. Your mother trusted Sam because he is a good man, no, he is a great man and knew he is a man of valor. God trusted Sam with this because He knew Sam could handle it. I know you did not have anyone in your life before that would defend you. Your mom didn't do it and your dad didn't either, God has blessed you with two absolute strangers that will cross borders to come and defend your Lily. If that isn't love, I don't know what is."

Lilith looks at Lola.

"Yes, we crossed international borders for you Lily. My husband been doing it, but he did it for you. We would do it all again, just to defend you. No matter where you run, just know, Sam and I will always be here for you Lily. There is no place we won't come to see about you."

"Gracias, Lola!"

While watching, Sam goes over to pick them both up off the ground to give them a hug. Lilith begins to have these complex feelings. While she does not want anything bad to happen to Sam or Lola, it feels delightful to be around people that makes you feel like you are family.

"Lily, what will you do now? Do you want us to take you back to MaryBeth?" said Sam.

"I really don't. I just saw them for the first time since I was a little girl."

"Could it be that it was not your father, but the guy he works for and that is who was tracking you? I mean you said it yourself that your dad's family was part of the Light Bearers and they wanted your mother to marry your dad because of their connection. So, it would make sense if someone in your family were in it as well."

Lilith sits in the back seat for a minute and begins to ponder what Sam has said. "If that is the case, then I really need to leave the country because I'm not safe. I have to go on the run again."

Lilith proceeds to get on her phone to find the earliest flight out of Winnipeg.

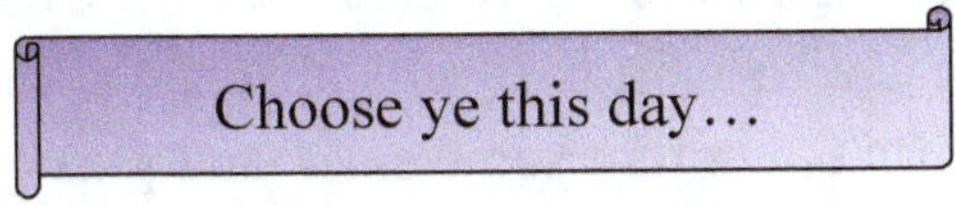

Tiffany continues to watch the game, but her mind is far from what is happening in front of her. She cannot believe that Damian pushed up their timetable to take out Lucius so soon. This was sudden and that must mean have happened to cause Damian to react like this. Whatever it was, she is hoping they will succeed because if they do not, the Light Bearers will stop at nothing to kill them all, including William. Looking at William in his game, she has never been prouder of him. She never thought she would be the one that would be good with children, but she really does look at William as if he is her own. As William makes the game winning shot, the crowd erupts in a loud cheer. This shakes her out of her own thoughts to cheer for him as well. William looks up, seeing her face and smiles. He looks over to her right, seeing Madison and Kate smiling even harder.

Damian makes the necessary phone calls for tonight, letting them know that this is the time that he is taking the necessary action and that they had better fulfill their end of the bargain or he will make them suffer. He sees a text from Tiffany, letting him know the score and that William's team won. Knowing that the time is near for them to meet, Damian gathers his things to leave.

Tiffany goes to William, giving him a big hug. She tells him how proud she is of him and that she is happy for him.

"So, let me guess, Dad had another excuse for why he couldn't come?"

"There was an emergency at work, he had to attend to it."

"Uh huh, of course he did. Why didn't I expect anything less of him?"

"Listen William, your dad is working on something right now that will change all of our lives. Every person in our family, this room, the entire world. It will all change, and it will be because of him. So, cut him some slack and plus, your dad isn't as cool as me anyway."

William laughs and agrees. As they are laughing and talking, Madison walks over to speak to William.

"Hey Bill, I guess you are amazing. I mean, you told me you are good, but wow. I don't think you even missed a shot. I don't even know how that is possible."

"Um, and you are…"

William introduces Madison to Tiffany. Tiffany shakes Madison's hand and can tell she is really into her son.

"I gotta meet with your father anyway. Don't stay out too long or you will be in big trouble. I bailed you out this time, but I won't be able to do it again if you mess up this time."

"Okay I won't."

Tiffany gives him a playful punch in the arm, telling him to stay out of jail too and he assures her that it won't ever happen again.

As Damian arrives at the meeting place, he sees everyone he has talked to that sides with him and some others that he knows are his enemies. While the meeting is being prepared, he messages Tiffany to find out where she is. He looks over to see Lucius coming with Urkin. Just seeing Lucius fuels the rage within him. As he sees them ready for tonight's activities, he hears the voice of Tiffany behind him.

"Why do you sound out of breath?"

"I practically ran here from outside. Are you ready?"

"As I will ever be."

As the final people come in, Damian begins to see what he saw all those years ago when he officially became one of them. He sees what could only be described as shadow figures and the room feels very cold, but the difference between then and now is that he now feels as if he is embracing the dark. As they get started, Urkin begins to speak up.

"We have someone here that has gone into business for himself. If our plans for the world are to work, we must all be on the same page. That includes some of our newest members, like Damian."

"If you have something you would like to say, then say it old man."

"Fine! We brought you into the fold because we thought you were better than your father, but we see that you are worse. You are a traitor and a cancer."

"Is any of this true, Damian?" Lucius asks.

Thinking about it for a moment, Damian begins to look around the room and he looks Lucius in the eye and says, "Yes, it is all true."

"You all come to these meetings, make your plans for the world in the dark, but have done little to carry out these things. You even dabble in your little witchcraft and sacrifices and still nothing is done. You take these small steps that mean absolutely nothing. This world is ours to mold and you all are either too afraid do what it or our leadership is just far too weak to do what I know the powers that be want us to do now. So, I did what you all won't do."

"Stupid boy!"

"If you call me boy one more time…"

Tiffany surveys the room to see if the people who said they will side with her and Damian look to be trying to back out. She can also feel the room getting colder for some odd reason. She looks at Lucius and Urkin, stepping in to speak.

"I have worked for you Lucius and I can honestly say you are ill fit for the power that you have. Damian is the one that we need now."

"You witch! Does he know that you hated his dead wife since you met her, that you always wanted her demise?"

"Leave my wife out of this Lucius. This is your only warning."

"What? Afraid of the truth?"

"Let's talk about the truth, Lucius. You had horrible things done to me, things that I have nightmares about. I did things I regret just to be a part of this. I hate you for all the things you did to me."

"You knew what it took to be join us at this level Tiffany. Sounds like you are having buyer's remorse."

Filled with rage and to the shock of everyone in the room, Damian takes out a gun. He shoots Urkin and shoots Lucius in the chest. Damian walks over the body of Urkin and puts multiple bullets into him.

Struggling to get out his words, Lucius asks Damian, "Why? After everything I have done for you."

Looking up, Damian sees multiple demonic figures in the room with them and as he sees more of them appear, the wrath and bloodlust builds more and more.

Damian answers Lucius' question, "That was for disrespecting Tiffany and everything you did to her."

Shooting him again, Damian says, "That is for Lily and Rebecca." Lucius, on death's door, begins laughing.

Angrily, Damian asks him, "What's so freaking funny?"

With Lucius' dying breath, he says to him, "Lilith is alive."

Epilogue

It has been five months since Damian's takeover of the Light Bearers. It all seemed like a dream, but it is Lucius' dying words that haunt him.

"Lilith is alive."

Could it really be possible that Lilith survived the fire all this time? If she did survive, he wonders why she had not come to find him. It is with these dying words that shake to his core.

Tiffany tries her best to find any traces of Lilith using her connections, but nothing. She explains to him that it could be a lie, but Damian fears that Lucius was indeed telling the truth about her fate.

"Are you going to tell William?"

"No…not until I find her."

"I hope you are aware that if you do this, he will never forgive you for hiding this from him."

Walking into his meeting, Damian looks at all the members of the Light Bearers still around after his treachery. With a smirk, he says, "Our time is near, Let's begin our work."

Choose ye this day…

For the last few months, Madison has developed a connection with William. She never thought that she could be as close as she is with a guy, considering everything she has gone through. She has exposed herself to him, in ways she never thought she ever would. As they wind down their school year, she notices that William is becoming distant towards her. She does not want to believe that he would ever break her heart, but she cannot help but wonder. She sees William coming down the hallway.

"Hey Babe, Um…we need to talk."

"Oh hey…do you think that we could do this later? I a—"

William becomes distracted by a young lady that walks past him, talking to him about a class assignment.

"Excuse you?! Are you flirting with her?"

"What? No. She knows me because I mean, everybody knows me Maddy. It comes with being me and you being my girl."

Getting close to her, he seductively says, "You know I only want you, right?"

"Yeah." Madison says, bashfully. She goes on to say, "However, we have to talk. We have been doing things lately and I ha—"

William cuts her off, explaining that he must get to class to get ready for his presentation, but that they will talk soon. Madison agrees and asks to meet up after class. William agrees and leaves. Madison sees Jamie and begins talking to him.

"Hey Jamie!"

"Hey, you seen Bill? We are supposed to meet up to hang out."

"He went to class."

"He does not have class now. He probably with some gir—"

Jamie stops himself, realizing that he made a mistake.

"Where were you supposed to meet, Jamie?!"

"I shouldn—"

"Where?!"

"Right outside the football field."

Madison storms away from Jamie. As she and Jamie make their way to the field, to her dismay, she sees William kissing the young lady he spoke to while with her. She locks eyes with him and with anger in her eyes, she screams out that she hates him. He tries to go after her, but she gets in the car to drive off.

Later that night, she arrives home with tears in her eyes. Still reeling from William's betrayal, she lays in her bed, crying. After everything she has gone through lately, she cannot believe he would do this. She lifts her hand up to look at the strips to see that her suspicions were indeed correct, she is pregnant with William's baby.

Afterword

The Gospel of Jesus Christ is the most priceless message that one can ever hear. The bible records in I Corinthians 1:21 that God is pleased by the foolishness of preaching to save them that believe. Biblical salvation starts with the hearing of the Gospel. Once one has heard the preached word of God as it begins to permeate in their spirit, a choice must now be made to continue to walk in the flesh (the world of sin) or begin to walk in the newness of life.

How does one walk in the newness of life, you may ask? Hebrews the sixth chapter gives one the first principles of the oracles of God that every born-again believer should have. Please take note of the first three principles found at the end of verse one and the beginning of verse two. The first being repentance from dead works. The word *"repentance"* is a change of mind or a change in the inner man. The change must happen from these *"dead works"* or the actions that have kept you from being in a place of favor with God previously.

What would constitute these dead works? Pretty much anything that does not build up your spiritual man or anything that increases your chances of not building your spiritual man. This can range based on who the person is. One must decide to no longer make excuses for why we do not want to walk a path of righteousness. The Bible says that "the way of the transgressor is hard" (Proverbs 13:15). The more you find yourself trying to be like the world, the more you will find yourself in trouble, in despair, in pain, in misery, etc. but Jesus said take my yoke upon you, and learn of me for my yoke is easy, and my burden is light. When you make the decision to repent from dead works you are one step closer to allowing Jesus to do the heavy lifting in your life.

The next principle is faith towards God. There are three faiths in the bible. There is faith "in" God or believing that he can do the impossible. There is "the faith" or the belief/teachings of Jesus Christ (Eph. 4:3-6) and the one we are focused on today, faith towards God. Think about your dream goals and aspirations like a career or achieving an advanced degree. Those things just do not fall out the sky and land in your lap, but because you have the goal type of mind, you work "toward" achieving that goal. Having faith toward God after repenting from dead works is the assurance of mind that you will no longer focus on those things that are behind you but that you will press toward the mark of the high calling that is in Christ Jesus (Philippians 3:14). You're no longer focused on the goals you once had when you were in sin but now you focus on being more like Christ who knew no sin.

The third principle is the doctrine of baptisms. It is vital that once you have repented and believed the Gospel of Jesus Christ that one is water baptized in the name of Jesus Christ and receives the gift of the Holy Spirit. As we move on in this brief afterword, we will discuss the importance of how having the Holy Spirit makes a difference in how you deal with spiritual attacks much like we find in the novel. In the 8th chapter of the book of Acts around the 27th verse Phillip met an Ethiopian man who was reading in the scripture but did not understand what he was reading. The Bible says that Philip from that scripture preached unto him Jesus. He gave this man the opportunity to believe the Gospel and the Ethiopians' response in the subsequent verse when they had come upon some water said, "See, here is water; what doth hinder me to be baptized?" It is apparent that somewhere in their conversation Philip mentioned to him that he should be baptized for the remission of sins spoken in Acts 2:38. Philip replied to him saying that if he believed with all of his heart then he could be baptized. These parts (repentance, faith, baptism) all are congruent with Jesus' death on the cross. Repentance from dead works makes you now dead to those dead works just as Jesus died on the cross. As Jesus had spoken before to the disciples that he would rise the third day symbolizes the faith towards God that the act spoken would be performed. Water baptism symbolizes how the body of Jesus was buried and when you receive the Holy Spirit it symbolizes the body rising the third day with power.

We see now that biblical salvation affords the believer power as mentioned in the scripture (Acts 1:8 and Mark 16:16-18). Once we have gotten to this point, we can now be equipped with the necessary tools to battle in spiritual warfare.

What is spiritual warfare? It is the act of demonic forces constantly looking for ways to attack you so that you do not receive biblical salvation or that you would lose the salvation that you have received. The devil and demons are nothing to play with. They will use any method they can to thwart your progress in growing with Christ.

One point we must make clear, if you have not been born again of the water and Spirit, it is nearly impossible to fight back against demonic forces. It's like going to a gun fight with a knife. The unregenerated will constantly be at a loss every time the enemy attacks them. It is also not wise to cast demons out of people that are not going to yield themselves to the Holy Spirit. Why? The scripture says in Matthew 12:43-45 that when an unclean spirit leaves a vessel it will return with seven other spirits more wicked than itself. Unless Jesus is the inhabitant of the vessel (your body) one is at risk to be led or possessed by demons.

The possession of demons, referenced in the novel, means that your body, spirit, and soul are vexed by an evil spirit with an assignment to kill, steal and destroy your life. Your purpose will be stifled. Your assignments will be eliminated, and if you are not careful your soul will be lost. It is imperative that the people of God learn to fight this good fight of faith. Well, how do we fight? Well, the Bible tells us in I Corinthians 10:4-5 that the weapons of our warfare are not carnal, but mighty through God to the pulling down of strongholds. This tells us that the battle that we fight against demons and principalities are not ones that can be won utilizing materialistic tools. We cannot fight the demonic forces with a knife or a bazooka. We cannot battle with a metal sword or a swift boxing style. The only weapon that will be effective against the enemy is the Word of God. It is the same weapon that Jesus Christ used in Matthew chapter 4, and it will reap the same results as Jesus Christ had. You will rebuke the enemy and cause him to flee from you.

The enemy's job against the blood washed and purchased believer is to diminish them to a terrified, and hopeless state of ineffectiveness. If the enemy can cause you to not rebuke his lies, he can cause you to stop praying. If he can cause you to stop praying, then he can disable you from fasting. If he can interrupt your normalities of fasting and prayer, then he can prevent you from reading the Word of God, and if he can stop you from that, then my sister and my brother, you are in a miserable state of vulnerability.

How can the child of God submit ourselves to the wiles of the devil when the scriptures already tell us that we win? It is when the child of God lacks the spiritual fortitude to fight. Fighting is not just natural punching and kicking against an opponent. It is the continuous life of prayer, fasting, meditating, and pushing ourselves to believe the Word of God beyond what the enemy attempts to seduce us into believing. This is why the scriptures tell us in Philippians chapter 4 to think on these things that are true. Honest, just, pure, lovely and of good report. When we are thinking and meditating right, the enemy cannot slither his evil head, neck and hands into our lives.

This is why Eve was subtly manipulated by the serpent in the Garden of Eden. When we do not walk and declare the truth, even in the presence of our enemies without a second thought, we give way to the enemy to divide and conquer, which is what occurred in the Garden. This one instant led to a spiritual partition between God and mankind, until the man Christ Jesus came on the scene. He was submitted as a lamb preparing Himself for the slaughter all so that we can access eternal life through the eternal sacrifice of a perfect specimen of blood. This blood and sacrifice are the beacons of hope that every person on Earth must know that even when the enemy comes in like a flood that the spirit of God will lift up a standard. This is why we should have confidence that if God be for us, it is more than the whole world against. We have power that will heal the sick and raise the dead. We have power to lay hands on the sick and they recover. We have power to tread upon serpents and scorpions and no deadly thing can harm us, and guess what?

With the power of God inside of us, we have the power and authority to submit to God, resist the devil, and he will flee! Use your weapons, believe the Word and live in abundance.

Let's Connect

Thank you for joining me on this literary voyage. You have come this far, and I would like to extend the opportunity to keep you informed.

If you would like to continue the conversation in this book with me, you have questions or for speaking engagements, you can find me on these social media platforms:

Facebook:

Instagram:

Email: